LAST
SEEN
ALIVE

BOOKS BY CAROLYN ARNOLD

LAST SEEN ALIVE

CAROLYN ARNOLD

bookouture

Published by Bookouture in 2022

An imprint of Storyfire Ltd.
Carmelite House
50 Victoria Embankment
London EC4Y 0DZ

www.bookouture.com

ISBN: 978-1-80314-213-5
eBook ISBN: 978-1-80314-212-8

This book is a work of fiction. Names, characters, businesses, organizations,
places and events other than those clearly in the public domain, are either the
product of the author's imagination or are used fictitiously. Any resemblance
to actual persons, living or dead, events or locales is entirely coincidental.

PROLOGUE

The silver sedan slowed to a stop. The driver had been careful to keep his distance, but stress had stiffness building in the back of his neck. There was always the chance he'd messed up, that he'd been made. If he was going to act, it had better be soon.

But he'd never killed a kid before.

He cut the engine, and the silence of the summer night was almost deafening. He sat still, recalling the scene a half hour ago when the detective returned home with her daughter, a sweet little blond kid about six years old. The two of them were laughing as they had gotten out of the Honda Civic and walked to the front door. The girl had dropped a stuffed dog on the pavement and had nearly tripped over it, but mother and daughter found that funny and set off in a new batch of laughter.

But a scuffed and bruised knee would be the least of the girl's worries by the time he was finished with her. He'd make the mother watch while he strangled the child if she didn't comply with his wishes. And it was such a simple request he had to make of her. She just needed to drop the investigation, let the past stay buried. He'd been watching her for days as she worked alongside her partner. They were a nuisance the way they pushed, pushed, pushed.

Well, he'd finally figured out a way to get them to stop, to force their compliance. The female detective had a weak spot, and he planned to exploit it.

That little girl.

ONE

SIX NIGHTS EARLIER...

This was a bad idea. The warnings sounded in Amanda Steele's head, but she was ignoring them, thinking only with other parts of her anatomy that shouldn't have any say. But it had been so long since she'd let herself fall into the arms of a man, and it wasn't like he was a stranger. He was comforting and familiar. He was a presence from her past, and she trusted him.

Logan was smiling as he fumbled with his key to open the front door. She wanted him to hurry before she got cold feet and changed her mind about this. As it was, she blamed her best friend, Becky Tulson, for things getting to this point. She'd filled Amanda's head with nonsense about getting back into the world of dating and had dragged her out for more girls' nights in the last three months than she'd had in the seven years prior. And that's all tonight was supposed to be—a night for the girls at Tipsy Moose Alehouse in Woodbridge. But Logan had walked in, and the rest was history, as they say.

"There." Logan smiled at her triumphantly, like he'd won an Olympic gold medal, not just claimed victory over a deadbolt. He moved in for his reward and planted a kiss on her that had her insides flushing hot in an instant and her toes curling.

It had been far too long...

Logan opened the door and gestured for her to go on ahead of him. She stepped inside. She was really doing this—spending the night with Logan. And while logic told her to call it a night and head home, she had needs. She'd also like to blame the small glass of wine she'd had for her lapse in judgment, but it had hardly been enough to make her drop her inhibitions. She missed being with a man and not just sexually, but the satisfying feeling of having a man's large arms wrapped around her, preferably ones belonging to a man who knew her. She'd dated Logan for a few months last year and their relationship hadn't progressed much further than being casual, but it had given her a small taste of what she had with her husband, Kevin, before he had died nearly seven years ago.

And why was she so wrapped up in her head right now? She deserved this indulgence. Just this once. And it was the right time. Zoe, her six-year-old daughter, was with Amanda's sister Kristen and her family all night.

She spun, and Logan was right there—their chests pressed together. He put his hands on her arms, then swept them over her body. His cologne smelled like a campfire, the scent intoxicating and earthy. She made the first move and pawed urgently at his belt buckle with one hand while she wrapped her other arm around his neck and pulled his mouth to hers.

They kissed as they slipped out of their shoes and walked through the house, pieces of clothing being tossed as they moved. His shirt went first, and he fumbled with the buttons on hers before tugging it open. Buttons ripped from the fabric and pinged to the floor.

"Hey." She drew back from him just long enough to say, "I would have you know this shirt cost me eighty bucks."

"Forgive me." He nuzzled into her neck, sending her mind into a tailspin, dizzy and euphoric.

They were about ten feet from his bedroom, and she caught the whiff of something above the notes of his cologne.

An odor she knew well.

She put her hands on Logan's chest, panting. "Just..." The rest of her words were unsaid, but she was going to say *stop*.

"What the heck is that?" Logan asked, sniffing the air, his mouth turning down in disgust.

She held up a hand to him. "Stay there."

"What is—"

"Stay." Her cop instincts were at full alert. The smell was unmistakable, and she knew it heralded death.

Blood.

She stepped into Logan's bedroom and saw a woman lying on top of the comforter, sprawled out and dressed in lingerie. There was no need to check for a pulse. Her right wrist dangled over the edge of the bed, and her face was turned toward the door. Her eyes were unseeing. At least one bullet had ripped through her chest and a pool of red stained the white silk and the bedding.

Amanda gripped the front of her shirt together to cover her chest, feeling exposed and vulnerable. *Who the hell is the woman, and what is she doing here?* She retreated from the room and ran into Logan. "Don't—"

He lunged, and she tried to stop him by holding out an arm, but he pushed through. The force of his movement jarred her shoulder and had her crying out in pain.

"Claire!" he yelled, frozen inside the doorway, looking from the bed to Amanda and back, as if torn where to go.

"You need to leave her alone and get out of that room." Her adrenaline and experience were kicking in. Amanda worked in Homicide for the Prince William County Police Department. Solving murders was what she did, but she'd never found herself in a situation like this one. Still, the basic principles applied. Touch nothing and call it in—immediately. She gathered her jeans off the hallway floor, pulled them on, and swiftly took out her cell phone from a pocket.

She called in direct to dispatch and as she made the report, she wished she'd had the common sense to listen to her intuition and go home instead of here. If only she could reverse the clock and tell Logan that their hooking up for even one night wasn't a good idea. But, no, she'd had to forge ahead, full of hormones like a teenager on prom night.

"Police units will be here in a few minutes." She made one more call before she stuffed her phone back into her pocket and did up her shirt's remaining buttons. Thankfully, only two had popped off. She looked around quickly and spotted one, which she picked up. "We should wait outside." Their presence alone could have contaminated the scene, but they could prevent more damage being done.

Logan was staring blankly at the floor.

"Logan," she prompted.

His eyes were wet when they met hers. "This can't be happening. She... she's..."

"Come on, let's go outside." She put an arm around him. "The police will figure out what happened and who did this, okay?"

He nodded so subtly it was barely perceivable.

They sat side by side on the front step. She looked over at him. He was in complete shock and pale, like he'd seen a ghost. He kept blinking, and his breathing was shallow.

She wanted to console him and offer comfort, but there was a part of her that held back. It was her job clashing with her personal inclination. But she had to protect herself too—until she figured out exactly why that woman was murdered in Logan's bed. "You knew her."

"Yeah." He rolled his bottom lip through his teeth.

"You called her Claire. Who is she?"

"My wife."

TWO

Amanda knew Logan was married, but he had told her they'd been separated for years and that he'd hired private investigators to find her—without success. "What is she doing in your house?"

"I have... no idea." His head was hung low, his knees up, elbows resting on them. His gaze was on his feet.

"That's not good enough, Logan."

He looked at her. "What do you want from me?"

"The truth. You're going to have to tell me everything because this isn't looking good." She was having a hard time balancing all the emotions she was feeling—two of which she hated, namely the twinges of betrayal and jealousy. "Were you back together?"

"No. I haven't seen her since— You know what? Never mind." He shot off the step and onto the pathway where he stood, hugging himself and periodically raking a hand through his hair.

The night was warm and humid. Except for the song of crickets, the neighborhood was quiet. It would have been a beautiful evening if not for the dead woman inside the house behind them.

Amanda got up and went to Logan, kept at a distance to give him space. Give *herself* space. "You're going to have to talk eventually. She didn't just show up that way."

"No shit." He met her gaze, his eyes cold and his jaw clenched.

Anger flushed through her. She was just trying to help him, to get a handle on the situation herself and he was pushing her away. Well, he could suit himself then. She didn't need to defend him—and why should she if he wasn't interested in doing that for himself?

Three cruisers pulled down the street, their colored strobing lights reaching her before the hum of their engines and the crackling of their tires as they rolled across the hot asphalt. Night or not, this June was one for the record books with its high temperatures. Behind the cruisers was the SUV for the PWCPD's interim Homicide sergeant.

Amanda drew a deep breath, wishing for things to return to the way they used to be before Sergeant Malone had developed a tumor in his brain. At least he was on the mend, and while she held out hope he'd come back to the post, life had taught her to never get her hopes up too high.

"Let me do the talking."

Logan waved a hand, immersed in his own world, likely tangled in thoughts, but were they of guilt and remorse or simply shock?

Sergeant Katherine Graves was the first out of the entourage. Not that Amanda was surprised. In the last few months of working with her, she'd realized the woman was proud and domineering, and the type of boss who led with fear and intimidation instead of with a firm hand balanced with compassion and understanding.

Graves headed straight for them, her stride chewing up

everything in her path. Her legs were long and slender, like the rest of her near six-foot frame. For ten thirty at night, she was dressed impeccably in a black pantsuit paired with a white collared shirt and dress boots with two-inch heels. Did the woman ever let go and relax? The only thing remotely soft about her appearance was that her dark hair was wavy and left to fall over her shoulders.

"Steele?" Just her name and a nudge of Graves's head had Amanda stepping into the driveway with the sergeant. "What are you doing here?" She crossed her arms, her face a mask of seriousness as if she were prepared to scold Amanda for her presence.

Amanda stiffened, wanting to tell this woman that what she was doing at Logan's was none of her business, but mouthing off to Graves wouldn't be the wise choice. "Logan Hunter is a friend of mine."

"And that's..." Graves looked over at Logan, who was now standing with two officers.

"Yes."

"All right then." Graves didn't voice her disapproval, but her tone and eye contact passed judgment.

"What I do in my free time is up to me." The words slipped out, and Amanda wished she could reel them back. She was defending herself, the very thing she'd just told herself wasn't necessary.

"It sure is, Detective. Unless that's committing a crime or abetting one."

Amanda bit her bottom lip, trying to quell the urge to continue defending herself while pointing out how ridiculous Graves sounded. If Amanda wasn't careful, whatever came from her mouth would be a CLM—a career-limiting move.

"Tell me what's happened here." Amanda got the sense there was more Graves wasn't saying, given how she peered into her eyes.

"As I told dispatch, there's a DB—"

"Right. *As you told dispatch.* May I remind you that as your sergeant, you should also call me?"

And there it was... the true gripe. "I knew they would have informed you."

Graves tightened her arms, testing the fabric of her suit jacket.

She must be sweating like hell!

"There may be things you got away with when Malone was in charge, but I want to be kept current. Am I understood?"

If she was asking if Amanda realized the woman had an issue relinquishing any *perceived* control, then yes, Amanda understood her perfectly.

"Detective?" she prompted.

"I heard you, and yes, I will keep you informed."

"Now that's out of the way, run me through what happened here."

"Logan and I were here for a nightcap when we found the body."

"A nightcap?" Skeptical, and Graves didn't seem to try to conceal that fact.

"Yes." As if Amanda were going to come right out with the fact that she and Logan were going to hook up.

"And how well do you know this..."

"Logan Hunter." Amanda provided his name again.

Graves gestured for Amanda to proceed.

"We've been acquainted for a year and half but haven't seen each other in several months." She would keep her answers simple and vague. Besides, she didn't know much about what had taken place here. And as much as she wanted to rush to Logan's defense, she also had her career and future to think about. Zoe's future too, as it was linked to hers.

"Friends? Lovers?"

"I'm not sure why that matters." But Amanda knew that it

very well did where a homicide investigation was concerned. "Former lovers," she eventually offered.

"Yes, well, that explains some things then." Graves flicked a finger toward Amanda's shirt, indicating the missing buttons.

Amanda resisted the urge to cross her arms in some display of modesty. She was a grown woman and if she wanted to hook up with a guy, why should she care what anyone else thought?

"And the woman inside...? Who is she?"

Amanda gave thought to how to respond. It was always best to be forthright, but no matter how she could think to spin her response, it didn't come out sounding good for Logan—or her. But it was best she stick to the truth. "She's his wife, but they are estranged."

"Huh. Doesn't seem like they are much *estranged* now, does it?" Graves didn't give Amanda a chance to respond and charged toward the house. She stopped at the doorway to say something to Officer Wyatt before going inside.

Amanda was grateful for a few seconds alone and for being obscured by shadows. She was scowling and had one hand balled into a fist at her side. Malone really couldn't get back to the job fast enough. She took a deep breath and headed to the front door.

Wyatt held up his hand to stop her. "Sorry, Detective, but I can't let you in there."

"What do you mean you can't?"

"Just following Sergeant Graves's orders." Wyatt wasn't even meeting her eye.

"You and I know each other and—"

"I'm not sure what you expect me to do. She'll have my badge."

Amanda was practically vibrating with rage. It wasn't like she was some first-day rookie who didn't understand the fragility of a crime scene. She was with the Homicide Unit.

She pivoted to join Logan, at least feeling like she might be useful there. But there was a voice inside cautioning her again. That same voice she should have listened to earlier. She had witnessed Logan's face when he saw the body; she didn't think he was the killer, but the fact remained that his wife was shot in his bedroom. And wearing very little. She needed far more information than she had before she could race to his defense in good conscience.

Another vehicle pulled to a stop in front of Logan's house, and Trent Stenson was in a half-jog coming toward her. Trent was her partner on the job. Trent was the other call Amanda had made, but she wasn't feeling so confident he'd be allowed inside either. After all, Amanda and Trent worked as a team. With Amanda blocked, Trent likely would be too, but it was worth a try...

She walked down the driveway.

"You all right?" Trent stopped in front of her.

"Yeah, I'm fine."

He angled his head. "You're tapping a foot, your hand is on your hip, and you're tense like a jungle cat."

"Graves." One word should be all it took for him to get the picture.

"Ah. She's put up the wall."

"Yep. Won't let me inside."

Trent glanced over at Logan, back at her. "This is Logan's place?" They'd met, and Trent knew they were seeing each other before.

"Yep." She realized how limited her vocabulary had suddenly become, but whatever.

A few seconds passed in silence. Maybe he didn't know what to say, as no doubt, the imagery played out in his mind.

"It's not what you think," she rushed out, hoping to stop him before his imagination got too carried away.

"Well, unless you came here for book club and the other

members are just running behind..." Trent's words disappeared to nothing.

"Fine, it is what it looks like," she hissed. "But I've got nothing to feel bad about." And here she was defending herself again, like it was some knee-jerk reaction.

Trent made a funny face that had his lips pressing together, almost as if he found her rebuttal strange. "No one says you do."

"I know that. It's just... You know what? Never mind. You're here. Go in and take a good look and update me, would you?"

"I'll see what I can do, but don't be surprised if I'm tossed out."

"Just go. Give it a try." She was so uncomfortable standing there with Trent, given that she was busted with Logan. *Busted?*

"First, tell me what I need to know."

"Logan says the woman is Claire Hunter, his wife." She paused there, giving Trent the opportunity to say something as opposed to talking over her if she'd carried on, but he said nothing. She continued. "She was shot in the bedroom, on the bed."

"What's Logan saying?"

"Not much." She could have said *nothing* for the number of useful syllables that had left his mouth since their macabre discovery.

"All right, well, I'll go in, take a look around. Hang in there."

"Yep." Apparently, that was her word of choice for the moment, but it was about all she had the energy for. She was bombarded with shock, indifference, betrayal, empathy, and on the list of conflicting emotions went.

She wanted to go to Logan, stand by his side, but her legs wouldn't move. He glanced at her, even waved her over, but she stayed put. Until she knew more, she was best to stand as neutral as Switzerland and not give her loyalty to any side.

THREE

Trent wished he'd handled things with Amanda a bit differently, offered some reassurance, said something that might make her feel better. But he didn't know Logan, beyond being aware that Amanda had dated him for a while, and as far as he knew, they'd broken things off a long time ago. Whatever the case, it would appear their relationship had heated back up. That's if her mussed-up hair and missing buttons were any indication.

He did his best to respect her privacy, but there might come a time he'd have to push a little more. That was if Sergeant Graves didn't send him back out the front door on his ass.

He slipped some plastic booties over his shoes before entering the home, striving to preserve what he could of the crime scene. He heard Graves talking and followed the sound of her voice down a hallway. He found her just inside the door of the primary bedroom, holding her cell phone to an ear. She barely passed him a glance and ended the call.

"Detective Stenson," she said coolly.

"Sarge."

"Did Steele update you on the circumstances of this discovery?"

"She did."

"Then you know that she's likely sleeping with the man who owns this house."

"I wouldn't know." And, God, he hated to think about Amanda and Logan together.

Graves angled her head as if she wasn't buying his response. "Any good detective could put two and two together here. Steele's too close to this, and by extension, so are you. I'm going to assign this investigation to Detectives Ryan and Hudson."

Some called Ryan "Cougar" around the department, a rather juvenile nickname in Trent's opinion. Hudson was a good guy and rather new to the Prince William County Police Department, but not new to the badge. Like Hudson, Graves was a transplant too, but she came from the big city of New York. Trent could understand why Graves would desire the peacefulness offered by a smaller community, but Trent had a feeling her reasons for moving stunk to high heaven.

He stepped into the room and noted the scene. Dead woman supine on a king-size bed, dressed in scanty lingerie, shot to the chest, female clothing scattered on the floor. Trent scribbled these details in his notepad. There was a nightstand next to the bed, a lamp on it. A length of its cord was coiled up on the tabletop.

He moved farther into the room, looking up at the victim from the base of the bed. Her left arm was slightly curled over her torso. She had long fingers, and there was a gold band on her ring finger. *Oh, Amanda...*

At the far end of the room, there was a window, the curtains drawn. He swept his gaze right.

Graves stepped in front of him, but she didn't block every-thing, even though she was almost as tall as him. He could see over her shoulders. A long dresser, a match to the single night-stand, dark wood, chrome hardware.

"Detective Stenson, did you hear me? This isn't your case. You're excused."

Trent was about to turn and leave when his eyes landed on the corner of the dresser. A handgun. He couldn't tell what make and model, but it was all black.

"Detective," Graves said sternly.

"Ah, yeah"—he folded his notepad shut and tucked the pen in its coils—"I'm leaving."

He led the way back out of the house, but took in the layout as he went. It was like Amanda's place, with another bedroom on the right and a bathroom. The kitchen was at the rear of the home. Moving toward the front from there was the dining room, with the hallway shooting off to the right, the living room next to the entry.

He walked slowly, deliberately, even though the sergeant was right on his heels. He saw a button on the floor, but from what he'd quickly seen of the victim's clothing, it didn't belong with her. He had a feeling he knew where it had come from, and he didn't care for how the realization had his stomach turning to lead and his chest squeezing with something resembling jealousy.

"Detective, could you move any slower?" Graves urged him.

He picked up his pace. Guess that was the problem when someone transplanted from the city to the country—they hadn't yet clued in that life didn't need to be lived as a drive-by.

He stepped outside and took a deep breath, trying to cleanse his mind of what he'd just seen and the situation. Amanda was back together with Logan. One night, dating him regularly; it made little difference. He was happy for her. Or he should be.

She was standing next to Logan, but her body language was rigid, and she kept space between them. They were with two uniformed officers, and Detectives Ryan and Hudson. They certainly got there fast enough.

Amanda turned, met his gaze, and closed her eyes slowly. Silent communication—something they had worked out, given that they'd been partners for a year and a half. In this moment, he read she was pissed by the way everything was playing out. While he understood her point of view, he also could appreciate Graves's.

He went to Amanda. "Can I talk to you a minute?"

"Yeah." She gave one look to Logan, who was watching her with these pleading eyes. "I'll be right back," she assured him, touching his forearm just before walking away.

An intimate touch...

Trent went to the end of the driveway and waited for her to catch up.

"What's going on? Ryan and Hudson have been assigned the case?" she blurted out.

He nodded, wishing he'd had the chance to break it to Amanda before they arrived.

"Crap."

"You must see that you're close to this one."

"Seriously?" She glared at him, her mouth tightening.

He hated being at odds with Amanda; her fiery temper lived up well to the stereotype assigned to redheads. But there were times he needed to stand his ground. He even thought she admired him when he did. "You must see it? You are involved with Logan, and the dead woman was his wife."

"You make it sound like we're together."

"Well, aren't you?" he fired back.

Her cheeks went a bright red.

"Even if it was only for tonight, Amanda, you and Logan have a history. But can I ask you this, do you really know him?"

"I dated him for a few months."

"Then you know everything about his relationship with his

wife? What went wrong, for instance?" He waited, but she didn't respond. Not in words, anyhow. Her body language and facial expression were saying plenty. She'd crossed her arms and her lips were pressed together, the corner of her mouth angled downward. Closed off, defensive. "And that's a no."

"Trent, just stay out of it."

"Listen, this is a mess."

"You don't think I know that? His ex-wife is in there—"

"Ex? I thought they were still married?" His mind went immediately to the gold wedding band on the woman's finger, but he couldn't bring himself to say it to Amanda just yet. Besides, she may have noticed it for herself. Why pour salt on her wound?

"They are... but he hasn't seen her in a very long time."

"How long?"

"I don't know... a few years."

"A guess then? You don't really know?"

"I just admitted that much."

"Then, how do you know what's happened here—with absolute certainty?"

"I don't, but no one does yet."

"Logan might."

"If he killed her, yeah, but he didn't."

"And you know that for sure?"

"You know what?" She threw her arms in the air. "I'm done talking." She left him standing there and returned to Logan.

The detectives were gone now, probably having entered the home to look around. A van from Crime Scene pulled up and parked, and investigators unloaded with their gear. Trent watched them, but his mind was on Amanda. What the hell sort of mess had she gotten herself mixed up in?

FOUR

Amanda hated the way Trent was looking at her—like she had done something wrong. And why should he care if she was at Logan's tonight? They worked together, and that was all. Friends too, by extension, but that was *it*. He dated people, and she had every right to do the same. And why should she feel pressured by his scrutiny about how well she knew Logan? She knew him *enough*. For whatever that meant, but it would have to do.

He'd asked about Logan's relationship with his ex. Honestly, all she knew was what he'd told her when she'd first found out he was married, and it hadn't been much. Just that he hadn't seen her in a couple of years. And that was a year ago, so it was safe to guess it had now been at least three years since Claire was in his life. But there were niggling doubts at the back of her mind because he had to have seen her more recently. Otherwise, how could she have ended up dead in his house, in such intimate attire at that? She could let most of this go, excuse it, figure there was some innocent explanation, if not for that lingerie. It was when her thoughts wandered to all that lace that she felt a prick of jealousy and betrayal. It was laughable, really, as she had no claims on Logan's affections. They were going to sleep together. One night over and done, fun for simply old-times' sake. There were no emotional entanglements or commitments made, nor did she want any.

Sergeant Graves drew her eyes over Amanda as soon as she returned to Logan's side. Amanda was determined to offer what advice she could and stand by him for as long as it remained logical to do so, but she still erected a barrier of sorts. Again, it was the missing pieces from the picture that gnawed on her.

Logan's estranged wife shows up after years, murdered in his bedroom. Did he have a motive to want her dead? After all, Amanda didn't know the details surrounding their breakup. Why did she leave him in the first place?

"When did you last see your wife, Mr. Hunter?" One of the uniformed officers had a pen poised over a notepad, ready to record Logan's response. The officer must have been tasked with completing Logan's initial statement while Ryan and Hudson were looking at the crime scene. No doubt this question would be repeated by the detectives.

"I don't know... A few years ago."

"You're not sure?" This came from Graves, the accusation alive in her voice.

"No, I... We broke up a while ago."

"Not exactly definitive," Graves said to him, her gaze briefly carrying over to Amanda.

"Fine. Four years, one month ago."

That had Amanda going cold. He could have rounded down. *Four years.* But he knew the month count. The days too, which he just didn't share? She now vaguely remembered when they'd first broached the topic of his wife that he had included the number of days. She laid a hand over her stomach. Even though he'd dated Amanda, it couldn't be ignored that he had a bit of an obsession with his wife. That didn't bode well. Had obsession blossomed to rage and revenge?

Had Claire shown up at his doorstep and Logan snapped? But that wouldn't explain the lingerie. That would suggest forgiveness and reconciliation. But where had things gone wrong?

"And this breakup... was it mutual?" Graves asked.

Logan glanced at Amanda, pain alive in his eyes, but she also saw fear—probably for good reason. Graves watched Logan as if she were hungry to catch him in a lie. Maybe it had to do with one of her detectives being entangled with the victim's estranged husband. Graves would probably want to make sure that everything was by the book and beyond reproach so there couldn't be any claims of favoritism to one of PWCPD's own. In doing so, she might be heavy-handed in her judgment.

"Officers, Sergeant Graves, Mr. Hunter may want to secure a lawyer before he says any more." She heard her advice hit her ears and could hardly believe she'd uttered those words. It wasn't something she normally encouraged.

"Detective Steele." Graves waved for her to follow. She stopped about five feet away from the group.

The woman didn't even need to open her mouth, as Amanda could have guessed what was going to spew out. But, whatever, let her expend her energy.

"It's time for you to leave."

Huh. She thought for sure she'd be in for a lecture about encouraging a suspect to seek legal counsel. "I'm not going anywhere."

"You are if you want to keep your job."

"What—?" Amanda snapped her mouth shut. Seriously, Malone couldn't return fast enough. She took a few deep breaths. "You took me off the case. Fine. Your prerogative, but I am involved one way or another. I was here, and I made the discovery."

"You are advising a suspect to lawyer up. Whose side are you on, exactly?"

"I'm on the side of justice, on the side of remaining objective and unbiased."

"Really? Then are you considering the possibility that Mr. Hunter could have killed his wife?"

The question slammed into her as a physical blow.

Graves went on. "It is also possible that he did this and then used you and your presence to aid his case."

"No. He wouldn't do that." Amanda was quick to come to Logan's defense or was it more to salve her pride? Surely if he'd killed his wife, he wouldn't drag Amanda into his mess. Or would he? Logan likely wasn't under any misconception that feelings were involved in their reconnecting. Did he see her as easy to manipulate? Had he planned to exploit her because of the perceived influence she might offer with her job?

"Your eyes give you away, Detective. Even you are starting to wonder. I need you to go home, sit tight until morning."

"Is no one going to take *my* statement?"

"Yes. In the morning. Be at the station by eight AM. We'll talk then too. But right now, you need to remove yourself from this crime scene, Detective. And that's an order."

Amanda stared the woman down, but she knew there would be no give. The sergeant had won this round.

Amanda dropped her keys in the bowl inside her entry. She had gotten out a quick goodbye to Logan and told him to call if he needed anything. She had hated leaving him there to Graves, who was eager to impress in her new position with the PWCPD. Yet even with all the woman's efforts, Amanda hadn't found reason to respect her. She had held some top post within the New York City Police Department, but so what? Surely, she'd experienced a fall from grace to bring her to Prince William County. Not that it wasn't a nice place to live, but it wouldn't come close to competing with the excitement of the city.

Amanda brewed herself a decaf coffee, to make it possible to salvage a few hours' sleep before sunrise, and settled at the kitchen peninsula with her ancient relic of a laptop. As long as it continued to power up and let her log on to the internet, it had a home.

She'd just hit enter on her Google search when there was a knock at the door. Guess intel-gathering on Graves would have to wait. She shut the lid on her computer and got up to answer.

She sure as hell hoped Graves hadn't changed her mind and wanted to talk now. She had said Amanda's statement would be taken in the morning. Saturday too, of all days. She could think of a thousand better ways to spend it other than going into the station for that purpose. Next time Becky asked her out for a girls' night, she'd opt to stay in.

She opened the door, not too fearful of who she might find on the other side, as her neighborhood was a relatively safe one. She backed up when she saw it was Trent on her doorstep. He walked in and shut the door.

"What you doing here?" She would love to put this night behind her, forget it even happened would be nicer still. Upon seeing him, she realized she hadn't even said a word to him before leaving Logan's. She was too angry to see straight. Honestly, it was amazing she had enough wherewithal to say parting words to Logan.

"I thought you might want to talk."

"Not really."

"They took him in," Trent said anyway. "Logan."

"Yeah, I figured they would. Do you know if he requested a lawyer?"

"He did. Graves is livid, by the way."

"Good for her."

"I heard you suggested the lawyer?"

"It is his constitutional right." She headed for the kitchen.

"Sure, but it's just... It's not something we usually encourage suspects to do."

"He deserves to be protected. Graves is going to come after him. Hard. All because I was there. She'll want to make sure she's really coming across as handling this by the book. *Better than* the book." She looked over a shoulder at Trent. "Want something to drink?"

"A beer would be great if you have any."

"I do." Go back a few months even, and Amanda wouldn't have had any alcohol in her house, but she had started to crave it again. She'd given it up after her husband, Kevin, and their six-year-old daughter, Lindsey, had been killed by a drunk driver. Amanda had barely walked away with her life, but she'd also found out she'd been pregnant and that child had been lost too. And due to her injuries, Amanda could never have a baby again. It was hard to believe the accident was seven years ago next month—July eighteenth. She'd been beyond devastated by all the blows, but by the grace of some good fortune, Zoe Parker had entered her life and Amanda had adopted her last year.

She grabbed two Coors Lights, their mountains blue, from the fridge.

"Thanks." Trent lifted his in a toast gesture before putting the bottle to his lips and taking a long draw.

She drank hers too, but much slower. "Want to go outside?"

"Sure." He smiled at her and in that instant, she could almost imagine him adding that it was a nice night, if a bit humid. But there was nothing *nice* about tonight at all. And Amanda had a sickening feeling that the ride to hell had just begun, like a roller coaster clicking up that first hill.

She flicked the back light on and got the patio door for them, and Trent led the way out. There was just a modest slab of concrete that served as her patio. She and Kevin had it put in the year before he died. The barbecue was practically growing rust before her eyes, but she never used the thing. It was a remnant of her past, far more Kevin's thing than hers. While she'd been forced to clear out some of his things and Lindsey's to make room for Zoe, there was still a lot around the house that spoke to her former life.

Trent set his bottle on the barbecue and grabbed two of the four gravity chairs she had folded and leaning against the house.

"Oh, what do we have here?" Trent moved toward his chair and drew back with something in the palm of his hand. "Mr. Spider." He held it toward her, possibly expecting a reaction, but she grew up with an older brother and had been put through a lot worse.

"How do you know it isn't *Mrs.* Spider?"

He smiled. "Guess it could be." He set it free on the lawn and grabbed his beer before sitting.

She dropped down, letting out a deep breath as she did. Neither of them said anything for several minutes. The night sky was clear and there was a blanket of diamonds overhead. The moon was up there somewhere, but it must have been on the other side of the house.

She sipped her beer, enjoying the flavor, surprised by how much she had missed it in the years that had passed. *Nothing like it on a hot day*, Kevin would often say. She used to agree.

"So why are you here?" She looked over at Trent, her question not intended to insult him or make him feel unwelcome, but she hadn't exactly been that nice to him at Logan's place. She could justify it, of course. Trent's questions about Logan made her uncomfortable. Not because she was shy about admitting to the rendezvous, so much as she was embarrassed that she knew so little about the man she was going to sleep with—and who she had dated.

He lowered his bottle, licked his lips. "How good of a look did you get at the scene?"

"Not a very good one. Guess you could say I was in a bit of

shock at the time." The confession pained her to admit. She'd been a cop her entire adult life, and she was thirty-seven now. She should have compartmentalizing down pat.

"Understandable."

"Yeah. Tell me what you saw. Your thoughts?"

"The scene was intimate." He stopped there as if considering her feelings.

"She was in lingerie. I know."

"I'm not saying this is the case, but was Logan back together with her?"

She hated how yet again she didn't have the answer. She shrugged and put her bottle to her lips.

He was watching her like he wanted to speak—his mouth slightly twitching. She'd save him from saying something they might both regret.

"We hadn't even seen each other for months." She leaned back in her chair, her focus once again on the sky, and there was the hope that she could just go to a galaxy far, far away, like in *Star Wars*. "Graves said that maybe Logan used me, you know to be there, when her body was found."

"To suggest his innocence?"

"Yeah."

Again, his mouth twitched.

"Go ahead. We both know what you're thinking."

"I know. You can only guess."

"Logan wouldn't use me like that."

"If"—he held up a hand—"and I'm not saying he killed that woman. But *if* he did, would he be concerned about your feelings in all this? He'd want to protect his own ass. That's all he'd be thinking about. And from the looks of things—from the surface—the murder wasn't planned. Likely more in the moment."

She was getting warmer by the second, and it wasn't because of the weather. She felt affronted by the scenario he'd just painted. "We bumped into each other at the Tipsy Moose. He couldn't have known I'd be there. And with him there, how could he have killed her?" Such a weak defense. It all depended on when Claire had died and where Logan had been at *that* time. "Let's say Logan killed her, why leave her in his bedroom in the first place? Why kill her there? Why not someplace else and/or hide her body?"

"All good questions. But then it raises another one. If Logan didn't do this, who had reason to make it look like he did?"

"You mean, why frame him?" She looked over at him, and he was facing her.

"Exactly."

She didn't have an answer for that and the only person who might was Logan, but she doubted she was going to get near him any time soon.

"I don't know exactly how to tell you this, just that I should."

"What is it?" Whatever he had to say couldn't be good, being served with that caveat. But she'd been through so much in life, it emboldened her. What news could be worse than what she'd faced years ago?

"She was still wearing a diamond on her ring finger."

"Claire was..." That had her speechless for a few seconds, but there could be an innocent explanation. Logan had made it sound like Claire left him, but maybe there was a good reason—something large at stake—and it had her ending things even though she loved him. "It doesn't necessarily mean anything." *Like they were reunited and getting back together...*

"It might not, but I wanted you to know."

She wasn't about to thank him, but she appreciated he was considering her feelings.

"Also, there was a gun on the dresser. Graves asked me to leave not long after they took Logan in, but I was around to hear that it was a SIG Sauer P320, one bullet missing from the magazine."

Amanda had nothing she wanted to say to that. Things were looking damning for Logan. But if the SIG Sauer was the murder weapon, why would the killer—Logan or someone else —leave it behind?

FIVE

It wasn't until around one in the morning that Trent went home. Amanda got in some sleep but was at PWCPD Central Station where the Homicide Unit was housed by seven fifteen. It was in Woodbridge, about a ten-minute drive from Dumfries where she lived.

Central served as one of three stations belonging to the PWCPD. The building itself was mostly a single-story redbrick structure except for one second-story office tower, sided with formed aluminum panels. It was on a country lot surrounded by trees and would have been a serene setting if not for the investigations that went on within the brick walls. Besides Homicide, there were bureaucratic offices, including the one that belonged to the police chief.

Amanda's first interest this morning was in the holding cells. "I'm here to see Logan Hunter," she said to the officer at the counter.

He said nothing at first, just stared at her blankly like she had three heads. "Detective Steele, I can't let you back to see him."

"Why not?"

"Orders from Sergeant Graves."

You've got to be kidding me! She took a few seconds to calm her temper. The woman had gone over and above this time. "She specifically said not to let me see Hunter? That was her precise order?"

"It was. I'm sorry."

"You can let me back. She doesn't need to know." She proposed defying a direct order, but desperate times and all that...

The officer, *Roberts*, based on his name tag, angled his head. "Yeah, I'm not letting you back there."

It was apparent that Graves had put the fear of God—or at least the fear of losing his job—into the officer. "All right. Guess it is what it is." She turned to leave but was struck by a thought. "Do you know if he called for a lawyer?"

"Yes, ma'am. That one there." The officer pointed to a name on the list of attorneys posted on the counter.

Peter Wilson. Amanda was familiar with him, and they'd crossed paths as recently as last fall. Peter worked with a defense firm in Woodbridge and had created quite a formidable reputation for himself as an attorney. But he didn't exactly come cheap. "Do you know when he's expected to arrive?"

The officer shook his head. "Though, I suspect this morning sometime."

"Okay. Thanks."

"Wish I could help more."

"Me too." She left. At least she knew Logan's interests should be looked after. Still, her insides were quaking with rage. It was one thing for Graves to send her home last night like she'd done something wrong, but now she was keeping Amanda away from Logan. She could understand it if she were a suspect but surely Graves didn't view *her* as a criminal? Again, it probably just came down to Graves trying to protect her ass.

Amanda went to her desk, wishing for a coffee from

Hannah's Diner. It was an independently owned and operated business, and they had the best coffee of anywhere local. She looked at the clock. 7:45 AM.

Graves had told her to be at the station for eight. That meant Amanda had fifteen minutes. Not enough time to slip out for coffee and return on time. Being late wasn't an option; she'd have to do with what they had here. And that meant brewing a pot as the Homicide Unit was currently a ghost town. Even Ryan and Hudson weren't in yet, which was surprising considering they'd be the ones taking her statement in less than fifteen minutes.

The smell of the roasted beans was just making its way to Amanda's nose from the coffee machine when Detective Natalie Ryan approached. A fancy purse was slung over her shoulder and her perfume, a floral number, was at its peak potency. *Five minutes to eight...*

"Good morning, Amanda."

"Hi." Curt, but Amanda had her guard up. She couldn't afford not to. Natalie stopped next to Amanda like she wanted to say something, her mouth opening and shutting, but she went to her cubicle without another word. It couldn't be easy to think about taking a statement from your fellow officer, but this job brought the undesirable to your face most days. You learned to live with it or changed careers.

The coffee was ready, and Amanda poured herself some in a mug that was hanging around with the words *World's Greatest Golfer* stamped on the side. It was the only remnant that remained of Detective Dennis Bishop, aka Cud, a nickname earned by his nonstop gum chewing. He'd left PWCPD a year ago this past January. Long story there.

Amanda went to her cubicle, a six-foot cell if viewed in a negative light. Each workstation had partitions on three sides that were high enough to afford some privacy, but they also made it easy enough to talk over if—and when—necessary. She dropped into her chair and stared at her monitor and tried to calm herself down. She just had to give her statement and leave. Simple. Except for being bombarded by thoughts of Logan in the cells. She couldn't just leave him to the wolves—or *wolf*, Sergeant Katherine Graves. But Amanda was probably being paranoid for no reason. Surely, Logan would be cleared of any perceived wrongdoing, the evidence exonerating him. He'd be released, Ryan and Hudson would continue the investigation into the murder, and Amanda would be free to go, pick up Zoe, and salvage what was left of the weekend. She and Trent would pick up another case on Monday.

Detective Fred Hudson walked by her space with a dip of his head, not even a verbal greeting. She and him hadn't exactly had a chance to bond, but he was normally friendlier than that. *All business*, she supposed, but that gave her a bad feeling. After all, the only reason he had to be that way was if she was suspected of something. Then maybe he was just playing the role expected of him. Just as she was guarded, he needed to be.

She drank her entire coffee before Fred and Natalie sidled up outside her cubicle and said, "Ready?"

She was *ready* to get this the hell over with and get on with her life.

They were taking her statement in a small conference room. She sat at one end of the table and Natalie and Fred sat on each side of her.

"This will be recorded." Fred nudged his head to indicate the video camera in the corner and clicked the record button on a remote.

It seemed over-the-top considering who she was, but she said, "Wouldn't expect otherwise."

"Right then." Fred opened a folder and clicked a pen.

Natalie wasn't looking at her.

Again, a bad feeling.

"How do you know Logan Hunter?" Fred asked.

"We met last year." She would do her best to keep every-thing succinct and on point. No allowance for detours and rambling. She had a feeling she was being treated as a suspect, which she didn't like one freaking bit.

"Where was that?"

"I met him at the Tipsy Moose Alehouse in Woodbridge."

"And since then how would you describe your relationship with him?"

Amanda's mind went back in time, how there wasn't supposed to be any sort of relationship between her and Logan. He had been a one-night stand, and that's all he was ever supposed to be. But life had other plans, and they had dated for a while. They'd been separated for months though.

"Detective?" Fred prompted.

"We started dating." There was no way she'd be sharing her initial indiscretion. Those in the department were quick about assigning nicknames and showed no mercy. Take Cougar here, for example. She was mid-forties, single, with an inclination toward men about half her age. What a cop did in their off time was never truly off the clock.

"How long did you date?"

"A couple of months."

"Why did you break up?"

"He didn't like the risks I faced with the job." She'd leave it there without noting how she had other priorities weighing on her. Her heart was claimed by a little girl who needed a home—and she took precedence.

"I see. And while you were dating, did he tell you about his wife, Claire Hunter?"

"He mentioned her." Technically, Logan mentioned Claire before he and Amanda started dating. Though her discovery of his marriage through a background check had prompted the conversation.

"What did he say?"

"Just that they were separated, and he didn't know where she was."

"Do you know a Deb Smith?"

"Ah, no." Her brows furrowed. Confused. "Who is that?"

"She was the dead woman in Mr. Hunter's bed."

"No. It was his wife, Claire."

"Yeah, that's what he's telling us too. Swearing by it, in fact. But ID from her wallet tells us her name was Deb Smith."

That made no sense, but she hesitated to say as much out loud. She'd rather discuss this with Logan directly. Maybe he was mistaken about who the dead woman had been. It had been years since he'd seen his wife. But could he really forget what she looked like? Then again, Fred had just said Logan was adamant it was Claire.

"Why don't you walk us through what happened last night... you know, from your perspective," Fred said.

She did just that, not that there was a lot to tell. She left out the parts about her and Logan's urgent rush to the bedroom.

"And she was just lying there when you walked into the room?" Natalie asked, her first time speaking during this interview.

"That's right. I told Logan we had to get outside, call it in."

"And that's what he did? He didn't touch anything?" Fred had his pen poised over the page.

"That's right." She was almost leery to say as much even though it was the truth, as if her words would be twisted and used against her somehow.

"He went nowhere near the gun that you saw?"

"The gun?" She'd play stupid.

Fred smirked and scribbled something down. "What was Mr. Hunter's reaction to the scene?"

"Genuine shock." She hadn't missed that Fred ignored her question.

"*Genuine*," Fred parroted, his focus on his notepad as he wrote more.

He fired additional questions at her. When did she and Logan connect last night? Where? When? How? These were followed by ones more focused on Logan's character. An hour and a half after entering the room, Fred closed his folder.

"Cop to cop, I'm going to tell you that things aren't looking good for your friend," Fred disclosed. "There was a SIG Sauer P320 left on the dresser. Logan has already confirmed it is his gun. Registration records back up his claim."

Tingles spread across the back of her neck, down her arms. "And when did he say this?"

"When we asked if he owned one."

"Before he requested a lawyer?"

"Of course."

"So you manipulated things. What did you do... ask him in a conversational manner? Stress how important it was he be honest with you?"

"We didn't *manipulate* anything," Fred said, "but the situation seems pretty damning against your friend."

Situation... It hardly seemed strong enough a word. "You said her ID was Deb Smith. Any connection between Logan and a woman of that name?"

"Yeah. She was found dead in his bed," Fred volleyed back, his gaze hardened.

This investigation was feeling pigeonholed, with everyone already pointing their finger at Logan. "You can't just take some circumstantial evidence and run with it. You need to build a case."

"Believe me, we've got one."

"I would need to hear more to believe that," she snapped.

"What more is there? His gun, his bed, dead woman in it. His prints are going to be all over the weapon."

"Possibly, but it is his gun. That would make sense. But

maybe... Now just entertain the possibility that someone is trying to frame him."

Fred groaned. "I can understand you'd want to believe the best about this guy but, Amanda, you need to see it from our perspective—"

"Yours or Sergeant Graves's?" She wished she could backpedal that one. Both detectives' faces fell. Amanda toyed with the collar of her shirt, dropped her hand when she realized what she was doing. "I see the importance of handling this case by the book. A PWCPD detective was on scene, and there can't be any media speculation of playing favorites, but Logan Hunter shouldn't have to pay for my being at his home."

"Amanda," Natalie said gently, "even if you weren't there, this would be where we are with the investigation. Mr. Hunter's gun, a woman he claims is his estranged wife. There's likely motive. He also doesn't have an alibi for the time of her death."

Amanda sat there, taking in all that Natalie had just said. Surely there had to be some mistake, something they were missing. She swallowed roughly. *Think*, she coached herself. All this emphasis being placed on Logan's gun... "Has Mr. Hunter's gun been confirmed as the murder weapon?"

"The vic was shot with a nine mil. Same as Hunter's SIG Sauer, *that was on scene*." Fred put special emphasis on the latter bit.

"Sounds convenient, but that doesn't mean that it was the one used to kill her."

"Just a matter of time before ballistics confirm." Fred glanced at Natalie, and the glint in his eyes and the set of his mouth pissed Amanda off even more.

"You are rather confident, but I'm interested in solid evidence. I haven't heard any yet. Cop instinct and common sense are telling me that." She didn't care if she offended either of them. Let Fred and Natalie take her words as they wished. She went on. "There hasn't even been an autopsy conducted yet. The round that killed her might not have come from Hunter's gun."

"If it's not that one, it may be the one we found in her purse," Natalie said, though she didn't sound committed to her words. She added, "I'm sorry."

"The one that you... There was a gun found in her purse?"

"That's right."

"So two guns on scene?" Her heart was pounding.

"Uh-huh," Fred responded, as if she was some sort of idiot for not knowing. But why would she?

"What caliber of bullet in it?" she countered.

"Nine mil, but don't make too much out of it."

"Don't make—" She snapped her mouth shut, took a few calming breaths. "So both Hunter's gun and one found on the vic were loaded with nine mil ammo. How can you be so certain the bullet that killed her came from Hunter's gun? No autopsy, no ballistics," she repeated. "Wow, Detective Hudson, you must be some sort of all-powerful, all-knowing being."

"No bullets were missing from her gun," Fred said coolly.

"Huh, so case closed then. You really don't find it strange that there were two guns, and Hunter's was left in the open for us to find. Down one bullet, no less." She didn't even know what she saw in that, but it raised questions. If the woman had a gun, why hadn't she returned fire? Did she not have a chance to defend herself?

"Oh, Amanda," Natalie murmured, but Amanda ignored her and continued.

"You have a dead woman who is ID'd by sight as Claire Hunter, but by license, Deb Smith."

"Yes, I think we've been through this." Fred sighed.

"Was the gun in her purse registered? If it is, that could confirm her ID."

"Nope."

"All right, and you don't see an issue with any of this? It's not raising any flags?"

"None. And we're done here." Fred stood and left the room.

Natalie stayed put, and Amanda leveled her gaze at her. "You see it, right? Something more complex took place?"

Natalie pursed her painted lips and tugged on the gold chain she always wore around her neck, sliding her fingers along it. "Sergeant Graves is pushing us to press murder charges against Logan Hunter. I'm not sure what else you expect Fred and I to do."

"I expect you to do your job, Natalie. For frick's sake." Amanda jumped up and pushed her chair into the table so hard it tipped back.

SIX

Amanda went straight to Malone's office—at least that's how she'd always see it. These days it had been invaded by Graves. She was in, as Amanda had expected, probably there to make sure her minions were playing their part and doing her bidding. And Graves had said last night she wanted to speak with her this morning.

Amanda rapped her knuckles on the window in the door, and Graves signaled for her to enter.

"Go ahead and sit." Graves gestured toward the chair opposite her desk.

Good morning to you too... Amanda wanted to steamroll ahead, but she'd learned a long time ago to let the superiors talk first.

"I take it you've finished giving your statement to Hudson and Ryan?"

"Yep."

"They may have told you"—Graves clasped her hands on her desk, leaning slightly forward—"but murder charges are going to be brought against Mr. Hunter."

The fact they were going ahead with charges was news—

and ludicrous. "Without factual evidence," she muttered, unable to bite her tongue. If this was how Graves ran her department, Amanda wasn't sure she even wanted to be a part of it.

A small smile, more predatory in style. "Really? I would have expected more of you."

The feeling was entirely mutual, but Amanda tamped down a sharp response. She pulled from the patience and tolerance she got from her mother. "Maybe I should have said they didn't share any *factual* evidence with me. Would you be so kind as to do so?"

Graves listed off exactly what she'd just heard from Hudson and Ryan. Nothing *factual* about any of it.

"When is the autopsy scheduled on... Ms. Smith?" She'd use the name on the ID.

"You don't need to concern yourself with that, Detective Steele, as it's not your case."

"Sure, but Logan Hunter is still an acquaintance of mine."

"Huh, I would have pegged your relationship as much more than that."

Amanda took a beat and let the sergeant's remark roll off her. "Sure, we're friends, and because of that I know he didn't kill that woman." The declaration was out, and while she'd been leery to take sides so adamantly last night, she felt sure that there was something hinky with this case. She certainly didn't agree with the way it was being handled. The two guns, the different ID when Logan swore it was Claire... the unclear motive. None of it was being questioned.

"We like to think we know the people we are sleeping with. Trust me, I understand."

Amanda wasn't about to touch on the sergeant's *I understand*. "Why are you so set against Mr. Hunter?"

"I assure you it's nothing personal at all. I'm looking at the evidence, and with you being so close to the situation it would make sense if you can't see clearly."

"I can see perfectly." Her redheaded temper was at the boiling point now. "I want to take this case."

"No way is that going to happen. You should just be happy that I didn't have you brought in last night too."

Wow. Amanda took a few deep breaths. Nothing would be accomplished by verbally attacking Graves like a raving lunatic. "I went to talk to him this morning. You told the officers not to let me."

"That's right. You can't be jeopardizing this case, Steele. It's abhorrent enough that you suggested a suspect request a lawyer."

"You made your stand on that clear last night."

"Perhaps not clear enough. If you ever recommend a suspect lawyer up again, you'll be turning in your badge." Graves held eye contact and then shuffled some paperwork in front of her. "That's all."

Amanda got up and left. She was steaming mad. Threatened with losing her job twice in less than twelve hours. First, if she didn't leave Logan's at Graves's request last night, and now if she ever suggested a suspect get a lawyer again. Where the hell did the woman get off? But she couldn't keep Amanda from Logan forever, and she wasn't without recourse. She could go right to the top and appeal to Chief Buchanan, but she would prefer to hear more of what Logan had to say before she did that. There were oddities in this case, and they couldn't be ignored.

The ID was the burning mystery in Amanda's mind. If the dead woman was Logan's wife, which Amanda believed she was, that meant the ID was a fake. But why had she needed it? Logan had mentioned that the private investigators he'd hired to find her had failed at every turn. It was like she hadn't wanted to be found. And why would that be? Had she been running from something—*someone*—that had finally caught up with her?

Amanda went back to her cubicle when she should have gone to her sister's to pick up Zoe. But there was no way she could relax knowing what Logan was up against.

She googled Claire Hunter, keeping off the police database. Graves could see who her detectives pulled backgrounds on, and Amanda supposed if she were desperate enough, she could track search history too. Oh well, she'd take the risk.

No results.

Amanda keyed in *Deb Smith*. Nada.

Two women, possibly the same one, with no online presence. It was curious in the least. These days it took effort to exist without any online presence, and those who did usually had their reasons. Were Claire's nefarious ones? Or did she want to be invisible because she was hiding from someone? Could fear explain her departure from Logan's life? Who *was* Claire Hunter? And was it her secrets that got her killed?

There was a shadow in the opening of her cubicle. Amanda looked up to see Natalie.

"Mr. Hunter's lawyer has requested a meeting with you and his client."

Amanda got off the internet, flicked her monitor off, and stood. "Lead the way."

Natalie did just that and took Amanda to the same conference room in which she'd given her statement. Natalie got the door and shut it behind Amanda, staying outside in the hall.

"Amanda, thank God." Logan let out a deep breath and raked a hand through his hair. He got to his feet and hugged her. She let him and put her arms around him too. She didn't want their embrace to end because when it did, she knew the nightmarish reality would return with a thud. Still, it couldn't be put off forever. She stepped back and looked at him.

He had dark shadows under his eyes, and they were blood-shot. She'd guess he hadn't slept that well, if at all, last night.

Peter Wilson, the lawyer, dipped his head at her. "Detective Steele."

"Hello."

Logan returned to the table where he'd been sitting when Amanda arrived, and she sat across from him. She wanted to claim some independent space to help her stay objective. Though at the rate the investigation was progressing, she felt she was the only one with any interest in doing so.

"Tell me what they're saying," Amanda said to Peter.

"They've laid charges of murder in the third degree."

"I didn't do this, Mandy, I swear I didn't." Logan's eyes were wide and wet.

She wanted to tell him she knew that, but she couldn't. Not just yet. "What's the evidence against him?" She put the question to the lawyer.

"His gun, which they believe is the murder weapon, but it's loose at best."

Amanda nodded. "Yes, I get that. Autopsy has yet to take place, as has ballistics testing."

"That's right. They don't know for certain that Logan's gun was used to kill her."

"I'm sure you can fight that."

"Oh, I will be. As you know we'll appear before a judge, but given that it's Saturday, not until Monday."

"I have to stay here, locked up, until then?" Logan's eyes widened.

Her heart ached for him. Until he saw a judge, a holding cell was his destination. Even the lab would be delayed processing the ballistics with it being the weekend. The timing of this was utter crap for Logan—and the integrity of the investigation. Assuming Logan wasn't the killer, that person was out there running around free and clear. "I understand there were two guns found. Logan's and one in the victim's purse." She assumed that this had been shared with him and his attorney already and didn't think she was crossing any line.

"That's right."

"And both nine mil, making either a possible match to the round in her chest?"

Logan sniffled, and Amanda realized how hard it must be for him to hear her talk about his wife's death so bluntly.

"Not just the same caliber, but the same ammo," Peter said.

Amanda inched forward on her chair. If things didn't sound off before, they certainly did now. What were the chances both guns were loaded with the same bullets? At least they were different makes and models. Once they retrieved fragments from the body, ballistics testing should be able to confirm which weapon was a match. Still, there had to be a message in two guns found on scene with the same ammo. When she didn't speak, Peter spoke again.

"The ammo was Logan's too."

What the hell?

"I'm guessing they aren't sharing much with you?"

"I'm pretty much in the dark. Do you know time of death?"

"Initial findings peg it between the hours of six and nine PM yesterday."

Amanda looked at Logan. It had been after nine when they'd run into each other at the bar and about ten when they'd arrived at his house. She looked at Logan. "And you don't have an alibi? I was told that," she added.

"I was at home getting ready to go out around six. By the time I had a shower and a bite to eat it was seven thirty."

Her stomach knotted into concrete. That meant whoever had killed Claire, running with the assumption it wasn't Logan, did it between seven thirty and nine. "Where did you go at seven thirty? Anywhere someone could verify?"

"I drove around until about nine—sometimes I do that to clear my mind—and ended up at the bar. That's when we bumped into each other."

"You see how that doesn't look good?" Peter said.

She leaned back in her chair. Logan was up the proverbial creek. "Okay, we'll figure something out."

"I didn't kill her. You do believe me?"

"I want to, Logan."

He looked up at the ceiling, back to her. "That hurts. You know me."

"I do, but I need to know more about everything. For one, they're saying it was a woman named Deb Smith, not Claire."

Logan met her gaze, a flash of anger briefly sparking light in his eyes. "It was Claire. I know my wife."

Amanda considered how to put her next words as delicately as possible. "It's been a while since you saw her..."

He scoffed. "You don't think I would recognize my own wife?"

"I never said that."

"Amanda, that woman was Claire Hunter."

"Why did she have ID that said Deb Smith?" she countered.

Logan flailed his arms in the air. "No freaking clue. Your guess is as good as mine."

He was obviously angry and frustrated, and she couldn't blame him on either count. "Why would she have a gun?"

"Again, I have no idea. Look, all I know is that my wife is dead, and I didn't kill her. Are you going to help me?"

Seeing the desperation scoring his features Amanda was hurled into the past when a serial killer had taken Logan hostage and she'd found him. He was as terrified now as he'd been then. "Where do you keep your gun and ammo?" If Logan didn't shoot the woman, and someone was trying to frame him, the next question would be how did they know where to get his weapon and ammo?

"In my bedroom closet, top shelf."

Somewhere easy enough for anyone determined to find. Still, she asked, "Anyone else know that?"

He shook his head. "It's never been a topic of conversation."

"Do you keep your SIG in a gun box?"

"Yes."

"And it's always locked?"

This is where Logan hesitated and glanced at his lawyer.

"It's not," Peter answered on Logan's behalf. "That's one element working in our defense. Easy picking."

Amanda wanted to grasp onto the lawyer's optimism. Hopefully, it would cast enough doubt for a judge to find charges of murder against Logan dismissible. But the scenario of a random killer happening upon Logan's gun—in his bedroom closet, no less—would be a tough sale. Tag on the victim being his estranged wife, and it would be near impossible. "And where do you keep your ammo?"

"In the open next to the gun box."

Every time someone opened their mouth, Logan was damned further.

"Are you going to help me, Amanda, or am I on my own here?" Logan was searching her eyes.

"You have Peter."

Logan angled his head, prompting her for some sort of assurance that she had his back.

She wanted to help him, but without full access to all the facts she wasn't sure how she could. "I want to, but there's more I need to know."

"Whatever it is."

She was stonewalled by Graves, and that put forensics findings out of her reach, but Amanda could look at motive.

"Tell me about Claire and your marriage, how it ended, all of it."

"I'll give you the short version. Claire and I met through a dating app. Her best friend and a friend of mine had the same hare-brained idea to set up accounts for us and then dared us to go on a date."

"When was this?" she asked.

"I was thirty. I'm thirty-seven now. So seven years ago. Thereabouts."

"And that was here in Prince William County?"

"Yeah, Dumfries specifically. She's from there originally, and so am I."

It was embarrassing that Amanda hadn't known that much. It was also surprising that they hadn't met when they were younger.

He went on. "Anyway, we thought the night was going to be an epic disaster, but we hit it off. We fell hard."

It was strange for Amanda to hear Logan talk like this because the man she knew was much more guarded. That may be due to Claire.

Logan continued. "We got married about three months after we met."

"Three months?"

"I was a little more impulsive when I was younger. Anyway, pretty much right after we got married, Claire got this job offer in Nebraska."

"What did she do?"

"She procured artwork for the wealthy—paintings, sculpture, all kinds of things—and she was great at it too. Someone up there supposedly wanted her full time to help build their collection."

Amanda nodded, not sure what response she'd expected, but it hadn't been that one.

"Claire went on ahead of me, while I sorted out our affairs

here. Then, I followed about a week later. We were happy there for two-and-a-half years. Then she was gone. Just like that." He snapped his fingers.

"No letter or anything? No sign of what went wrong?"

"A letter, yes. But it was more for her than me."

"What did it say?" Amanda inched forward on her chair.

"The gist? She wasn't the woman I thought she was, and that she was sorry to hurt me this way."

"You didn't hold on to this letter, did you?"

"Wishing I had, but I was pissed off at the time. I tossed it into the fireplace and watched the ashes fly."

There went a possible clue—literally up in smoke. Amanda let the words from Claire's letter sink in and slumped back. *Wasn't the woman he thought she was.* Assumed ID, carried around an unregistered firearm, nonexistent online. It would seem she certainly had things to hide.

Logan went on. "And it gets better. The client she supposedly carted us across the country for didn't even exist. After Claire disappeared, I looked him up and got nowhere. One PI found a man with that name sometime later, but he'd never seen or heard of Claire."

"Huh." Add that tidbit to the list of the unexplained when it came to Claire.

"I was speechless at the time too."

"She must have made money somehow or you would have noticed, right? I assume she contributed to the household income."

"She did, but we held separate accounts."

"She obviously had secrets she wanted to hide. Do you have any idea what they might have been?"

"Nope. I still haven't figured them out, and it's not like I haven't given it a lot of thought over the years."

She imagined he would have been borderline obsessed. In his place, she would be. "Do you think she was afraid of something... someone?" It could explain Claire's lack of an online presence as it had occurred to her before.

He shook his head. "If she was, it's not like she said anything to me about it."

"So she left, and then you...?"

"I packed up and moved back to Dumfries, thinking I'd visit our old haunts and see if I could find her. No luck at all. And now, she... *she* turns up dead in my house." Logan let out a deep sigh.

None of what he was saying added up to him killing her. Why had she upped and left Logan when she had? Assuming her past transgression took place before her relationship with him, what had changed or spooked her? Something had to have triggered her not long after marrying Logan. That's when she first lied about a rich man who wanted her as his private curator, necessitating a move across the country. "Anything happen that you can recall around the time she brought up the move to Nebraska?"

"No."

"What about when she left? Did you notice any changes in her?"

Logan gave it obvious thought, then said, "Well the timing sucked because I had been in a car accident the week before. I was in a cast, and it was a bitch trying to take care of myself. It certainly would have been easier if she'd stuck around."

Pile on the mystery. Could that tie into Claire's running or was it merely coincidental? "Tell me about the accident."

"Was just driving along and needed to slow for a bend in the road. The brakes failed, and I ended up flipping in a ditch. Claire was freaked out about that."

Was it just because her husband could have died or was there more to it? "Sounds like you were lucky to walk away."

"I guess. But things happen. I just took her concern as being because she loved me, and the accident had her worried about the what ifs. Not that any of that would explain her leaving."

Had it simply been a matter of the accident happening? It seemed oddly coincidental that Claire chose then to leave. And that note about her not being the woman he thought... Did Claire see Logan's accident as a message? Running with the assumption she was carrying a secret and hiding offline from someone, did she think they'd found her? If so, who was this person? Why were they after Claire? And had they gone for Logan? Then again, maybe Amanda was so desperate to see Logan as innocent of Claire's murder, she was inventing conspiracy theories.

"You're going to help, right, Amanda?" Logan asked her.

"I'll do what I can." That was the most she could promise.

"The detectives aren't listening to me. Neither is your boss. That Graves lady. All of them have convicted me already, and honestly, I don't have faith that the evidence won't be twisted to meet their agenda."

Amanda hated she agreed with him on that point. She glanced at the lawyer who had mostly remained witness to her conversation with Logan.

"We're both on your side," Peter said to Logan, who kept his gaze locked on her.

"Just let Claire's sister know, would you? I don't think those detectives have. They're all caught up with this Deb Smith ID."

"Her sister live in town?" Amanda asked.

"She does. Her name's Michelle. Maxwell is her married name; Ramsey was her and Claire's maiden name."

"And their parents?" she asked.

"The father's in prison, and the mom's dead. Murdered by the father."

"Wow." Amanda exhaled.

"Yeah, her life was crap growing up. She was only sixteen when it happened."

Amanda witnessed firsthand the emotional roller coaster that Zoe was on having lost both her parents to murder, and the girl had just turned six years old the month before it had happened. Also, the person responsible for their deaths had been a stranger. Claire had been a teenager, old enough to understand the finality of death, and her mother had been taken out by Claire's own flesh and blood. That had to have messed with the young woman's mind. But how much did it affect her life choices, and did this loss factor in to why she was killed?

SEVEN

Her mom and dad were screaming at each other when she left. She cupped her hands over her ears—anything to try drowning out their voices and the nasty words they hurled at each other. There would be no retracting what was said. The damage was done and continued to be inflicted. Every time they got into these moods, which was happening more often lately, it was best to get out of their way. When her father tipped the bottle, it transformed him into another man. He wasn't the soft-spoken son of a farmer anymore. He became a belligerent know-it-all who demanded everything go his way.

Her older sister had her own life going on. Michelle hung out with the "tough" kids, down on the footbridge in the woods, smoking weed, but that wasn't something that appealed to her. She liked peace and quiet and reading, but her parents never gave her money for books. And she'd read everything she was interested in from the small library in town—twice over.

She grabbed her bicycle from where it leaned against the mobile home and pedaled as fast and hard as she could. Eventually the sound of her parents fighting faded, then disappeared in the afternoon air.

The silver lining to the day was there wasn't a cloud in the sky. She took herself to the closest bookstore and set her bike in the stand out front. She gave herself a quick once-over and was satisfied she looked presentable enough. Her faded blue jeans were tattered at the knees, but they were clean and her T-shirt, having been yet another of many hand-me-downs from her sister, fit her snuggly, hugging her curves in a complementary way. She'd developed young and was always told she looked older than sixteen. She did what she could to wield that to her advantage.

A handsome man, about her father's age—ancient—got the door for her and smiled. It was an innocent expression, though, the way it softened his face and smoothed the fine lines around his eyes. He wasn't a perv like so many men were toward her. It was a rare day she could walk down the street without being subjected to hollers and honking horns.

She went to her favorite section of the store. Fantasy. Worlds existed within these covers, born from an author's mind, just far enough from reality to provide a real escape. And when she read, that's exactly what she wanted. To leave her life and slip into another one.

She touched the spines of a few, her fingers drawing out one by Paul J. Bennett. His was a new name to her, but she was attracted to the cover—a woman in armor. Strong female leads were a must. And the series name, Power Ascending, sent a bit of a thrill through her. She read the blurb and, intrigued by it, opened the book and scanned the first few pages. She wanted to read the entire thing, but she hadn't a dime to her name.

She looked down the aisle to her left. A man was browsing the shelves, absorbed in his own cares. He pulled out a few books and read their back covers but always seemed to replace them. To her right was no one.

She hugged the novel to her chest and rounded the bend. She would be leaving the store with this book one way or another.

And since paying for it wasn't an option, she'd be stealing it. She'd done it before and gotten away with it, but would she again?

Her heart pounded just thinking about the rush that came with the thought.

Usually she brought her backpack with her and expertly slipped her intended quarry inside. She'd done it three times already. But today, she'd wanted out of that house so badly she hadn't even thought about her bag. And her attire didn't exactly allow for much concealment. She had to consider the cameras that were likely all over the place too. Even if she tucked the book under her shirt, she'd be busted in an instant. And if not from the video surveillance, then a suspicious clerk who might notice a strange bulge under her snug shirt.

The man who had been browsing rounded the corner and smiled at her as he passed her. He was cute. Dimples so deep she could press her fingertip into them.

And she wasn't even the boy-crazy one. That had always been Michelle.

Enough. She needed to figure out her escape. She looked back at the man. He must have settled on a few titles as he was holding a cloth shopping bag that sat heavy, the load pulling down on the handles.

Then came the spark of an idea.

She followed him through the store, careful to keep at a distance until they neared the checkout. She busied herself looking at the myriads of journals and cloth bags branded with the store's logo by the front door. But she was more interested in keeping a close eye on the man.

Just as he was thanking the clerk, she toppled the journal display and did so in such a way that got the man involved with the mess. The scattered items blocked his path.

He bent to help her tidy up, and she was certain to look him in the eye. "Thank you so much." She tucked a strand of hair behind an ear.

"Not a problem."

"Really, I'm such a bumbling idiot." She bit her bottom lip. Threw in a pout. She might be young, but she knew how the world worked already—money and sex equaled power.

"No problem," he stressed, smiling and flashing those dimples. He was flattered she was interested in him; her plan was working.

The clerk joined them in cleaning up too, and with them both distracted she slid her book into a new bag and continued to return items to the rack.

The clerk was just happy that the shelves were restored to their former glory and returned to her post. The man held the door for her on the way out.

She held her prize—the coveted book in a new bag—as she rode her bike for the nearest park. She had her reading spot picked out. It was her favorite place near the Potomac River, under the shade of a willow tree. She settled there, her back against the trunk, and cracked open the cover.

"Is it any good?" A man's voice, and it had her turning around.

The man from the bookstore. She shot to her feet. "It's not what it... It isn't what it looks like." She nudged out her chin defiantly.

"Quite the impressive stunt you pulled back there."

She scowled. "I don't know what you're talking about."

"Yes, you do. You stole that." He pointed to the book she held; her finger was inserted between the pages so as not to lose her spot.

"I did no such thing."

He smiled, his blasted dimples showing again.

"So what if I did? What are you going to do about it? You a cop or something?"

He laughed, and her heart skipped off rhythm at the sound. She'd had her share of crushes, but this one felt different. He was older than her, by at least five years. He'd be experienced and know how to treat her, how to touch her. She warmed as her thoughts took a sexual turn. She hadn't even been with a boy yet. Nothing past third base anyway. This guy could be the one.

"So you're not a cop." She rushed now to fill the growing silence.

"No way. Anything but. You and I, though... we could make a good team."

He looked her right in the eye, and it had her cheeks growing warm. It also prompted other reactions in her body that she hadn't experienced before. And it was like he could see right through her, like he knew the effect he was having on her and was wielding it to his advantage. He had to be working an angle. She stiffened. "I don't even know who you are."

"My first mistake." He held out his hand toward her. "Nick Clayton."

"Claire Ramsey." His hand was strong and warm, and she felt firecrackers ignite when they touched. But his touch had been brief, and she was left to wonder if she'd imagined it.

"Beautiful name."

"Thanks." She could feel her cheeks growing a brighter red and cursed her immaturity. Michelle wouldn't flush; she knew how to handle boys. But Nick, he was all man to Claire.

"You know you could really make a lot of money with the skills you have... under the right guidance."

"You're trying to tell me I could become—what?—a professional thief?" The thought of that was both thrilling and shocking.

"Why not? You have the skills as I mentioned, and you have the looks. If you put your mind to it, I'm sure you could get a hold of whatever you wanted."

Whatever I want... That sounded freaking amazing! It

certainly didn't sum up her life currently, which was more a living nightmare. Tiptoeing around her parents, desiring to be seen and heard, and feeling worthless no matter how hard she tried in school. Needing to steal books because she didn't have a few bucks in her pocket.

"What do you say? Want to get to know each other better?" He showcased his dimples again, and her legs went weak.

"You really think I could have whatever I wanted?" She was afraid to trust and to believe that she had that type of power.

"I do."

She smiled at him.

They spent the afternoon talking, getting to know one another, and by the time they parted ways, the seed of hope for a bright future had been planted in Claire's mind.

But it wasn't to last long.

She returned home, just as the sun was sinking in the sky. Police cruisers were out front of her home, their lights strobing.

She wanted to race ahead and find out what was going on, but fear froze her. She hopped off the bike and nestled up close to a tree, watching as her father was led out of the front door cuffed and fed into the back of a police car.

"It was an accident, I swear," her father yelled out. It seemed for anyone who would bother to listen.

Her heart was pounding and thundering in her ears. She was having a hard time catching a full breath.

A hand on her shoulder had her spinning around—Michelle. Claire let go of her bike. The chain clinked as the pedals slammed against the ground and carried loudly in the early evening air. Police officers looked over and saw her and Michelle and started walking toward them.

There was nothing that could have prepared her for the news coming her way or how her life would change that day. Maybe if she had known that was the last time that she'd see her mother alive, she would have stayed, tried something different. Done her *part to intervene and save her. But then there was also the possibility she would be dead too.*

There were two options in front of her: burrow in her grief and live in the past, or lean forward.

Nick just may have been a guardian angel sent to save her.

EIGHT

Amanda had heard enough. The case felt like an out-of-control vehicle with Logan in its headlights. Her phone rang, and she saw it was her sister Kristen. "Hey, everything good with Zoe?"

"That's one way of answering the phone. But, yes, she's fine. How are you this fine Saturday morning?" Kristen was obviously high on life, but there were rarely times when she wasn't.

"Things could be better."

"Oh. That doesn't sound good."

"It's not." Amanda didn't really want to get into the fact that a man she used to see was being charged with murder. *Really, why go there...?*

"Anything I can do to help?"

"Are you okay to keep Zoe for longer?"

"Sure, no problem." Curiosity was nestled in her sister's voice, but Amanda wasn't about to satisfy it.

"Thanks. Could I talk to her for a minute?"

"One second." Her sister's rings clicked against the mike in her phone, and then came a slightly muffled, "Zoe!"

A few moments later, "Mandy?" It was Zoe, little beam of light.

"Hey, sweetie. How are you? Are you having fun?"

"*Yeeaaah.*" She dragged it out like it was a no-brainer. She was with Ava, Kristen's teenage daughter, and one of Zoe's favorite people on the planet.

"I may be a little later getting to you. Is that going to be all right?" If this girl told her no, Amanda would leave that minute.

"We're playing Barbies."

So that's a yes, she'll be fine. "All right, good. You have lots of fun, and later I'll take you to dinner at Petey's Patties." It was Zoe's favorite burger joint.

"Sweet." That was followed by a chuckle, and the most tender, "Loveyoubye." Three words rushed together like they were one.

"You get that? *Swweeeeeet?*" It was Kristen back on the line, and she was laughing.

"I got it. All is under control."

"Yes, it is. Call if you need anything else. Love ya." With that her sister hung up without even waiting for a response. Typical Kristen.

Under control... She was deluding herself. Those two words alluded to confidence, but they were a badge of denial. Nothing was under control—ever. She'd told Logan she'd do what she could to help him, but her hands were rather tied. Graves had seen to that. There were two options, and neither was pleasant: one, sleuth around; two, go to the top and speak to Chief Buchanan. And if she wanted anything she discovered to hold up in court, to be of help to Logan, she had to go about this the legitimate route. Even if it wouldn't be a particularly pleasant path to take.

And it was Saturday. The police chief was likely enjoying the day on a patio somewhere or out on a golf course. And how could she expect a favorable response when she'd be going over her superior's head *and* doing so while invading the chief's personal time? It probably wasn't the fastest track to his good side.

She dropped into her desk chair and flicked the monitor on again. This time she googled the name Claire Ramsey. That netted results and a Facebook profile. It wasn't locked from public view, but it hadn't been active for about seven years—around the time Logan and Claire first met. Claire would have been twenty-nine, though she looked like she could be younger than that.

Her profile picture showed a pretty woman with brown hair and long bangs—the same style and looks as the woman in Logan's bed. The last post was a picture of her with Logan. She was kissing his cheek, and he was smiling. The expression reached his eyes, only confirming how he had felt for her. How he might *still* possibly feel.

There was no way he killed her.

Amanda had to help everyone else see that too.

This is a bad idea. The thought ricocheted around Amanda's head. She'd thought the same thing last night when she went to Logan's. She should have listened to that little voice inside her. But like then—and *like an idiot*—she was ignoring it again.

She knocked on Chief Buchanan's front door. He had a nice two-story brick house in Woodbridge, which he shared with his wife, and apparently a yappy little dog. Its high-pitched barks —*yap, yap, yap*—rang out like heavy artillery fire, as did its sharp little claws that ticked against the back of the door.

Buchanan didn't need a doorbell with that fur ball on duty.

The sound of a woman's voice carried over the animal. Then it stopped. All went quiet. The door cracked open to a woman with a slight build, on the shorter side, with a pleasant demeanor. She was holding onto a Pomeranian—all eight pounds of him if it weighed that much—aka *the security system*.

"Sorry to bother you on a Saturday," Amanda said. "Mrs. Buchanan?" She had yet to meet her and was certain showing up at the woman's home would make one hell of an impression.

"That's me."

"I'm Amanda Steele. I work for the PWCPD in Homicide, as a detective."

"Holly. Nice to meet you."

"Thanks. And who's this?" Amanda held out a hand toward the dog, but it lunged for her, his jaw snapping.

"Bad, Frufru." Holly tapped its nose. "You'll have to excuse him. He doesn't like people that much. Come in." She backed up to let Amanda inside.

Maybe he was bitter about his name. Poor dog. "Thanks again. I appreciate your understanding."

"I learned a long time ago that a cop's hours aren't set, no matter how far up the ranks one climbs." She smiled kindly at Amanda. "If you want to follow me, Jeff's out back."

"I hope I'm not disturbing anything."

"He's just drinking a beer and reading a biography."

Amanda's steps slowed. She had hesitated to interrupt the chief's Saturday, and now that it sounded so low-key and peaceful, she really should have listened to her instinct. But how could she not come when her inaction might seal Logan's fate? It was feeling like she was the only way he'd get a shot at a fair investigation.

"Here you go." Holly gestured toward a patio door, through which Amanda could see that Buchanan was seated under an umbrella, legs crossed, a thick hardcover in his lap, a beer bottle on the table next to him. "Go on," Holly prompted.

Amanda dipped her head and slid the door open and stepped outside. She really should have left well enough alone. At least until Monday.

Buchanan looked up, an irritated grimace on his face, but it quickly transformed to confusion. "Detective Steele?"

"Yeah, it's me. Sorry to disturb you." She waved toward his book and the setup he had going. It looked relaxing, and their yard was a haven with neatly cut grass, a flagstone firepit area in the back, and flower beds bursting with color on all sides.

"Nonsense. It must be important to have you coming here. Go ahead. Sit." He snatched a bookmark off the table next to him and stuck it into his book. "What is it?"

She dropped into the chair next to his, and her gaze went to his beer bottle, dabbled with condensation.

"Oh, how rude of me," he said. "Would you like one?"

"No, that's... I'm fine. I was just thinking again how sorry I am to be barging in here. You have a nice place." She rushed out the latter bit hoping her flattery, though sincere, would cover her transgression of coming here.

"Thanks. So what is it you need?" Buchanan had been hospitable, but it seemed that his patience had reached its limit.

"I'm not sure if you heard about the murder in Dumfries last night. A woman was found in the residence of a Logan Hunter." She'd phrased everything with professional detachment.

"I heard. Also heard you were there." He lifted his sunglasses to rest on his head and squinted in the bright sun.

"I was. Mr. Hunter is a friend of mine. He was brought in under suspicion, and this morning was charged with murder."

"I'm sorry to hear that. It can't be easy being close to the situation."

His response silenced her for a few seconds. He would have heard about her past, surely. How her mother had murdered a man. How Amanda had still done her job and turned her in. Had he responded as he had to throw her off balance? She'd have to choose her next words carefully. It wouldn't do her any favors to point an accusatory finger at a fellow brother in blue without proof. And while she hoped she could trust Buchanan, he was a fairly new presence around PWCPD. But if she was going to help Logan, she might need to cross the line a bit... "There are factors in the investigation which are suspect."

"What are you saying?" His voice went deeper. Shadows darkened his face.

"In my opinion, the evidence against Hunter is circumstantial at best."

"I heard the murder weapon was left on scene. It was his gun."

Graves certainly hadn't wasted any time filling in the police chief. "There were two guns," she rushed out, then cleared her throat.

His features, normally relaxed, tightened. "What are you saying, Detective?"

"It hasn't been confirmed as the murder weapon, sir." She stiffened, feeling uncomfortable under his gaze, but if she was reading him right, his anger wasn't directed at her. She wondered if he'd heard of the second gun.

"Huh."

"I'm taking it you heard something different?" She was probably pushing things too far, taking advantage of the liberties he was already extending her by simply hearing her out and giving her an audience.

"What is it you're here to ask?" His tone was all business, and he was unmistakably ticked off—at her, Graves, the interruption to his weekend? All of it?

"This case has been assigned to Detectives Ryan and Hudson," she began.

"Yes. You have a connection to the suspect, thereby creating a conflict of interest."

"If looked at one way, but I haven't seen Logan for months. Haven't even kept in contact."

He didn't say anything.

She continued. "We just ran into each other at the Tipsy Moose Alehouse in Woodbridge last night."

"Uh-huh, I know the place."

He wasn't going to make this easy... "Well, one thing led to another, and we decided to go back to his place."

"And that's when you found this woman shot in his bed?"

"That's right."

"And you're sure he didn't arrange the entire thing to make it look like he was innocent?"

It sounded like he was reading a book Graves had written. "I believe he *is* innocent." There was the lack of an alibi and Logan's gun, but to her they were all that was working against him. The unknown, the unanswered questions raised by anomalies in the case, supported Logan's claim of innocence.

"It's natural to want to believe in those close to us."

"As I said, Hunter and I aren't close." She halted at the flicker dancing across his eyes. How she must look—about to sleep with a man she didn't consider herself close to. She'd stick to the business at hand. If she was going to get anywhere with Buchanan, she needed to share some enigmas. "Claire Hunter was the victim, though ID in her purse said she was Deb Smith."

"All right. Not sure where you're going with this."

"Logan's quite certain the woman was his wife, Claire Hunter. Well, she and Logan had a complicated history." She shared how Claire had uprooted from Dumfries to Nebraska for a fictional job, only to disappear two-and-a-half years later, after Logan had an accident that could have killed him. She also filled him in on Logan's return to Dumfries and that he'd hired private investigators. She summed up with, "And now you have an ID saying one thing, while Mr. Hunter positively identifies her as his wife. There was a note she left Mr. Hunter back in Nebraska about not being the woman he thought she was. To me, this sounds like a woman with a past to hide. Then there's the unregistered gun in her purse, which coincidentally was loaded with the same ammo as Mr. Hunter's gun." She bit back the urge to add, *That's a stretch on its own.*

"Okay," Buchanan eventually said. "But what brought her to Logan's house? If they weren't in contact at all, how did she even know where it was? You said that Mr. Hunter returned to Dumfries, did he buy the house he'd shared briefly with his wife?"

Amanda hadn't even thought to ask about that, but she'd guess if it had been the case Logan would have said as much. In the least if someone was trying to frame Logan, that person knew where he lived. "That's a good question, and I don't have the answer."

She let silence fall between them, but all was not quiet. Birdsong filled the air, along with the nattering of squirrels close by.

"I want this investigation, sir," she said, cutting through nature's symphony.

"You are close to the situation."

The way he said it now, she sensed there was some wiggle room. "I know Logan Hunter, yes, but I also don't have tunnel vision about the case. I can see there's a lot more here than what first meets the eye. The autopsy hasn't even been conducted, and he's been charged? We want to close cases, but we want them to stay shut. And, honestly, I think the real killer is still out there, and who knows what his or her plans are now? Claire may have been their only target, but maybe someone else is in danger? And even if her murder was a single, isolated incident, she deserves justice. So does Logan Hunter." Her little speech flowed with ease, and she hoped grace.

Buchanan's mouth twitched, a trait she'd observed gave him away as being deep in thought.

"It took a lot for me to come here, to ask this of you," she said. "The only reason I did is because there are too many unanswered questions. I want the answers. It's our job as the police to get them." Talking to him for this length of time had apparently emboldened her.

"I appreciate your forthrightness, Steele, and I admire your courage."

She sensed a *but* was coming and felt a cold dread run through her.

"But at the same time, it's important that I'm able to trust the people who work under me."

Her chest tightened. "You can trust me. I assure you." She didn't want to pull out mention of her father, former police chief for the PWCPD, but she would if it would help.

"I feel I can trust you, Detective."

With those words, she could breathe again.

He went on. "But what I've been told by others about this case doesn't completely line up with what you're saying."

Tight ball... right in her chest. She didn't like Graves, but her intention here wasn't to steamroll her. "I'm sure whatever you were told was said with good intentions."

"Not necessarily sure about that. Some are very concerned with how things look, not how they actually are." He paused and sipped his beer, stared across the lawn for a few seconds. "If I requested that Sergeant Graves assign you this case, would you be able to remain objective?"

She'd been asked that question so many times in her career —would likely hear it again. Small towns... Suppose the odds were in favor of stumbling across a person she knew during a murder investigation. "I would."

"See, I thought you'd say that, and I believe you"—he tipped the top of the bottle toward her—"not because that's what you're telling me, but because I've seen you in action. I know you've been put in unpleasant personal situations before that tested your resolve to the badge."

"I have been." At least two instances came to mind. The

first had been eighteen months ago, give or take, when her mother had admitted to murdering a man. Amanda could have tried to hide it, but she'd been there to turn her mother in. Then in March, she had solved an investigation involving a former friend whose wife was murdered.

Buchanan set his bottle back on the table and steepled his fingers. "Leave this with me. Hunter won't go before a judge any sooner than Monday."

"He won't, but he's in the cells. Isn't there anything we can do?"

"Unfortunately, not yet. I need to talk to Sergeant Graves and do some thinking. I trust you will accept that." Delivered dry and matter-of-fact. His decision wasn't open for debate. She'd pushed this as far as she could.

"Thank you." She got up and could have left it there, but she couldn't help but ask, "When do you think you'll have made a decision?"

"By Monday, latest."

In case she had any question about the finality of his resolve, him putting his sunglasses back over his eyes signaled their conversation was over. She saw herself out, going through a side gate to the front. What the heck was she supposed to do now? Her hands were tied any way she looked at it. Even as she thought of Logan and his pleas, pictured him trapped in a jail cell, there was nothing she could do. She couldn't even take care of his wish to inform Claire's sister about her murder. Amanda's mind was screaming for her to back up from that cliff, and this time she was going to listen. After all, what if the woman didn't turn out to be Claire Hunter but someone else altogether? And what if Logan had killed her? Then Amanda's career would be over, and she'd have no one else but herself to blame.

NINE

Amanda had no choice but to pick up Zoe and leave the case alone. She didn't want to jeopardize the investigation in any way. Notifying Claire's sister was out, as was tracking down her father in prison. A visit to him might provide insight into Claire's past, but she didn't even know his full name, never mind where he was serving time. Finding that out would require running a report, which Graves could track, and then would the father even speak to Amanda or offer anything helpful to the current investigation? Regardless, for now, she was done. It was the respectful decision. After all, Buchanan had asked her to wait until Monday. She should just put the murder and Logan out of her mind and spend time with Zoe and other members of her family.

She pulled away from the Buchanans' house, planning to drive to Kristen's. Her phone rang. Becky.

"So, did you get laid?"

"I wish."

"Oh no, what happened? Everything seemed to be going so well between you."

To answer Becky's question right now would suck too much

energy, and even though Becky was a police officer with the Dumfries Police Department, Claire's murder was an open investigation as far as Amanda was concerned. "Possibly another time."

"Possibly? I'm your best friend."

"I'll tell you, just not now. Have a great weekend, Beck. We'll talk next week."

"I'll hold you to it."

Amanda hung up, wishing there was a workaround to her predicament. A way to do something productive to help Logan, but she had to be smart about things too. Little good it would do him, or her, or Zoe, if Amanda lost her job. Then they'd all be up that proverbial creek.

She drove to Kristen's, only feeling a little guilt at the thought of Logan in a cell. His being there wasn't her fault. And she was doing whatever she could to help him. Right now that meant doing nothing.

She pulled into her sister's driveway and went through the front door, after knocking softly and calling out, "Kristen!"

Footsteps pounded throughout the house—on the main level and second story. From the sound of it only one set was coming her way.

It was her sister Kristen and, as always, she looked flawless. Amanda couldn't remember catching her looking bad once—well, maybe *once* when she was down with a bad cold.

"Wow. I didn't expect to see you for hours," Kristen said.

"Change of plans."

Kristen smiled. "I like it. Have time to sit out back, soak up the sun?"

"Sure. Why not?" Amanda smiled, but she was curious why Zoe hadn't come to say hello. Kids really grew up too quickly, and maybe it was already happening. Amanda being home wasn't the huge highlight it used to be. *Bummer.*

"Want anything to drink? I'm having iced tea, and I just made a big jug. I can get you a glass..."

"Sounds good." There were still steps moving overhead, some Amanda would swear belonged to Zoe. None came toward the stairs. "I'm just going to go check on her." Amanda made a move to do just that, but Kristen caught Amanda's arm on a back swing. Amanda turned. "What?"

"Just let her have some space. Trust me. She gets to be Ava's age, and you'll be happy she's grown up to be independent. You don't want Zoe to become clingy, do you?"

Yes... "No, of course not."

Kristen smiled. "I know it's hard to let go, but it's best for everyone." She got a large glass pitcher from the fridge that was mostly full of iced tea, slices of orange and lemon floating on top. Kristen poured a glass for Amanda and topped up her own.

They went out back and settled on the patio. They talked about a myriad of things and nothing at all. Kristen's husband, Erik, was golfing with friends, and she had been enjoying the peace of the yard.

Kristen let out a long, deep sigh, and looked up at the sun and the cloudless sky. "What a beaut today."

"It is." Amanda had her sunglasses on, but it was so bright, it was possible to forget they were there. She might look into getting darker lenses.

"So what changed? First you were going to be late, and now you're here and it's just after lunch."

That reminded Amanda's stomach it needed food. A loud rumble.

"Oh, someone hasn't eaten." Kristen laughed.

Amanda smiled. "That obvious, eh?"

"You can help yourself to leftover hot dogs in the fridge. Buns are on the counter." Kristen spoke and pointed toward the house.

"I'm good for now."

"Not from the sound of that stomach. You need a muffler for that thing."

"Very funny." With all the talk of food, Amanda was starving, but she was also comfortable sitting there with her sister. It was familiar. It was safe. It was free of conflict. She could almost forget what else was going on in her life.

"So, Mandy, what changed? You're here sooner than I expected." Kristen looked over at her, peering into Amanda's eyes like a skilled therapist.

"Last night just didn't go according to plan."

"I kind of picked up on that given our earlier phone call."

"Yeah..." Amanda would love to leave it there, one word dangling until the end of time.

"It was really that bad?" Kristen took a sip of her drink and licked her lips. If Amanda were anyone else, she might be fooled by her sister's cavalier approach, but she was dying for information.

"You probably wouldn't believe me if I told you."

"Try me."

Amanda drank some of her iced tea, for a distraction and a delay—and *damn* this stuff was delicious. The perfect balance of sweet and tangy. "I went out with Becky."

"I know that much." Kristen was getting impatient now.

"Fine, I'll skip ahead to the shitty parts. I ran into an old boyfriend, we headed back to his place—"

"Oh..." Kristen shuffled up straighter in her chair. "An old boyfriend? I didn't even know you saw anyone after Kevin."

"I had no reason to tell you." Just like her sister had no clue Amanda went through a time when one-night stands were a regular occurrence, as if falling into the arms of a stranger could fix a broken heart. In hindsight, it was more like Amanda was punishing herself, judging herself unworthy of love. After all, God or the universe saw fit to strip her of her husband and her daughter.

"Amanda," Kristen prompted, a grin on her face.

"It was nothing. Very casual, and it only lasted a few months."

"A *few* months? When was this?"

"We broke up not long after I met Zoe, so last September."

"Why did you split?"

Her sister, the head of the great inquisition. "Things fall apart sometimes. It was mutual."

"But last night you went back to his place and... dot-dot-dot?" Kristen bobbed her eyebrows, the terminology a tribute to the movie *Mamma Mia!* Her sister had probably watched the film a hundred and one times.

"Not exactly." Amanda gulped back more iced tea. She was hoping that her sister would relinquish her interrogation, shoot off in another direction. And was it too much to hope for Zoe to come outside now and completely throw the direction of the conversation? Her sister wouldn't accept a rain check on this conversation the way Becky had complied. Amanda would just stick to the bare basics and not trespass into territory that would violate the confidentiality of the case. After what felt like minutes of silence, Amanda eventually said, "There was a dead woman in his bed." Best to get it out fast, and hearing it hit her ears it almost sounded like she'd made it up.

"A dead woman?" her sister parroted. "For real? What the f—"

"Mandy!" Zoe shot across the patio and hugged Amanda. She hadn't even heard the patio door open and close.

"Hey, sweetie." Amanda swept the girl's blond hair back. "You having fun with Ava and your aunt Kristen?"

Zoe stood in front of Amanda. "Ah, yeah. Always."

Amanda could imagine her adding *duh* to that in a few years. "Tell me what you've been doing."

Zoe rolled her eyes in dramatic fashion. "Too, too much to say." And with that she was gone, running back inside.

Yep, they grow up too quickly, Amanda thought.

"All right, talk to me." Kristen leaned forward, her iced tea forgotten on the table. "Who was this woman?"

"This is between us?" A pact made between sisters was a strong one.

"Of course."

"She was his wife, but it's not like it sounds," she hurried out at the widening of her sister's eyes.

"Still though..." Kristen pulled back and gave Amanda this sharp glare that was so their mother. It impaled the receiver of said look with a spike of guilt.

"They've been separated for years."

"If you say so."

Amanda's back tightened. "I do."

"You trust this guy?"

"Yes. And I like to think I'm a pretty good judge of character."

"That might be, but how do you explain his estranged wife showing up dead in his bed? And how did she die? I mean, did she have a heart attack or...?"

Amanda shook her head, not about to disclose too much.

"Was she murdered?"

Amanda sipped her iced tea.

"Oh." Kristen's mouth widened into an O just like her eyes. "She was."

"He didn't do it, but he was arrested for it."

"Are you sure he didn't? There may be things you don't know about."

Amanda supposed that was possible, but she still found it near impossible to see Logan as a killer—and to murder Claire? Amanda could see he still loved her, and honestly that hurt a bit. Like she was just realizing that she was competing with a memory since she'd met Logan, and now she was up against a ghost. But Amanda could appreciate the bond that was made when two people exchanged nuptials. There was none like it. She supposed Logan faced the same challenge when it came to Kevin.

"You heard what I said?" Kristen asked, and Amanda nodded.

Her mind was too full of thoughts to say anything coherent. Foremost was the replay of Kristen's words, *There may be things you don't know about.*

TEN

Amanda's weekend passed in a blur that included a lot of family, but that was fine by her. It was like she was making up for the time she lost when she'd pulled back from them after losing Kevin and Lindsey. Amanda had four younger sisters and one older brother. And of her five siblings only the two youngest didn't have kids of their own.

On Monday morning though, she was up and ready to go. She was even armed with a coffee from Hannah's Diner. She brought in one for Trent too and threw in a glazed donut.

She was setting both on his desk when he came in. "Thought you might like a morning dose of sugar."

"Oh, tell me it's chocolate." Trent peered eagerly at her offerings.

"Next time." She went to her cubicle, practically slinking away. Somehow coming face to face with him, her trip to the chief's house came hurtling back with intense clarity. She'd done what she felt she needed to do, but Trent was her partner and there could be repercussions that affected him. It just all depended on how the next few hours panned out. She had a feeling that she'd know Buchanan's decision sooner rather than later.

The phone on her desk rang, and she answered. Sergeant Graves, requesting that Amanda join her in her office.

"I'll be right there," Amanda said and hung up.

The knot in her stomach didn't necessarily mean bad news was coming... right? She swallowed roughly and informed Trent that she was going to see Graves.

"Happy Monday." He lifted his cup in a toast gesture.

"Yep. Lucky me." She probably should confess about her trip to the chief, just to prepare him in case he caught flak for it too. But she was out of time.

She headed down the hall, bringing her coffee, clutching it to her as if it could give her courage to stand her ground with Graves. She didn't want to give true consideration to losing her job. Sure, she'd survive financially. The house was paid off, and there was money in her account from Kevin's life insurance to keep her and Zoe going for a while until she found a new job, and it wasn't like her family would ever let them go without. In addition to that, Zoe's parents, who had been murdered, had left their sizable fortune to Zoe, including an allowance to assist her guardian should they die while she was a minor. They'd be fine. Maybe if Amanda repeated it enough times, she'd believe it. But what the hell would she do if she didn't get up and don the badge in the morning? Heck, it was so much more than an accessory to her wardrobe; it was a part of her. It gave her purpose.

Graves's door was open, but Amanda rapped her knuckles on the frame.

Graves waved her in without looking up. "Close the door behind you."

Amanda did that and dropped into the chair across from the sergeant.

"There's been a development," Graves started, looking at

Amanda for the first time since she entered the woman's office. "First, I want you to know that your friend Logan Hunter is going in front of a judge today. The charges against him stand."

A wave of nausea flushed through her. "On what grounds?" Somehow, she found her voice.

Graves straightened her posture and clamped her hands together. The picture of prim and proper—and defensive. "As you may know, the autopsy on the victim was conducted on Saturday. Bullet fragments were pulled from the victim. One round, but the ammunition caliber *and* manufacturer match what was loaded in Hunter's gun."

"From my understanding, there were two guns that were loaded with the same ammo."

"Huh. I see you've been keeping yourself in the loop even though this isn't your case."

Isn't... Had the chief decided to leave things with Hudson and Ryan?

"Only one was missing a bullet," Graves hissed.

Amanda literally bit her bottom lip to refrain from pointing out the oddity that both guns—including one in the victim's purse—were loaded with identical ammo. But why waste her breath?

Graves went on. "Let me be crystal clear. There was no sign of forced entry. There are prints on Hunter's gun belonging to him and Claire. They must have had a struggle over getting control of the weapon. Hunter won."

Just one more thing working against Logan. When would the hits stop coming? Or was she being blind to the situation and Logan had killed Claire? The absence of a third set of prints, ones belonging to the true killer, was explicable. He or she had worn gloves.

"Maybe you're not so convinced of his innocence anymore yourself." Graves scanned Amanda's face.

Amanda peacocked her stance. "I believe there are too

many anomalies that need to be explained if the investigation is to be conducted fairly."

Graves angled her head. "And what's that supposed to mean exactly?"

"I appreciate that you must consider the reputation of this department, of your detectives. I was on scene so there can't be anything that hints at any favoritism, but an innocent man shouldn't have to pay the price."

Graves smiled, her lips in a thin strip, making Amanda think of a reptile. "So you're sitting there, essentially accusing me of lining up the evidence against Hunter, while you are doing the exact same thing—just you are stubbornly convinced he's innocent. Even when the evidence is indicating otherwise."

Amanda tightened her grip on her cup, and the plastic lid popped up. She reset it. "There are unanswered questions, and everything seems too... perfect."

"Now you've lost me."

"I've worked a lot of homicide cases, and rarely is everything as it appears. And that's the case here."

"Without even giving you a reaction to your insinuation—that I'm some inexperienced rookie—you're suggesting Hunter was set up to take the fall?"

"Why not?" Amanda volleyed back.

"Why would anyone do that? *Who* would?"

"I don't know yet, but that's what a thorough investigation would reveal."

"So you have time to burn following assumptions? A deep desire to prove yourself right and everyone else wrong?" Graves sat back in her chair and swiveled.

"It has nothing to do with that. Do you even know the victim's true identity yet?" It was taking all her self-control not to lash out at Graves.

"Deb Smith."

"That's what her license said. Sure. But that's not who she's been physically ID'd as. That would be Claire Hunter."

"Says the man who killed her."

Amanda opened her mouth, shut it, her temper flaring. She took a moment to calm down before speaking. "Why would he lie about that? And let's say it was a woman named Deb Smith, what was her relationship to Logan Hunter?"

"Do you need it spelled out for you, Detective? She was shot in his bed, wearing lingerie."

Amanda was ready to throw something or hit someone, but she went inward and talked herself back from the ledge.

Silence passed between them for several minutes before Graves spoke.

"I can see that you feel quite strongly about this case," she said, stalling there as if she expected Amanda to interject something. When Amanda didn't, Graves went on. "We have a strong enough case against Hunter, but I'd rather have you on our side than see you stand up for the defense. I'm not interested in seeing this department take the hit for that."

Amanda met her gaze but remained quiet. She had a good feeling and didn't want to jinx it.

"With that said, I'm reassigning this investigation to you and Detective Stenson, *but*"—Graves gestured toward her—"you need to keep me in the loop along the way. We'll discuss and approach this as a team."

Amanda found it interesting how Graves made it sound like this was her idea, after accusing Amanda mere minutes ago of following assumptions that would waste department time. But whatever allowed her to keep her pride was fine with Amanda, as long as she got the case. She tried not to smile too broadly. "You won't regret this."

"Make sure I don't."

"In the meantime, though, what about Hunter?"

"As I said, there is evidence against him. Things will proceed with his hearing before a judge."

That niggled at Amanda, but surely Logan's lawyer would see him released until trial. And they had time to turn things around well before then. "Have Detectives Ryan and Hudson been informed of your decision?"

There was a flicker in Graves's eyes, as if she'd picked up on the *your* decision part and how Amanda had given her credit. "They have been. Now, what are your next intended steps? I'm assuming you already have some lined up in your head."

"We need to confirm the victim's identity once and for all." Not that Amanda doubted for one second she was Claire Hunter.

"Good idea. How do you intend to do that?"

She'd have next of kin confirm identity—Claire's sister. But there was another route she was willing to share with Graves. "Has the gun in the vic's purse been sent for ballistics testing?"

"I'm not sure why we would do that. She was the victim."

"Uh-huh, but that victim has secrets any way I look at it. Her unregistered gun alone tells me that much. Why was it in her possession? Is it connected to a previous crime?" The ID that was most likely fake told Amanda that was quite possible.

Graves nodded, though subtly, and there was an energy Amanda sensed coming from her, like she wished she'd thought of that. "It is curious."

Wow, she gave me an inch! "I'd like to get that gun tested. Not just for ballistics, also for prints."

"I'll approve that."

Amanda went on. "Was the victim's phone recovered?"

"No."

"Really? There wasn't one in her purse or the pockets of her discarded clothing?" There wouldn't be room to hide anything in the lacy number she was wearing.

"Nope."

"That would help us, but Claire Hunter has a sister, who lives in Dumfries. I think we should serve notification and have her go to the morgue to see if she can identify the body."

"Fine."

"Trent and I will also need to bring ourselves up to speed on all the evidence that was logged: crime scene photos, autopsy findings, officer interviews with Logan's neighbors, any forensics. Then we'll go from there."

"All approved. Get to it."

Amanda walked out of the office feeling taller than when she'd arrived there. Then it had been a bravado that she'd put on, but now she felt it deep inside. She and Trent were free to work the case. Hopefully, Amanda could plug the holes in this investigation—of which there were many. If she didn't, she had the feeling Graves would be far too happy to see her downfall.

ELEVEN

"Hope you're happy, Steele, when you're left to admit your boyfriend's a killer," Fred said as he brushed past Amanda with Natalie. She'd just reached her cubicle, and the detective's words had Trent popping his head over the divider.

"What's he talking about?"

She went into Trent's cubicle. "The Hunter case has been reassigned to us."

"It... Really? How did that happen?"

"Let's not get weighed down with that."

"I think we should. Last I knew we weren't allowed near the investigation, and now it's ours. And what's up with Hudson?"

"The murder charge against Logan is still proceeding."

"Now I'm really lost. The case is closed, but we're working it anyway?"

She counted to three in her head. Did she set off into a tirade, listing off all the things that didn't line up with the so-called evidence? She'd save that—for now. It was time to come clean about her visit to the police chief. "I went to Chief Buchanan and requested the case."

"You went over Graves's head?" Trent let out a low whistle. "That takes balls."

"Whatever, Trent. Logan wasn't receiving a fair shot. It was like they'd pegged him as guilty and shut out everything else."

"Everything else being what?"

"The woman's sudden emergence, two guns on scene— loaded with Logan's ammo. Then there's the fact Logan's SIG has his *and* Claire's prints on it. As if to suggest a struggle for control of the gun. And if Logan was clever enough to get me there to find her body, why would he be that stupid with the gun? Also, there's the discrepancy with her name. They haven't bothered to dig into any of this. They ran with what they saw, face value, and Logan could go to prison for life because of incompetence." She panted for breath, frustrated, angry.

Trent said nothing for a few beats. "All right, so what do you suggest we do first?"

She ran through it as she had with Graves and told him they had to get the victim's gun tested for ballistics and prints. She took the time to make that request immediately and made a quick phone call to the crime lab. She was put right through to crime scene investigator Emma Blair, one of the senior investigators, who said she'd make sure that happened.

She hung up, and Trent was watching her. "I suggest our initial steps need to be familiarizing ourselves with the autopsy report and the crime scene," she said. "Also what the canvassing officers in Logan's neighborhood might have found."

"Good idea."

They started with a quick look at the officers' notes, but nothing struck as immediately useful.

She ended up wheeling her chair beside Trent's when they'd finished with them. He brought up the autopsy findings compiled by Hans Rideout, one of Amanda's favorite medical examiners from the Office of the Chief Medical Examiner in

Manassas. Cause of death was as expected. Gunshot wound direct to the heart. Death would have been instant.

"The heart," Trent mumbled. "Whenever that happens, I wonder if the killer is sending a message. Is it indicative of a romantic relationship between them and the victim?"

"I think it's possible to read too much into it. A shot to the heart is also a surefire way to successfully kill someone quick."

"True enough, but look at this." Trent pointed at the screen. "This is interesting. The victim's lymphatic system was full of cancer. Rideout noted that if it wasn't the bullet, cancer would have killed her soon."

"Wow." Amanda let that news sink in. Running with the victim being Claire Hunter, was it her terminal diagnosis that had her returning to Dumfries after all these years? She shared her thinking with Trent. "She may have wanted to see Logan and make amends."

"Possible, but just a guess. Her being in Logan's house, or even back in Dumfries, doesn't confirm for me that Claire was going for any sort of soul-cleansing or reconciliation. And she might not have known about the cancer."

"I suppose you're right."

"I love it when you say that." Trent gave her a bright smile that touched his eyes. Then he turned to the monitor. "Rideout didn't note any signs of self-defense or epithelium under her nails, nothing like that. No sign of intercourse either. But there was a contusion on her forehead. Based on its coloration, Rideout noted it would have happened right around time of death. It's unclear whether she was hit with an object or fist."

"Okay, she was struck, but who gets hit and doesn't fight back?" Her mind went to the latest news—Claire's prints on Logan's gun along with his. Had there been a struggle for the gun, after all? "I don't recall the crime scene showing anything to indicate a struggle. You? You were there longer."

"No."

"So what? She was hit in surprise and possibly knocked out from the blow? Where was Claire struck?"

"Her temple."

"Hit there hard enough, and it's possible she might have passed out. Bring up the photos of the crime scene."

Trent did as she asked. They shuffled through photo after photo.

Amanda sat back in her chair. She was hunting for something to prove her suspicion—that Logan was set up. Nothing was standing out until— A photo snapped from the end of the room, looking toward the bed's headboard and the nightstand. The woman's clothing could be seen in a heap on the floor. *One large heap.* "Look at that," she said pointing it out.

"What about it?"

"If she took the time to put on lingerie, is she going to leave her street clothes lying around like that? Why not put them somewhere out of sight?"

"Might not mean anything."

"And it might. The evidence against Logan is too convenient—his house, his wife, his gun, his ammo. What if the killer also dressed Claire in the lingerie?"

"Not sure how we'd go about proving that."

"All right..." She had it straight in her head; it was just talking about such things with Trent that was uncomfortable. "Let's say that Logan and Claire were reunited. Years had passed, but they still had feelings for each other. Hence, she was wearing her ring. But things between them would be heated. They've just been reunited, sparks are flying, clothes are being ripped off in a trail to the bedroom." Her cheeks heated as her words struck close to her own truth—the way Friday night was headed before the dead woman.

"I can sort of get what you're saying." He was peering into her eyes, and she shifted uncomfortably. "Now, you might not want to hear this, but maybe Logan is lying, and they've been together for a while. They already did the whole 'rip the clothes off' thing. The night she was shot, maybe they took their time, made it romantic."

If her cheeks burned any hotter, they might catch fire. Giving his counter-argument credit would blow up her theory but she wasn't ready to relinquish her grip on it yet. "Maybe there isn't proof, then, basing it on lingerie, *but* it still seems odd she'd be dressed that way. It's indicative of a romantic evening, but then Logan shoots her? Why?"

"A man's pride can be a fragile thing. Claire would have deeply hurt Logan. Let's say she returns, and they reconcile. His hurt is still festering beneath the surface..."

"No, I'm not seeing that. I believe the killer staged things to make it look like a romantic liaison. They gave the police what they wanted them to see—a domestic affair that turned dark." She pointed to the screen, anything to direct Trent's focus off her. His gaze eventually broke from hers and followed the direction of her finger. "I think the killer did a good job."

"I'm not saying you're wrong, but you want to know what stood out to me at the scene?"

"You know I do."

He moved through a few photos and zoomed in on the nightstand. "See that?"

"The lamp cord?"

"Yes."

"What about it?"

"This might mean nothing, but look at how it's bunched on the tabletop. Why? I tuck mine behind the table, so the top is clear."

"Huh. I see what you mean."

"But there could have been a struggle, and the lamp was responsible for the bruise on the vic's head. Though, I suppose it could have been anything, even the butt of a gun."

She looked closer at the photo and picked up on something else of interest. "Huh. Usually that lamp has a shade."

"I wondered about that when I saw the lamp at the scene but dismissed it. Sometimes they get damaged."

"As I said, it normally has one. Used to anyway. We'll need to ask Logan to know for sure."

"The killer took it then. But why?" Trent bunched up his face.

"One reason I can think of—maybe they feared leaving trace on it. Maybe Claire used it to defend herself. She wielded the lamp as a weapon..."

"We need to get that lamp tested for prints and DNA."

"Agreed."

"Take us to the evidence log. Maybe it was done already."

Trent brought up the list and scrolled through. He shook his head a few minutes later. "Doesn't look like that was done."

"We'll make sure it happens. Go back to her personal effects. I just know about the gun in her purse and the fact she didn't have a phone."

"That latter bit is more than I knew. Let's see here... Designer jeans, a collared silk shirt, and black boots."

"Boots. Where were they?"

"Next to the bed with the rest of her clothing and her purse."

"Now that is strange. She went all the way to the bedroom before taking them off? Sounds more and more to me like the scene was staged. You said she had a purse. What was inside?"

"A wallet with fifty dollars in cash, no credit cards or bank card, a driver's license belonging to Deb Smith, and a half-heart charm. In the open section, there were two tubes of lipstick, one of gloss, a nail file, a brass key, a hotel key card, and the gun you already knew about. A Glock 19."

No credit cards fit with Claire living off the grid, but money was necessary, so where did Claire get hers? And how did fifty bucks fit with designer jeans? There was another anomaly. "You said a heart charm?"

"Yeah."

"Seems an odd thing for a woman in her late thirties to be carting around. I'm guessing it must have sentimental value. What does it look like?"

Trent brought up a picture of the trinket. "It's small, like a charm you'd put on a bracelet or necklace."

Amanda used to have one similar to it in high school, but instead of a charm, it was a pin she put on the collar of her jean jacket. "You split it between friends. Each person gets half. Guessing there's an inscription on it?"

Trent enlarged the photo, and there was engraving. *BEST*, in a scrolled font.

"The other half, wherever it is, I'll bet that says 'FRIEND.'"

"I doubt it's in Logan's possession. Not really a guy thing... splitting up a heart charm."

"I don't think so either. That means that Claire was close to at least one other person. And close enough to potentially hang on to this for years. I doubt she picked it up recently. If we can find the person with the other half, we might get some answers we're looking for."

"Just how do we find that person?"

"Oh... Logan had said that Claire's best friend got her on the dating app. That person could have the other half of the charm. I'll ask about the friend. Now, you mentioned Claire had two keys, including one belonging to a hotel?"

Trent brought up the picture of the key card. "Lux Suites. Right here in Dumfries."

"As its name implies, that hotel isn't exactly the place you go when money's tight. Guessing she's got more than the fifty bucks somewhere."

"But where?" He smiled. "And we have more questions."

"It's time to get some answers. Let's have a talk with Claire's sister. Logan asked that I notify her anyway. She could also ID the body as Claire, to support what Logan's already told us."

"The sister's name? I'll get the address, and we can hit the road."

"Michelle Maxwell."

Trent's mouth fell open. "You're kidding me, right?"

"Ah, no. Why are you looking like you've been sideswiped by a Mack truck?"

"Michelle Maxwell is my buddy's wife and a friend of mine."

TWELVE

That heart charm had looked very familiar to Trent and upon hearing Michelle's name, he knew why. But, boy, had the world just gotten smaller. Trent had stood up as best man for Michelle's husband, John, and he still hung out with them once or twice a month.

He looked over at Amanda from behind the wheel of the department car. They were parked out front of his friends' house. "Let me handle this in there, okay."

"Absolutely."

Trent had already called his friend at work and told him to get home and round up Michelle too.

"So you never met Claire?" Amanda asked.

"I was more John's friend first. Still, I never knew Shell —*Michelle*—had a sister."

"She wasn't at their wedding?"

Trent shook his head. "No, and maybe given what we know about Claire, Michelle likely didn't know where to reach her. They just got married a couple of years ago."

"When Claire was who-knows-where. That must have been hard for Michelle not having her own sister at her wedding."

"Must have been, but as I said I didn't hear about her sister before." All Trent really knew about Shell's past was she hadn't had an easy childhood. All that entailed was never disclosed to him, and he respected his friend's privacy too much to pry.

Trent and Amanda got out of the car and headed to the front door. He lifted the brass knocker, but the door was opening before he let it go. John was standing there, and he let his gaze fall over Amanda.

"This is my partner, Detective Amanda Steele," Trent told him.

John bobbed his head. "I've heard a lot about you."

"All good, I hope." Amanda smiled, passed a glance to Trent.

"Amanda, John Maxwell," Trent rushed out, not wanting Amanda to make more out of his friend's reaction than necessary. But, of course, he'd talked about Amanda. She was a huge part of his life. "Michelle's here?" Trent asked. He just wanted to make sure. He hadn't seen her car in the driveway, but it could be tucked away in the garage.

"She's in the living room." John stepped out onto the porch. "What's this about, Trent? You're starting to really scare me."

There'd be no easy way to break this news, but it didn't feel right telling John first. "We need to talk to Michelle. You can be right by her side while we do."

John held eye contact, hesitant. He eventually nodded and took a heaving breath. He stepped inside, leaving the door wide open for Trent and Amanda to enter. They followed him to the living room. John stopped outside the door and turned. He was only inches from Trent. "Whatever it is... which I sense is bad news, please break it to her as gently as possible."

"You have my word," Trent assured his friend. He entered the living room ahead of John and Amanda. Shell was sitting on the couch, a cup on the table beside her with either tea or coffee, and her phone was in her hand. She looked up from it and smiled at Trent.

"What are you doing here?" Then her smile disappeared, like it had smashed into a wall. She put her phone down and reached her hand out toward John, who sat next to her on the couch. "Who is it? What happened?"

John threaded his fingers through his wife's and cupped the back of her hand with his other one.

Shell turned to John, rubbing her throat and tugging on the charm bracelet she always wore. "Do you know?"

John shook his head.

Trent had never asked her about the bracelet and could excuse himself for just being a guy on the matter. But now seemed like a good time to show interest. Trent pointed to Shell's bracelet. "Could I look at that?"

"Sure." She took it off her wrist, and Trent walked over to retrieve it.

He returned with it to Amanda who was now seated on a chair, so she could look at it with him. There were several charms. A book, a small ruby set in gold, a rabbit, a feather, a butterfly, and a half heart with the word *SISTER*. He pinched this one between his finger, so it laid flat for Amanda to read. She met his eyes briefly. It was enough to drive a stake into his heart. He took a calming breath and gave Shell her bracelet back. "Beautiful."

"Thanks." Her brow pinched down.

"Where did you get it?" It pained Trent to ask when he strongly suspected he knew the answer.

Shell slipped the chain back on her wrist. "My sister."

"Claire Hunter," he put out there affirmatively.

"Yes. But how do you know about her?"

Trent took a seat. "Late Friday, a woman was found murdered in a Dumfries home. We believe that woman was your sister, Claire Hunter." He repeated the name to aid the horrid news in sinking in. "Shell, I'm sorry." And he truly was. He wanted to believe the dead woman who had been in Hunter's house was some Deb Smith, but given the certainty of Hunter himself, and now the matching charm, Trent figured that was just wishful thinking.

"How was she...?"

"She was shot in the chest. Death would have been instant." He wasn't going to lie and say she hadn't suffered at all. The bruise to her head said that much, and that wasn't touching on the emotional and mental anguish she would have experienced.

Shell sniffled, her eyes staring into space. "Well... I can't say that hearing this is much of a surprise." She met Trent's gaze.

"Why do you say that?" This from Amanda, and her voice almost startled him, as if it were pulling him from another dimension.

"I'm sorry, but who are you?"

"Apologies. This is Detective Amanda Steele, my partner." Trent had spoken of Amanda to Shell before, just failed to make the introduction today.

Shell nodded. "Claire was always marching to her own beat, drummer, whatever, I stink at clichés."

"When was the last time you saw her?" Trent asked.

"The day after she returned from her honeymoon."

"Before she moved to Nebraska?" Amanda had filled him in on what Logan had told her about his relationship with Claire.

"The day before she left."

Something had Claire on the move right after her honeymoon. "Did she talk to you after the move?"

"Nope. I tried calling her. Always got voicemail. Then her number was disconnected. I reached out to Logan to get him to have Claire return my calls. This was all before she left him. Claire still didn't call me. I had wanted to invite her to our wedding"—she looked at John—"but by then, I really had no idea where she was. She'd left Logan by that point, essentially disappearing into thin air. Logan ended up moving back to Dumfries, but he was as much in the dark about where she went as me. I've spent the last few years letting her go." A single tear fell as if to debate her success at doing that.

It seemed evident that Claire had wanted to disappear. That begged an answer to why. It had to be a powerful motivator to have her leaving family and loved ones behind.

"Can you tell us about that last time you saw her?" Amanda said when Trent didn't say anything.

"She showed up at my apartment. I was single and living with a roommate at the time. Anyway, she said she was moving away, and she didn't know if she'd ever be back this way. I gave her a hard time, telling her she was being dramatic making it sound like she was falling off the face of the Earth. If I'd known..." Shell pinched the bridge of her nose, dropped her hand.

"Do you have any idea why she was acting that way?" Trent asked.

"No, and I've spent years trying to figure it out. I'd say she was running from something, but I don't have a clue what that could be."

"You two weren't close?" Amanda leaned in.

Shell toyed with the bracelet again. "We were connected. I thought we always would be."

Trent pointed to the gold chain on her wrist. "When did she give you that?"

"The last time we spoke. When she came over to basically say goodbye. I never thought it would be all I had left of her."

Trent couldn't imagine being in Shell's place. He had two sisters—one younger, one older—and they were close. They didn't get together in person a lot, but they messaged on social media at least once a week, even if it was about nothing important. For Shell, to have her sister just disappear—and with no real justification—it would be impossible to accept and get over.

Shell would always wonder about Claire—where she was, how she was, and who was to blame for the estrangement.

"You say you were connected," Amanda said. "It seems an interesting word choice to describe your relationship with your sister. Just being blood would give you a connection."

"There are a few years between us. I had my group of friends, and embarrassing to say now, but I spent a lot of my time hanging out in the woods smoking weed. It was what it was, though. Not like we had an easy home life. You do what you think is necessary to either numb or escape reality."

"While you did that, where was Claire?" Trent asked.

Shell shrugged. "She was always rather reclusive, private. She often had her nose in a book. She was very smart and did well in school. Put me to shame anyhow. You might know as much as John at this point, Trent." Shell ran her fingers over one trinket on the bracelet—a small golden book. "Our father was charged with killing our mother. Life was crap. We lived in a mobile home. Dad spent most of our money on booze. Mom did her best, but she wasn't strong enough. And she wasn't what you'd call independent. Her parents spoiled her, and she probably expected Dad to take care of her like her father had. Dad just wasn't that type of man. He needed her to lift him up."

Trent noted how robotically Shell had dispensed such painful details of her past. "Your father killed your mom?" If Amanda had known that she hadn't passed it along to him.

"He says it was an accident, but that's not what the charge on his record is. Murder in the third degree. He'll be in prison most of his natural life."

Shock, quickly followed by anger, rushed through Trent. He had an aunt he cared deeply for and after his uncle's death she'd gotten herself embroiled with some loser who beat on her. Trent and the rest of his family tried to get her to break loose and see she deserved better, but it hadn't sunk in yet. Given that years had passed, Trent wasn't sure she'd ever rid herself of the loser. "He beat on her?"

"He had a drinking problem. Mom had a way of pushing his buttons." She held up a hand. "Not an excuse, I know. Just telling you what I saw. Besides, what doesn't kill you makes you stronger, right?" Her voice, that had started off firm and resolute, became softer as she spoke and nearly disappeared with the word *kill*. "Do you have any idea who did this to her?"

"Not yet. But Logan Hunter has been charged."

"He what?" Shell snapped. "There's no way he killed her. That man wouldn't hurt a freaking hair on her head."

Trent was curious what her reaction would be, and this one was telling. "Claire was found in his house, Shell."

"No. No way." Shell was shaking her head adamantly. "There must be another explanation. He loves Claire. From the first time they met. Those two, like me and John, they had something." She made a show of squeezing her husband's hand.

"What are your thoughts about Logan?" Trent asked John. It was surprising given how their worlds intersected that Trent hadn't met Logan long before now.

"Logan's a good guy, in my opinion."

Shell nodded as if to punctuate John's conclusion.

"Do you have any other suspects?" John asked.

"Not yet, but Amanda and I are taking a closer look at the... case." Somehow referring to the murder of Shell's sister as a *case* felt so cold and detached.

"Do you know of anyone that might have wanted to hurt her?" Amanda asked.

"As I said, I haven't exactly been a part of her life for a long time, but Claire was always good about keeping secrets. Who knows what she was hiding?"

That brought up something else Trent should mention. "She had a license in her purse with the name Deb Smith. Does that name mean anything to you? Do you know why she'd have a fake ID?"

"No freaking clue. Claire was the wind. No pinning her down. It shocked me she got married, but she and Logan were a great match. She broke his heart too." Shell frowned and a few tears fell, which she quickly swiped away as if embarrassed by the display of grief.

"After your father was arrested, I assume you and Claire landed in the foster system." This from Amanda, and Trent was happy that she was keeping her focus. His mind kept going back to how the father had killed the mother. Would his family ever get such a call about their aunt?

"I turned eighteen a few months after Dad's arrest, so I never landed in the system. But I wasn't in any position to take care of Claire. I could barely look after myself. Claire bounced around to a few homes in the first year. Staying nowhere longer than a couple of months, except for the last family she was with. She was with them close to a year before she aged out of the system."

"Their names?"

"Sylvia and Albert Hamilton."

"Were all the foster homes in the Dumfries area?" Trent asked.

"Yeah. The idea, I believe, was that she wouldn't be uprooted more than necessary and could continue going to the same school."

"Did she have any close friends? Boyfriends?" He was thinking that maybe by a stretch one of them had kept in contact with Claire over the years. Though it was unlikely as she cut her own sister out of her life.

"Not sure. If she hooked up with any guys, she wasn't a kiss-and-tell type of person. As for friends, she kept them to herself, but she had mentioned a Roo once or twice in passing. A nick-name, I suspect. Don't know the person's real name. Wish I did, especially if it would help you find who did this to her. But, please, I'm telling you, Logan never would have killed her. Ever." Her eyelashes were weighed with tears and as she blinked, they fell.

"We won't keep you much longer," Amanda started, "but do you know what Claire did for work? There's nothing much on record."

"Claire had a fine eye for art. She had a job at a gallery in Washington years ago, started not long after mom died. Stayed there until she got that *job* in Nebraska."

They'd discovered the art gallery, but nothing else. A search under the name Deb Smith netted nothing helpful either. Amanda had told Trent that Claire's job in Nebraska was fabricated, and it seemed Shell was aware of that fact too. She'd probably heard that from Logan.

"I don't even know what to believe about her anymore." She ran her hand over the bracelet again.

"You said she gave that to you," Trent started, "along with all the charms?"

"Yeah."

"Do they represent something to you?" He was thinking if Claire had chosen every charm for special meaning, he and Amanda might learn more about the person Claire used to be.

"Yeah. Me and Claire. The book, well that was her. Avid reader, as I said. The ruby is the gemstone for my birth month. The butterfly was to represent how she and I emerged from the cocoons of our miserable childhoods into independent women. The rabbit stands for luck and abundance. Claire also told me it would protect me when she was... gone." Her voice turned rough and gravely. "I thought she meant while she was in Nebraska, but I guess it carries even more weight now. She knew she was cutting me off, and now she's dead."

"And the rest?" Trent hated to burden Shell with memories, but some may arise that could help the investigation.

"The feather was to strengthen my intuition, to recognize the signs on my path. You need to understand that Claire was very much attuned with the universe." Shell's face wrinkled up, and Trent knew why. She was more about what she could see and touch than imagine in some invisible realm. Shell went on. "The half heart, that's self-explanatory. Claire was to keep the other half. Did she have it on her?"

"She did," he said, thinking that might be some small comfort.

Shell set off into a small crying jag.

"Michelle," Amanda started when she calmed, "as we've discussed, we have strong reasons to believe the murdered woman was Claire, but it would help strengthen the case if you would confirm her identity."

"I'll do whatever I have to. Just make sure you get her justice."

"We'll do all we can. The medical examiner's name is Hans Rideout, and he'll be the one contacting you about identification."

Shell nodded and glanced at John, who put his arm around her.

Trent turned to Amanda. "We should go." Back to Shell. "I'm so sorry." He went over and hugged her. She sagged against him.

A few minutes later, Trent and Amanda were loading back into a hot car. He started the AC, but it just kicked out more warm air. It would take a minute for the cool stuff to push through.

"As far as I'm concerned, we can stop second-guessing whether that woman was Claire. It's unlikely anything else would explain the matching charm in her wallet." She snapped her seat belt into place.

He was staring out the windshield.

"Trent? You heard me?"

He nodded, though he could barely get his head to move.

"That's a good thing. And if we can get a meeting with the foster parents, one of them might know who this Roo is."

"Did you know about the father?" He slowly looked over at her. She said nothing. "Did you know?" he repeated.

"Yes. Logan told me."

"You should have told me before we went in there. To at least prepare me." His insides were jumping with annoyance. "You want us to talk openly, to work as a team, then we need to lay everything out."

"It's not like I withheld it on purpose."

What was he going to do? Accuse her of lying to his face? But there was a part of him that was deeply offended, as if she had left this out on purpose. He'd told her about his aunt before. If she was trying to protect him from the ugliness of the world, too late. He'd already seen it many times over.

THIRTEEN

She didn't want this to be goodbye, but she knew very well that's exactly what it needed to be. If she was to move on successfully from her life, she had to make a clean break of it. She couldn't leave without at least talking to Shell, though. They were blood. They had been there together through most of the ugly. Side by side.

Their father's drinking.

Their parents fighting.

Their mother's murder—at their father's hand.

He could swear it was an accident all he wanted, but not even a jury bought it. The evidence and testimony from neighbors about her father's violent mood swings and his alcohol addiction damned him.

So she lived with it because she had no other choice. It was that or resist and spiral down into Crazy Town. But that day would always haunt her. There was no rationalization or justification. Only questions. The main one being three simple letters. W. H. Y.

Her future was doomed to be an endless cycle, doing what

she did with Nick, until that night at the bar. Enter Logan Hunter.

All because of a dare issued by her best friend, Roo, who thought it was time she meet a nice guy and settle down. She was twenty-nine, but marriage wasn't in her purview. Nick had grown more into the role of an older brother. He was adamant they keep their relationship professional. Romantic entanglements could threaten the entire operation.

Roo had signed Claire up for the dating app. When Logan's picture came on screen, Roo had grabbed her phone and set up a meet in person.

Logan was handsome in the strictest sense. Blond, muscular, and the way he peered into her eyes that first night made her question whether he could tap her darkest, most intimate secrets.

"I'm only here because of my friend," she told him as she sat in the booth across from him.

"You too?" He smiled. Flashing dimples. And how she had a thing for them.

"You're kidding me."

"Nope. My friend John thought I needed to get out more."

They laughed and what was to be one drink, then the door, ended up being three drinks, dinner, a nightcap, and an overnight at his place.

In the few weeks that followed, they became inseparable. She should have fought harder to push him away. Her life didn't allow for such an indulgence, and she certainly wasn't worthy of how he looked at her. And every time she saw him, she only felt it more. He loved her. She loved him. Maybe she could make it work—her secret life and Logan.

And it was fine for a while. They got married, a small but tasteful event. Her sister stood up for her, and John for Logan.

Kismet—that's how Michelle and John met and started dating.

But she felt like an impostor, living someone else's life, one *that shouldn't be hers. She had a father who was a killer—did that live in her DNA? She certainly wasn't the lily-white image that Logan seemed to see. She had her demons, and they were hers alone to entertain.*

All because of choices she'd made and one night that went so terribly wrong. There would be no turning back for her from that point; her life was forever changed.

The events of that time still came to her in flashes, the heaving, the blood, the last breath...

She had to get out of Prince William County. That was decided. She didn't want to leave Logan, hurt him, but maybe that was unrealistic. Still, she was nothing if not a dreamer with high hopes. Maybe if she got herself far enough away from her past, cut all ties, went somewhere completely unpredictable, everything would be fine.

She decided on Nebraska, five states over from Virginia. That ought to do the trick.

She didn't just want to leave Shell empty-handed, though. This would be the last time she'd probably see her or talk to her. It was just how it had to be. A complete sever from her life here to move forward with the man she loved. And in Nebraska, surely, she and Logan would be safe.

She went into a jeweler's and picked out a lovely charm bracelet, gold with tight links. Elegant, just like the woman her sister had become. She'd left the weed behind and came close to being a teetotaler. She was the prime example of how a child could rise above a shitty upbringing and make something of themselves. Her sister might disagree as she always downplayed her accomplishments. But she held a job at a local bank and had worked her way up from teller to manager.

"It's perfect. I'll take it." She told the jeweler and added assorted charms to the final purchase. Each of them was to mean something. That was more important than simply filling up the bracelet. She was especially pleased when she scored the ruby—

the real stone—and more extravagant than Shell would ever allow herself to buy.

"Anything else?" He smiled at her, and with his gaze dipping back into the glass cabinet, her eye followed the direction in which he was looking.

She pointed at a two-piece heart charm in the display case. "I'll take that, but please wrap one half with the other charms, and I'll take the other half."

"Here you go." He handed her the one half, which she put into a zippered section in her wallet, as he put the bracelet and other charms in tissue paper and inserted them into a bag with the jewelry store's name emblazoned on the side.

Claire walked out of the store, bag in hand, head held high. She was so proud that she could do this for her sister, even though she realized it wouldn't come close to compensating for her exit from Shell's life. Not that she was telling her sister that in so many words.

Shell might question where she got the money for such a gift. But that wasn't an answer her older sister would ever get—not if Claire could help it. All she knew, and that was probably too much, was that Claire worked part-time at an art gallery.

Thankfully, she'd never questioned Claire's sudden interest in the finer things, starting at sixteen. It certainly wasn't something they were accustomed to, living in the mobile park as children. But Claire took to the world of culture like a baby bird who left the nest only to soar to the high heavens. She was good at sniffing out the most exquisite pieces, whether they be gems, artwork, or sculptures. As Nick had told her more than once, she was a natural. And as far as she was concerned when you were blessed with a gift, you put it to use. Anything else would be a waste.

Claire knocked on Shell's apartment door and presented her gift. Her sister admired it and didn't even ask how she could afford such a thing. Still, Claire told Shell about the amazing job opportunity in Nebraska that she just couldn't turn down. She recycled the same story she'd given Logan and hoped Shell would buy it with as much confidence. But it was the look on her sister's face that would stay with her forever. She knew Claire wasn't telling her everything. And she was right.

FOURTEEN

Amanda felt about two inches tall. She hated it when Trent directed his anger at her, but it wasn't like she'd left out the bit about Claire's father on purpose. There'd just been so much to catch Trent up on as it was, and then they had the other information they'd mined that morning from the officer interviews, autopsy findings, evidence log, and crime scene photos. And her mind was spinning with her own drama. Logan's face constantly appeared, asking why the hell this was happening to him and why she wasn't doing anything about it.

And after sitting there with Michelle Maxwell, listening to her talk about Claire and how they'd become estranged, it had Amanda thinking about her own life. Claire had pulled herself away from her sister, just as Amanda cut out her family after Kevin and Lindsey had died. Amanda thought by doing so she could protect her heart from more pain. She lived under that illusion for the better part of six years.

Trent was driving to the hotel where Claire had been staying—or at least where the key card in her purse belonged. They'd discussed that much before dipping into a tense silence.

Amanda was sitting in the passenger seat trying to figure

out what she could say that would get through to him right now. But he had this hard edge to him. Could any words break through? She was trying to piece together why he was so upset that she left out telling him about the father. It really hadn't been intentional, but he wasn't buying that... so why? Was he really hurt she hadn't mentioned the father killing the mother, or was there more to it, something that smacked personal for him? She racked her brain, then recalled that Trent had told her some time ago about his aunt and how she'd married an abusive man. Could that have something to do with his reaction?

"What's really bugging you?" she asked.

"I don't want to talk about it."

So it was personal... "Does this have to do with your aunt?"

He didn't look over at her, but his cheeks flushed red. Silence.

Might as well be admittance. "My not mentioning the domestic violence wasn't intentional or left out to protect you."

"Good, because I don't need you to protect me." He shot a cool glance at her now, sending a chill through her.

"I know you can handle anything that comes your way. And I had every intention of telling you, but there was a lot we were learning about the case, most of it coming at us quickly."

"Is there anything else you might have left out?" he asked.

"Not that I can think of off the top."

He turned into the parking lot for Lux Suites.

"We good?" She hated how much she wanted to make things right between them, and with every syllable from her mouth, she felt her personal power slipping away.

"We're good."

Her phone rang, and caller ID told her it was Logan. She answered before the second ring. "I've got you on speaker. Trent's here. You're out?"

"I can't go home. It's still locked down as a crime scene."

"Right..." She felt for him, but he'd have to bunk at a

friend's place or get a hotel room. She couldn't offer her place for at least a couple reasons. One, it would confuse Zoe, and two, she was working the case he was involved with.

"Mandy, are you helping me? What's going on?"

"Trent and I have been assigned the case."

"Even though I've been charged? Doesn't that usually mean case closed?"

"Usually, but an exception is being made. I assure you we are doing everything to get to the truth."

"Did you see Michelle, tell her about Claire?"

Amanda glanced over at Trent, sensing that he'd withdrawn energetically. "We just left there."

"How is she? Heartbroken, I bet. She was just as devastated as me when Claire disappeared from her life. Only Claire had ghosted her years sooner. Michelle would call and ask me to have Claire call her. Claire talked as if she were in contact with Michelle. Why all the secrets and lies, Amanda?"

"We're working to get that answer." *Among many others...*

"Did Michelle tell you I wouldn't have done this, that there's no way I could have hurt Claire?"

"She did. She also told us about a good friend that Claire had. She didn't know her name, just the nickname Roo. Does that ring any bells?" If Claire had a close friend, one would think the man she loved and married would know about her.

A few beats of quiet, then, "Don't think so."

"Who was her maid of honor at your wedding?" Trent asked, and it had Amanda looking at him.

"Her sister, Michelle."

How strange. Where would that leave Roo—whoever she was? "You told me that Claire's friend got her on the dating app, how you two ended up meeting. Who was that?"

"Honestly? I never met her."

"You never met your girlfriend's best friend?" Trent let out a huff of disbelief and shook his head.

"I asked Claire about her, but she said she'd moved away. I let it go."

"And you figured she had only the one friend?" Trent again, his skepticism not hidden well.

"She told me she had a hard time getting close to people."

Another dead end... She and Trent would need to revisit Claire Ramsey's dormant Facebook account. They could check there and see if they could identify this best friend. "I found an old Facebook account belonging to Claire. You wouldn't happen to have her password? Access to Claire's private messages might be a big help."

"Wouldn't know where to begin."

"One more thing, Logan. Is the house you're living in now the one you shared with Claire before?"

"No, and before you ask, I have no idea how she got there."

Yet another mystery with this case... "Okay, well, I'm going to let you go for now. Just hang in there all right."

"Yeah." Sapped of all enthusiasm and bland acceptance.

They said their goodbyes and ended the call.

Trent parked in the hotel lot and got out without saying anything. Amanda followed his lead.

"That Facebook account I mentioned... We could see if we can get anywhere finding the best friend that way. Logan doesn't have the password, but we could get a judge to approve access."

"We can. And it might not get us anywhere."

Wasn't he just Mr. Positivity?

He got the door for her.

A man in a suit greeted them at the front desk. He swept his gaze over them, at first giving the impression he thought them to be a couple, but then his eyes dipped to the badges clipped to their waistbands. "What can I do for you?"

Amanda tapped a finger to her badge, just to emphasize their authority. "Do you have a Deb Smith staying with you?"

She'd roll with Claire's alias, figuring that's how she would have booked the room. It was curious how she got a room without a credit card to secure it, but sometimes a cash deposit was accepted. Again, Amanda wondered where Claire got her money and where she kept it.

"One minute." He clicked on a keyboard, and a few seconds later confirmed the booking.

"When did she arrive, and how long is she set to have the room?" Trent asked.

"I'm not sure how much I should tell you without a warrant."

"Deb Smith was found murdered last Friday evening," Amanda said.

"Oh, that explains it then."

Tingles spread over Amanda's body. "Explains what?"

"Why I haven't seen her. And the maids told me they haven't had to make up her room for the last few days."

"And that didn't strike you as odd?" she asked.

A twitch of irritation tugged at the corners of his mouth. "It's not our place to interfere with our customers or their schedules. As far as we're concerned, she dipped out for a couple of days. It was assumed she was returning as her possessions remained in her room."

Amanda was curious how long it would take before hotel staff became concerned. "Do you know if she had any visitors?"

"I never saw any. She left the hotel, though, a few times in taxis. Don't ask what cab companies. I wasn't looking that closely." He nudged his head to a phone on the end of the desk. "She used that to order the rides."

They could request the phone records for that line, but without more information to go on, narrowing it down would be impossible. But the use of public transportation raised another question. "Did she not arrive in her own car?"

The clerk glanced at the screen. "There's no request for parking."

It was possible Claire had taken a bus into town and then a taxi to the hotel. "When did she check in?"

His eyes flicked to the monitor. "She got here last Wednesday just after noon."

Two days before her murder... "Do you know where she was coming from?"

"No."

"Did she use a credit card to secure the room?"

"No, she didn't have one, but she provided us with a thousand dollars cash as security."

Trent looked at Amanda and raised his eyebrows. Claire had financial resources available to her.

"How long was she booked to stay?" Trent asked.

"Until this Wednesday." At least the clerk was being far more helpful than her first impression led her to expect.

So, one week. Taxi rides would suggest she had places to go, people to visit. And assuming Claire had been away from Prince William County all this time, what had her back and planning to stick around for seven days? Was it as she considered before—to come clean with loved ones before the cancer took her? "We'll need to know when—within approximation— that she left in taxis. Can you help with that?" They'd need to follow up from there and see if they could hunt down the drivers and find out Claire's destinations.

"I think so." He wiped his brow, which had become shiny with sweat.

"Great. Do you have surveillance cameras on the lot?" she asked.

"Yes, and in here."

"We'll want that footage."

"We'll also need access to her room," Trent interjected.

"I can help with both, but I'm going to need a warrant."

That word seemed to summon a broad-shouldered man in his fifties from a back office to join the clerk at the desk. "Is there a problem here?"

"No problem." Amanda lifted her badge for the new arrival. She ran through the highlights after he introduced himself as the manager.

"Yes, as you were just told, we'll need a warrant first, but then we'll be happy to assist."

"Thank you."

"Uh-huh."

Amanda and Trent stepped back outside. The day was getting away from them, and it was nearing four in the afternoon. She made a call to Sergeant Graves to fill her in on their progress and added, "I'd like to contact Judge Anderson for a verbal warrant so Detective Stenson and I can move on this immediately."

"Do what you must." With that, Graves hung up.

"She's a piece of work, I tell you."

"No need to tell me." He'd just ended a call too, but his was to Hans Rideout. "Rideout's going to reach out to Michelle and set up a time for her to ID Claire."

She nodded, almost absentmindedly. Her empathy going even more to Trent in this moment. She knew what it was like needing to notify a friend. She'd been in that exact position only a few months ago. "You all right?"

"I'll be fine. It is what it is, right? I mean all we can do now is get answers. Give Shell and Logan closure."

She squeezed his shoulder, offering comfort and reassurance, but she felt another energy surging beneath her hand. *Chemistry?* She drew back.

FIFTEEN

After making a call to the judge for a verbal warrant, Amanda and Trent went back inside to inform the hotel manager and his clerk. "We'll need to start with the room number assigned to Deb Smith," she said.

"Room eight fifty-two." The clerk handed her a key card.

"Thanks. And while we're up there, if you could get a list of the times she left and returned, along with the video for us to take, that would be great." It could be a painful process for her and Trent to wade through, but it might give them a solid lead.

"I'll write down what I remember," the clerk responded.

"One more thing before we head up," Trent interjected. "Did Ms. Smith receive any calls to her room or make any?"

Good thinking, Trent...

The clerk went to the computer, where the system must log incoming and outgoing calls. Made sense, as they'd need to know when long-distance charges applied. "Looks like she received one Wednesday afternoon around four. Don't know from *who*, but I have a phone number I can give you." The clerk prattled it off, and Trent scribbled it down in his notepad.

"Thanks." Trent tucked his book into his pocket again.

She and Trent left the manager and clerk and went up to room 852.

"We'll need to figure out who that number belongs to." A no-brainer and not even worth saying. She wasn't sure why but she felt on edge with Trent since their visit to the Maxwells, like she had to smooth things over with him. She just didn't have a clue how, and really, it wasn't her job to make sure he was okay.

The elevator pinged their arrival on the eighth floor. Signs on the wall directed them left to reach number 852, and they found it about midway down the hall.

She slid the key card into the reader, the light flashed green, and she twisted the handle. They were in. But what they were in *for* remained to be seen.

Straight across from the door was a window. Its drapes were open, but the sheers were drawn and the late afternoon sun was diffused. Amanda flipped the light switch next to her, and the shadows crept into the corners of the room to nest.

They both gloved up, though what remained was already potentially compromised as the cleaning staff had been here since Claire last left. She went into the bathroom while Trent spread out into the main part of the room.

She turned the light on in the bathroom and looked at the vanity. A cosmetic bag, a bottle of hairspray, perfume. The items were all gathered together and took up little counter space. Either the work of the maid, or Claire liked her things tight and organized.

She looked inside the bag, but it only contained makeup. She exited the bathroom. "Nothing exciting in there."

"Nothing much here so far either. No suitcase. Just this." He was elbows deep in a duffel bag and was taking everything out in an organized fashion and setting it on the bed. "A couple pairs of jeans—designer—a few T-shirts, socks, underwear, a bra..."

"Claire travels light. She just had the basics in the bathroom too." Amanda moved to the closet near the door. No jackets or other shoes, but there was a safe and its door was shut. She tugged on it. Locked. "Seems she has something in the safe." She got on the phone with the front desk and was given an override code. They assured her it was only used in cases such as this. She hung up and punched it in on the keypad. A clunk, and she was in. She opened the door, Trent now beside her.

She stepped back. So did he.

Stacks of cash. At least twenty grand.

"What the heck?" Trent gasped. "Where... how did she come into that much money?"

"My guess? Not doing anything legal." The fake ID, the secrecy, the disappearance from her sister's life, then Logan's, the unregistered gun in her possession, the fact she had been murdered, *and* all this dough. None of these things pointed anywhere good. But they also didn't provide the entire picture either.

"We've got to talk to your boyfriend again and see if he can give us anything to go on."

"First, he's not my boyfriend. Second, I am quite confident he would have nothing to offer about this." She flailed a hand toward the safe. "Even when they were living together, they kept separate accounts."

"We could still ask."

"Sure. Just don't expect to get anywhere." She leveled her gaze at him, and he eventually nodded.

"Okay, so we have cash, an unregistered gun, a fake ID... It's obvious whatever Claire was caught up in, landed her in over her head."

"I say we call in Crime Scene to process the room, bag the money. We get the video and see if it gives us anything about her last steps."

"There's not even a single receipt to help us with that. And if there ever was, it's gone now. The trash bins are empty."

"Just great."

"All right, just thinking what might get us our answers faster," Trent began. "We should look at Claire's Facebook account, see if we can find close friends of hers, but there's also an address that would be on the fake license. Where does Deb Smith supposedly live? Maybe that will help us get somewhere."

Amanda wished she'd thought of that before now, but she and Trent had been so caught up in other angles of the investigation. For a starter they had been more focused on Claire Hunter herself because they knew that was the victim's real name. "We'll check it out, see what turns up." She'd had high hopes of making it home tonight in time to have dinner with Zoe, but it wasn't looking like that was going to happen. She'd have to call Libby Dewinter, Zoe's godmother and effectively her aunt. Not related by blood, but in every other way that it counted. Libby often stayed with Zoe after school until Amanda got home. It worked well and was convenient for Libby as she was a teacher at Zoe's school. The start of summer break was only two weeks away, though, and Amanda would have to make arrangements for Zoe during the day.

"I'll call Crime Scene, probably the fastest way to get that address. Need to call them anyway to come here."

She nodded. "I've got a call to make too." A minute later, she was hanging up. As usual, Libby was a champ about just going with the flow. She'd make Zoe dinner and was happy to stay as long as she was needed. Next, Amanda called Graves and brought her up to speed. With each phone call Amanda made to her, the sergeant sounded less happy. She was probably realizing how rash she'd been about assuming Logan's guilt.

Trent pocketed his phone. "Crime Scene will be here within the hour."

That was fast considering they were likely coming from their headquarters in Manassas, which was a half hour away.

"I've got the address for Deb Smith. It's in Sun and Shade Mobile Home Park on the edge of town."

"Didn't Michelle say that she and Claire lived in a mobile home park when they were younger?"

"She did. I'll call and see if that's the park." He pulled out his phone again and made the call.

Amanda went to the window and swept back the drapes, affording Trent a little privacy while he spoke with his friend. She watched traffic on the street buzz by and then looked at the hotel parking lot beneath them. It was rather full. She could see their department car from here and noted an idling, silver sedan near the road access as two police cruisers entered the lot.

"It's the same park," Trent said, and it had her turning. "But a different number than where they lived."

"We'll pay the people there a visit once we can hand over the hotel room to Crime Scene and uniformed officers. Shouldn't be long. Just saw two cruisers pull in."

"Okay, good."

There was something in his tone. Sadness? Empathy? "How's Michelle holding up?"

"Not doing good. She's blaming herself. Said that she should have listened to her gut. It told her Claire wasn't being completely forthright the day she dropped by, but she didn't push because she figured she'd have all the time in the world to do that."

"That's rough." Amanda didn't know what else to say. She didn't want to point out what she learned a long time ago: One never knew when time would run out.

SIXTEEN

There was a two-tone brown beat-up truck in front of the trailer marked 2 1 7 at the Sun and Shade Mobile Home Park. The place itself had seen a fresh coat of paint, and Amanda would guess it might have been last month or the start of this one. Most of the places were in a decent state of repair and resembled tiny houses with their small, attached decks and flower gardens. The park felt homey and not as depressing as she'd built up in her mind based upon stereotypes.

Before coming here, they'd collected the hotel surveillance video and a list of times the clerk remembered seeing Claire leave the hotel. She also had Trent look up the name of the occupants of the mobile home.

Bill and Wendy Stevens both worked full-time jobs. Him at an auto supply store, and her in an insurance office.

The Stevens had a wood-carved sign that hung from a hook next to the front stairs that announced their surname to whoever happened by.

Amanda stepped up on the deck and knocked on the door. Rather quickly, footsteps could be felt in the boards beneath their feet as someone inside padded across the mobile home toward them.

The door creaked open. "Yes?"

Amanda held up her badge. "Detectives with the Prince William County PD, ma'am. Are you Wendy Stevens?"

"I am." Her tone was wary as was the way she was watching them.

"We have a few questions for you, if we could come inside for a minute."

"It's not exactly a good time right now."

Amanda was about to state her case a little more strongly when Wendy stepped outside with them. She was in her late fifties, of petite build, with graying hair. "What's this about?" she asked.

"Deb Smith." Amanda thought she'd get straight to the point, see if she could gauge a reaction—and she got one, all right. Confusion.

"Ah, who?" The sunlight had lost most of its power, but she still squinted as she crossed her arms. She set her gaze over Trent, then back to Amanda.

"This address is showing on record as belonging to her."

"Well, that's just ludicrous. I have no idea who Deb Smith is."

"What about your husband? Does he know her?" Trent asked.

"I don't like what you're implying. My husband might love his beer and hanging out at the bar with his friends, but he's not getting any on the side."

Trent held up a hand. "Never meant to insinuate that he was."

"Uh-huh. Now where in the blazons did you get this Deb having her address here? What record?"

"Her license," Amanda said.

"Nope."

"You ever get mail here for her?" Trent inquired.

"Not that I remember."

As if they didn't have enough to confirm the vic was Claire Hunter, this was yet further proof the license was fake. Otherwise they'd have received mail from the government. Amanda was about to thank Wendy for her time when she thought she'd try one more thing. "Do the names Claire or Michelle Ramsey mean anything to you?"

"Ramsey..." She tapped her chin. "That name I know. Isn't he the man who killed his wife? Those his girls?"

"Yes," Amanda said.

"That's all I know about the lot of 'em."

"All right. Thank you for your time," Amanda told her and was the first to turn to leave.

Back in the car, she said to Trent, "The license for Deb Smith was a complete forgery. Not legit on any level."

"Yeah, I got that feeling myself. She really had no idea who or what we were talking about." He turned on the car, and the vents belted them with cool air almost immediately as they hadn't been gone for long. "So back to the station for movie time?" He lifted the USB drive that contained the hotel's surveillance video.

"We'll get there, but since we're out, I want to look at the crime scene again."

He put the car into gear. "Whatever you'd like."

Guess any discussion on the topic wasn't going to happen. But just because he wasn't talking didn't mean that her mind wasn't nattering away. There was a strange feel to the air. Did he think returning to Logan's would be awkward for her? She'd survived stranger things than a one-night stand turning sideways. Or would it be uncomfortable for him being there with her? "We can stop for a bite to eat first."

"Sounds good. Pizza?"

"Usually I do that with Zoe on Tuesdays. We make them at home."

"Oh, right. I remember you telling me before. What about chicken wings?"

"That's fine. Tired of burgers, I take it?" They often took advantage of the drive-thru and ate in the parking lot.

"How did you guess?"

"A man tired of beef, that's a first," she teased.

"I know, and the barbecue season is just getting started." He glanced over at her when she didn't say anything. "For everyone except you. I saw that relic on your patio. It's all rusted out."

"It was more Kev's thing than mine." She wasn't going to admit that she had no idea how to use the thing even if she wanted to. It was embarrassing to think that at thirty-seven she didn't even know how to turn it on... well, maybe she could get that far.

"I hope I didn't upset you by making you think of him."

"No, not at all." There was a time that any memory or mention of her dead husband would have had her chest knotting in pain, but thankfully it seemed the worst of her grief had finally passed. Not that she wouldn't give almost anything to talk to him again, to see his face, to hear his laugh, but having Zoe in her life reminded her how things moved on.

"Good. So Dingawings it is then."

She laughed. The proprietor had certainly chosen the name of his business wisely—that's if he wanted to put a smile on his customers' faces. "That's fine." She wasn't a major fan of chicken wings, but she wasn't completely opposed either. It was Becky who cringed at the thought of gnawing on the little bones.

* * *

The wings were delicious. Perfectly cooked and coated with just the right amount of sauce. And Amanda might have eaten one or two more than she needed.

"Wow. You'd think you'd eat less considering you're forced to eat a little slower, but..." Amanda put a hand over her stomach.

Trent laughed. "They are addictive, though."

He pulled the department car into Logan's driveway. After eating, they'd dropped by the station and picked up Logan's key.

A cruiser was at the curb behind them, the officer there in case he was needed.

She got the door, cutting the crime seal tape. As she entered the house, Friday night flooded back. How anxious and excited she'd felt to be there with Logan after all this time. How they crashed together and couldn't get to the bedroom fast enough. Then how everything had turned to shit.

She turned the entry light on, and it cast enough illumination that it was easy to make out the living area to the immediate left and the walkway toward the back of the house. She slid the house key into her pants pocket and thought about how the killer and Claire had even gained entry.

"There was no sign of forced entry..." She retraced her steps to the front step, flicking the exterior light on as she walked. She inspected around the doorjamb. No nicks or evidence someone had tried to jimmy the door to get in. No obvious scrape marks around the keyhole either.

"Could be they came in through a window." Trent shrugged.

"I'd like to think that every possible entry point would have been inspected closely." She imagined the investigators combed every windowsill for any sign someone had pried them open.

"Well, they could have picked the lock."

"*They*... so did Claire and her killer arrive at the same time, or did he or she follow Claire?"

"Don't know, but you'd think at least one neighbor would have noticed different people around Logan's house."

"People are rather immersed in their own lives these days."

"Maybe they weren't hanging around outside long either. Does Logan keep a spare key outside?"

"It's possible. How would Claire and/or the killer know where it was, though?"

"Not usually too hard to figure that out." Trent went down the front stairs, turned to look back at the house. A few seconds later, he was beelining toward a rock in the garden bed. "I'm going to bet this one here." He lifted the rock. "Fiberglass." He examined the bottom, then brought it over to her and showed her the small compartment on the underside. "We have a hide-a-key."

"Well, look at you."

He flipped it open. No key. "We'll have to ask Logan if he kept one in there."

"For the moment, let's assume it's how Claire and the killer got inside."

"Or, just thought of something... If keeping a spare key outside was a long-time habit of Logan's, Claire might have known that. She could have let herself in, and the killer followed her in."

"Then we need to answer what brought her here. Also how she even knew where Logan lived. Why trespass?"

"You'd have to consult a spirit medium." He smiled at her.

"Yeah, yeah. Well, let's look inside, shall we, see if we can figure anything out." She led the way in, Friday night washing over her again, this time with less intensity. She did her best to put herself in Claire's mind. She hadn't seen Logan in years. Friday would have likely been her first time in his home, but it left the questions of how she knew where Logan's place was and what drew her there. "I think Claire still had feelings for Logan."

"Nah, you don't know that."

"Why else would she have entered his home? It had to be she was living in some nostalgic bubble."

"Or," he dragged out the word, "she could have been looking for something she left with him—what ended up getting her killed?"

"Could be. She's certainly shrouded in a hell of a lot of mystery. But what would Logan have that she wanted?"

"You might be the best person to answer that." He laughed.

She nudged his shoulder. "Mind out of the gutter."

"Yes, ma'am." He started walking through the house, bending over here and there, angling his head like he was searching for a specific thing. Then he stopped and hunched down, picked up something from under the front edge of the couch.

"What is it?" She stepped up next to him. He held a white, pearl button in his fingers. She could feel her cheeks heat. She snatched it. "Nothing to do with Claire."

He looked from her to his now bare hands, a small, amused smile resting on his lips.

She brushed past him to the hallway, headed for the bedroom. They could spend all night combing every inch of the place, but would it get them any closer to the answers they desperately needed? She stood in the bedroom doorway, letting her gaze take in the room. The investigators had taken a lot with them. The furniture remained, but the bedding had been stripped. Claire's blood had seeped through to the mattress. *Logan's* wife's *blood.*

Her head swooned, and she gripped the doorway. Trent had come up behind her at the same time and helped steady her. One of his hands was on her upper arm, the other on her hip. She looked over her shoulder at him. "I'm fine now. Thanks."

"What was it?" He had yet to remove his hands from her.

"Just thinking about how horrible this must have been for

Logan. Seeing her there like that." She turned, and Trent lowered his arms. They were face to face with about eight inches between them. "When I lost Kevin and Lindsey, it was the most horrible time of my life. The crash happened so fast, but it also felt like every second moved in slow motion. I saw their blood before I passed out myself. They were breathing, though. I had determined that much." She stopped speaking, an ache drilling into her chest. The thought of them suffering even for a second was too much to handle. And just when she thought that level of grief had left her, she realized it could be conjured at a moment's notice. It was lurking, ready to pounce. "Guess it just all came back."

Trent let a few seconds pass, then said, "Logan's lucky to have you as his friend, Amanda."

"Thanks." She took a deep breath. "Okay, let's look around." She entered the room, her eye drawn first to the night-stand and the lamp that they'd discussed at the station. It felt like that conversation had been weeks ago, but it was only that morning. There was some light coming in from the south-facing window, which for nearing seven at night was still casting enough illumination that turning on the ceiling light wasn't necessary. She took out her phone, though, and enabled the flashlight. She went over to the lamp and traced the beam over it.

"Claire very well could have grabbed the lamp and swung it at her attacker."

"And with the shade missing, I think our killer might have been concerned about leaving trace as we theorized before." She took a few seconds to peck a note into her phone to remind her to ask Logan if there had been a shade.

"Blood. Spit possibly? If she hit them, unexpected, I can imagine some drool flying through the air."

Amanda nodded. She turned back to the table and lamp. She leaned down and took a closer look, wishing for microscopic sight. Then stood, disappointed. "Nothing that's standing out to the naked eye, but this lamp needs to be thoroughly examined. The lab techs might even lift prints to advance the case."

"Well, I don't think there's going to be any that take us to our killer. No luck with that so far. I think it's safe to assume the killer wore gloves."

"Yeah, you're probably right, but they might lift Claire's prints, prove our theory." She tried to recreate the minutes before Claire's death. She ran through her mind their earlier notion about Claire letting herself in. There were at least two flaws with it. One, it didn't explain the lingerie. "We theorized the killer dressed Claire in the lingerie. It's occurring to me now that if that was the case, how did he or she know her size?"

"Good point, and where did they get it?"

"Uh-huh. I'm going to inquire about the piece, see if there's anything special about it. Maybe we can track the buyer."

"If the killer knew Claire's size, we're looking at someone close to her."

Amanda went cold. "It sure seems to indicate that." Of course, that theory hinged on their speculation that Claire didn't bring it herself for a romantic rendezvous with Logan. It suggested the killer—someone other than Logan—thought they'd use it to muddy the scene. She'd let that line of thought go and returned to the other hole in the theory about Claire coming on her own first. "We talked about Claire arriving ahead of the killer, that she found the hide-a-key and let herself in, but that wouldn't explain why the key wasn't in her things. Wait, there was a brass key."

Trent shook his head. "It was described as being small, like something for a chest."

"So then, the killer took the key to Logan's house? Why?"

"No clue why they would."

"Well... if the killer didn't take it and it wasn't in Claire's things, then it's in this house some— Oh, I know where." She rushed from the room toward the front door. In her house, she had a table with a bowl on it to catch her keys and whatever else she felt like tossing in there when she came home. Logan had a similar setup, but she didn't remember seeing a key. It could be that investigators collected it for whatever purpose.

But unlike her hall table, Logan's had three narrow drawers. She opened each one while thinking it would be strange for Claire to slip it into one. But maybe she wasn't a fan of the bowl or clutter? Her toiletries had been laid out neatly in her hotel bathroom. On the last drawer, she exclaimed, "Bingo." Inside was a single key. She took a quick picture of it with her phone, then snapped on gloves and picked it up. "Want to bet that it fits the front door?"

Trent gestured for her to try it. She did, and it fit like Cinderella's slipper.

"Let's say Claire let herself in, why put the key in the drawer, not a pocket to access quickly on the way out?"

"Habit?" That's all that came to Amanda's mind. "We might never know, just like why or how she ended up here. If on her own at first, maybe she wanted to feel close to him, build up her courage to see him face to face. As we talked about before with her dying from cancer, she might have wanted to clear the air between them."

"She probably had a reason to be nervous about facing Logan. If I were him, I'd be pissed with her."

"Sure, but he loves her. Can't help how you feel."

He met her gaze. "No you can't."

Her stomach fluttered. "We should go. I think we've got enough for now."

"Me too."

She put the key into an evidence bag that she got from a case in the trunk of the department car. She handed it over to the officer outside, made sure that a note of their visit was logged, and that the door would be sealed again. But not until he took the lamp in for evidence.

"Back to the station to watch the hotel video?" Trent said as he got behind the wheel, and she loaded onto the passenger seat.

The clock on the dash told her it was almost eight o'clock. They had hours of video to watch, and there would be more steps to follow from there. Not everything could get done tonight. "We've had a productive day. I say we call it. Start tomorrow at eight thirty, and see what answers we can get. I'd also like to know who called Claire at the hotel."

"Oh, let me google the number now." He pulled out his notepad and his phone, pecked the numbers into a Google search. "Bernstein at Law."

"A law firm," she said, though it was unnecessary. "Why?"

"To be continued tomorrow. Pleasant dreams." He smiled at her.

She laughed. Just as she'd thought, this case wouldn't be a quick one to solve. They'd likely be spinning for days yet. "Okay. Holding you to it."

"Fine by me." He put the car in gear and took them in the direction of the station where they'd get their own vehicles and head home.

Not that she'd be getting any sleep tonight. Why was Claire in contact with a law firm?

SEVENTEEN

Claire had led a secret life. To Amanda, that was the only thing about this case that seemed like a sure thing. The cash, the gun, the fake name, living off the grid, and now Claire was communicating with a lawyer's office. And it also couldn't be overlooked that Claire was walking around with a death sentence even before she was murdered. The big C, stalking her and readying to claim another victim itself. Claire could have just reached a lawyer to set her affairs in order. But what affairs did she have? Factoring in that private investigators couldn't find her, it could be assumed that she'd lived a rather nomadic lifestyle, bouncing around and never staying in one place for long.

On Tuesday morning, Amanda headed for her desk, but Sergeant Graves accosted her in the hallway. She asked that Amanda follow her to her office and bring her up to speed. Amanda obliged even though Graves would know most of it already. When she'd finished speaking, Graves stared at her blankly.

"That's all?" she said.

"I think that Trent and I made a lot of progress on the case for our first day. Sure, there are more unanswered questions, but that's par for the course. Evidence is telling me that Logan isn't guilty." *Just one little nudge...*

"Huh. I'm not sure it's saying that to me. She was in his house. Even if she let herself in with this key you mentioned, how did she know about it if she hadn't been in previous contact with Logan?"

Amanda smirked, turned away from the woman. She was exasperating and fixated. Her entire world must have been black and white with no allowance for shades of gray. "Claire was married to Logan for two-and-a-half years before she left him. In that time, I would assume they had a hide-a-key where they lived."

"An assumption," Graves served back, seemingly unable to see the irony as she was doing the same thing about Logan's guilt.

"I'll ask Logan if they used this fake rock when they were together."

"Be sure to do that. And this lamp... keep me posted on what the lab finds there too."

"Will do."

"Dismissed." Graves waved her hand, and Amanda shuffled to her feet, not wasting any time.

She called Logan as she walked to her desk. She had been wanting to allow him some time this morning to sleep, not sure whether he would have gotten much.

"Amanda? Tell me you know who killed her."

"There's a lot that Trent and I are finding out about Claire, but even more remains a mystery."

There was a groan followed by, "Mystery should have been her first name."

"Do you keep a key stored in a hideaway spot? Sometimes they are a little magnetic case that sticks to air conditioners, but they come in different forms." She wanted to make sure she asked without leading him.

"I sure do. You lock yourself out of your house once, you do what you can to ensure that it never happens again."

"So even when you were married to Claire?" She reached her cubicle and sat at her desk. Trent was at his, and she waved in greeting.

"Yes. She's the one who bought us a hide-a-key thingy."

"The one you still use?"

"Ah, yeah. I assume you found it—a fake rock about six inches by eight. There's an opening on the bottom. Why are you asking me about this?"

Claire had bought it. No questioning how Claire would know where to find the house key then. She probably spotted it in the garden bed and helped herself. "I can't answer that, but I have another question for you. Were you in the process of buying another shade for the lamp on your nightstand?"

"No. Seems a strange question to ask."

Adrenaline rushed through her. The theory she'd tossed around with Trent was likely exactly what had happened. Claire attacked her killer with the lamp, and that person took the shade with them.

"Mandy? Why are you asking me these things?"

"Again, I can't tell you. One more question for now. We found where Claire was staying, and there was a safe. There was at least twenty thousand dollars in cash in there. Do you have any idea why she'd have that kind of money?"

"Nope. I apparently knew nothing about my wife." There was pain laced with anger at his admission.

"Sorry, Logan."

"All the lies and secrets... hard to get my head around."

"You doing all right, though? Where are you staying?"

"With Michelle and her husband. They told me they know Trent. Good friends with him apparently."

"It's surprising you and Trent didn't meet at their wedding."

"Well I wasn't able to make it." A simple statement, but it

felt weighed down with regret. She didn't feel right about pushing him for a reason. It might have just been that it was hard being around Michelle with Claire in the wind.

"Take care, okay? Call if you need anything." She ended the call. Trent was looking at her over the divider between their cubicles. She filled him in on her conversation with Logan and where he was staying.

"It certainly is a small world. I never even heard them mention Logan's name before, but I guess they wouldn't have had much reason to bring him up. Not with how quiet Shell was about Claire. I mean I never even knew she had a sister."

"Family can be rough." She was blessed by a big, rather functional one. "So I just got back from speaking with Graves. She wanted an update."

"That explains that sour look you had on your face."

"She still thinks Logan killed her." She couldn't dwell on that for long or she'd get angry. "What have you been working on?"

"I called the law office, but they're not open until nine. Just got on Claire Ramsey's Facebook and was looking at her feed."

"Oh." Amanda walked to his cubicle. "Any friends named Roo by chance?"

"Nope, but there's definitely one person who Claire was in a fair amount of contact with."

"And you could find all this without logging into Claire's actual account?"

"She has her settings public."

"Doesn't really go with the rest of her life, how she typically took precautions."

"Well, nobody's perfect."

Amanda couldn't help but think maybe the social media site afforded the younger Claire some semblance of normality.

Trent continued. "Now, there were a lot of comments to Claire's posts by a woman named Rita Flynn."

"Click her profile, let's see who she is."

Trent did just that, and a quick look at the posts to her time-line had them staring back at each other.

"Condolences," she muttered. "Rita Flynn is dead too? When was this?" Tingles ran through her as the answer was in front of her. The sympathies were recent.

He scrolled down. "From what I'm gathering, I'd say she died in an accident in the last few days... Looks like the posts start last Friday."

"The day Claire was murdered. Quick. Type Rita's name into the system. See if you can get more information about when and how she died." *An accident...* It could be a coincidence that Claire and her friend were dead within a day or two of each other, but Amanda had a burning hunch it wasn't.

Trent pulled her background, and it showed her deceased as of last Thursday. "She died the day *before* Claire was murdered. Is this just a coincidence or...?"

His tone of voice relayed he didn't think there was anything coincidental about it either. "I don't think so."

"Were Claire and Rita involved in something illegal together, that finally caught up to them?"

"Could be, but how far back do we look? Years?"

"And it looks like there's an age gap between the two women of six years. How did they become connected? What bonded them?"

"Hard to say at this point. Cause of death?"

He pointed to his screen. "A car accident last Thursday afternoon. Looks like her vehicle careened off Interstate 95."

"Can you see anything about what caused the accident?"

"Not here."

"There's no way this was an accident," she said with conviction, although it must have presented as one for the state police to deem it as such.

"You think someone caused the vehicle to go off the road?"

She couldn't ignore the niggling in her gut, the one reminding her that Logan had a car accident not long before Claire left him. An accident Logan himself had said freaked Claire out. It was more than a wife fearing she could have lost her husband. It had to be. Claire ran away not long after, throwing away her marriage at the same time. Had she suspected someone tried to take out Logan? By extension, had Rita been targeted? "We need to find out what caused her car to lose control."

"I can call the officer on file with the state police."

"You could, but I want to talk to her next of kin. They might be able to tell us something about Claire while we're there too."

"Looks like Rita left behind a husband and two kids, a boy and girl."

Her heart splintered at the thought of disturbing their grieving process, but the intrusion could prove crucial for their case. "We don't have any other choice."

"Do you want to go now or head over to the lawyer's first?"

She shook her head. She knew the husband wouldn't be sleeping, and it was one visit she wanted to get over with. "We'll start with Mr. Flynn."

EIGHTEEN

There were two vehicles in the driveway, both middle-class suburban. One an SUV, the other a sedan.

Trent rang the doorbell and waited patiently. He understood Amanda wanting to come here after she had filled him in on Logan's accident and added that Claire took off not much later. Amanda had said Claire seemed spooked, according to Logan, but there was a chance it didn't have to do with the accident. He and Amanda could be chasing shadows.

The door was opened by a boy about ten, who gave him and Amanda the once-over, and from his face didn't really know what to make of them.

"Yeah?" he said, barely coherent.

"Would your father be home?" Trent asked him.

The boy nodded and let the door remain open, the invite for them to step inside unspoken but apparent. Trent stayed put, and so did Amanda. The boy's footsteps padded farther into the house.

A man came toward the front door, brow furrowed, gaze on Trent. "Can I help you?"

Trent held up his badge, and Amanda edged closer to him

so the man could see her and her badge too. "Detectives with Prince William County PD," Trent told him. "Are you Austin Flynn?"

"Yeah." Hesitant and uncertain.

"We have a few questions about your wife," Trent began. "If we could come in for a minute, we would appreciate it."

"Not sure what you'd have to ask... but sure. I can't spare much time, though. My parents are here."

"We won't be long. I promise."

The man dipped his head and gestured for Trent and Amanda to enter. The house was tidy and smelled strongly of flowers.

"Somewhere we could sit might be best." Trent phrased it more as a suggestion, not a requirement. They weren't here with further bad news but talk about his recently deceased wife would be upsetting.

He took them to a sitting room. There was no sign of the parents, but they could have been in another part of the house with the children. They hadn't seen the girl. A slight hissing sound had Trent turning, and he saw a scent diffuser in an outlet. A fresh dose of floral was pushed out.

Austin dropped into a chair directly across from a fireplace, and Trent and Amanda sat in chairs that had their backs to it.

"First of all, we're very sorry for the loss of your wife," Trent said.

"What is this about?"

Not the response that Trent had expected. Maybe he was tired of hearing sympathies. "We understand it was a car accident that took her life."

"That's right."

"What caused the car to lose control?" He was careful about putting the onus on the vehicle not the man's dead wife.

Austin rubbed his left temple. "Her brakes failed. Guess it happens."

Same thing that happened to Logan. But surely there needed to be more to rouse true suspicion. And, sure, Claire had a connection to both Rita and Logan, but that too was thin. But it was Austin's uncertainty that had the hairs rising on the back of Trent's neck. "Is there a part of you that believes something else caused her accident?"

Austin rubbed his forehead. "What do I know, but she had her car serviced a week ago." His eyes were full of anguish.

Trent refused to grant Amanda eye contact, but he could feel her burning a hole in the side of his head. It was starting to feel like the conspiracy was gaining some ground. "And they looked at her brakes specifically?"

"Yes."

Trent had heard of brake lines and knew if they were cut, it was bad news, but sabotage like that would likely be easy to spot.

"Do they know why the brakes failed?" Amanda asked.

"Some cap was missing from under the hood. I'm not a car guy so I'm sort of at their mercy and discretion." Austin looked back and forth at the two of them, as if he was finally suspecting there might be more.

"The cap on the master cylinder," Amanda said. "It's where the brake fluid goes. To work, the system needs to be under pressure. Without that cap, it wouldn't be. The brakes wouldn't fail completely, but they would be mostly ineffective, especially if your wife was moving at a fast speed."

"She was on the highway."

They knew she had been on the interstate, but the cause of the brake failure wasn't anything Trent had heard of before. Though he was certainly more handyman than he was mechanic. Set him free to work on home renovations—plumbing, wiring, construction—but don't ask him to touch anything under the hood of a vehicle. Amanda's knowledge on the matter was impressive, but was likely credited to her brother, Kyle, who was a licensed mechanic and from what Trent gathered, had always been into cars.

"That's all it would take," Amanda said, glancing at Trent. If he was reading her right, she had more to say on the topic and whatever it was, it would not be good.

"Is that something that just happens?" Austin's eyes were full of tears.

Amanda took a deep breath, so well hidden, it would have been easy to miss. "You said your wife recently had the car serviced. It's possible that they topped up the brake fluid but didn't tighten the lid."

Austin went pale. "My poor Rita."

Trent couldn't truly imagine what this man was going through right now. But he had a feeling there was more to this than Amanda was letting on to the widower. He'd ask her once they were back in the car. "We are investigating a case at the moment, Mr. Flynn. Have you heard of a Claire Hunter? You may have known her as Claire Ramsey."

Austin pointed behind Trent. He turned, not knowing what he was to be looking at. "The picture on the right," Austin added.

It was of Austin and Rita, and their wedding day with their party.

"Claire was Rita's maid of honor," Austin said.

Then Trent noticed the decade-younger Claire. She would have been in her early twenties at that point. Claire was smiling in the photo, but the expression didn't quite reach her eyes.

"They were the best of friends," Austin put in. "Nearly inseparable."

"Do you know how they met?" Trent was thinking of the age gap between Claire and Rita, again finding it strange they'd been so close. What had bonded them?

Austin shook his head. "Not really sure, but the friendship

pre-dated me by years." Tears pooled in his eyes. "I'm going to miss that woman."

"Do you know when Rita last saw Claire?" Trent watched as Austin's face shadowed, then he grimaced.

"Years ago. Claire just up and left without a word to Rita. It really hurt her."

There must have been some forgiveness, though, or Rita wouldn't have left a picture of the wedding party that included Claire on the mantle. "Is there some way maybe your wife and Claire stayed in touch without you knowing it?"

"We told each other everything."

Except details about her relationship with Claire... What necessitated the secrecy? And did it have anything to do with why they were both dead—one blatantly murdered, the other under suspicious circumstances?

"Did your wife have any nicknames?" Amanda inserted.

"A few, I guess. Why?"

"Was she ever called Roo?"

He pressed his lips and shook his head. "Never heard that one. Why are you here anyway? You mentioned an investigation and brought up Claire... And you never did say what unit you're with."

"Homicide." Trent had a feeling that was all it would take to get the wheels turning in Austin's mind.

"Homicide," Austin parroted as if he needed to say it out loud for it to sink in. He swallowed and licked his lips. "And you are asking about my wife's crash... Did someone cause her accident on purpose?" He grimaced like a sharp pain bit his side, and maybe one had.

"That we don't know. What we know is Claire was murdered last Friday night and your wife died Thursday. They were close, as you just told us. We think that there *may* be some connection between their deaths." Trent presented the possibility as tactfully as he could.

"Like I said, they haven't been in touch for years."

"We're still working to sort everything out," Amanda said.

Trent considered his next words carefully. "We have reason to believe that Claire may have been caught up in something illegal. Do you have any idea what that might have been?"

"No."

The next bit would require a skilled dance of diplomacy and persuasiveness. "It seems Claire was involved with something for several years. Your wife ever mention concern about her friend?"

"No, and if Rita had known Claire was up to something illegal, she would have turned her in. My wife was an honorable woman, a university professor, part of the parents' committee at our children's school, she volunteered at the homeless shelter—and not just during holidays."

"We're not saying your wife had nefarious dealings," Trent said.

"You're insinuating it." Austin stood. "I think it's time for you to go."

"We'll leave." Amanda stood and motioned for Trent to join her. He didn't want to go, feeling like they were just getting to the meat of things.

He pulled his card and handed it to Austin. "Call if you think of anything, no matter how small it might seem."

"Sure." The way Austin tossed out the word, Trent wouldn't be holding his breath for a phone call. The man might have suspicions about his wife's car accident, but he wasn't ready to navigate the rocky path to see them through.

They got in the car, Trent confirmed the lawyer's office was their next stop and started driving. "So what was with that look you gave me in there around the time you were talking about the brake failure? It was like there was more you wanted to say but not in front of Flynn."

"You're getting spooky-good at reading my mind, you know

that?" Her lips set in a thin, straight line, and she turned to him. "Those caps don't just come off. One, a mechanic is going to tighten the cap. Two, say if there was human error, the brake failure would have happened before her accident took place. Austin told us the car service was a week before. She has two young children and had a job. She would have driven that car several times before the brakes ended up failing."

"Someone tampered with her car."

Amanda nodded. "I'd say so."

"The same person who was behind Logan's crash in Nebraska?"

"I think so. Also the person who has shown up to kill Claire Hunter."

He took a right at the light and glanced in his rearview mirror. The sun bounced off the windshield of a silver sedan a few cars back, catching his eye. "What the hell is going on? And who else might be in danger?"

"Please don't even go there."

"Oh, I'm not thinking there's some mad serial killer out there." Lord knows they'd run into enough of them, and he was a little twitchy around the subject on the best of days. He'd been shot years ago when he'd assisted the FBI's Behavioral Analysis Unit in hunting one in Prince William County.

"Claire and Rita very well may be as far as this thing goes. Let's hope the killing stops with them."

"So who's behind the deaths and why?" He took another right, checked his mirror again, and saw the sedan take the turn on a red.

"The questions," she said. "Whoever it is, though, they are not beyond taking efforts to cast the light off themselves. Not the way they'd lined everything up to make Logan look guilty. We need to take a close look at everything left at that scene. I'll text CSI Blair about the lingerie, see if there's any potential lead there. Maybe we can determine where it was bought and who purchased it." Amanda pulled out her phone and started pecking away, presumably doing just that.

"Be nice to have ballistics and prints back on that gun in Claire's purse sooner rather than later too."

"I'll follow up with the lab if we don't hear by tomorrow, but that's probably pushing things."

Trent took a left, looked back in his mirror. No silver sedan within sight. It could be behind other vehicles. Either that or he was on edge, seeing things that weren't there. He'd blame the case—conspiracies around every corner. "Do you think the husband knows something he isn't telling us?"

"Gut feeling? No, I didn't get that from him. We can pull Rita's background, but I bet it will be clean."

"Think so too." He pulled into the lot for Bernstein at Law.

A silver Toyota Camry drove on past. Trent swore it slowed down just a little. He couldn't make out the plate, but reasoned he was just being paranoid.

NINETEEN

She loved him, and that's exactly why she had to leave him. And right away. Before any more "accidents" could occur. She ran around the house, gathering as much as she could and stuffing it into her duffel bag. All the while Logan was asleep in the guest room, where he went because he didn't want to keep her up. But she couldn't let herself give in to feeling sorry for herself, or Logan. This was how it had to be. She should be happy for the time she'd had with him.

She should have known her past would catch up with her— despite her precautions. How he had found her didn't even matter. He was here now—in Nebraska, breathing down her neck. All because she'd royally screwed up years ago. She had tipped her hand, her brilliant mind failing her when feelings for Logan had come into play. Well, now she was paying for being so stupid, for thinking she could drop the bomb she had and just walk away unscathed. Of course, he'd come after her—and just when she had given herself over to the fantasy that she might be free...

She pulled the door of the house shut behind her and threw the deadbolt. She tossed her bag onto the back seat of her BMW and gunned it down the road as fast as she could. She couldn't be tempted to go back, to entertain doubts, to question whether she was making the right decision. She was making the only one she could. She had to let Logan go if she wanted him to live.

Gravel kicked up from under her wheels in plumes of dust, shrouding her escape. But she still felt like eyes were watching her even though there was no one for miles around. There were no lights shining in her rearview mirror and not another vehicle on the road. She was alone. Just as life had intended for her. Alone and looking over a shoulder. All because of one bad decision that had led to several.

And it wasn't like she was a stranger to standing up for herself. She was all she really had in this world. That's what she told herself repeatedly as the guilt burrowed into her soul. Logan didn't deserve to be left this way, but she didn't see a way around it. She was certain he wouldn't walk away from the next accident.

The man stalking her would ensure that was the case. He'd use Logan as leverage to make her bend to his wishes without compunction. After all, he had proven himself a killer already. Don't they say after you take your first life, it gets easier from there?

The thing is, she'd been feeling watched for a while, but she'd just dismissed it as paranoia. Not now. Not when Logan could have been killed!

She had to think ahead to her future and make wise choices based on logic, not emotion. It had caused her flawed thinking to start with. She'd reasoned if she started living a good life, a pure one, it would compensate for past sins. That's how she had justified marrying Logan. Even if some of it was a lie. Not the "loving him" part. That was the real deal. And she could have had a future with him, if not for her past. The lie was the one where she told herself she was normal, like other people.

She pulled out a small brass key, thinking of the power it

held. *What it unlocked was what the man wanted, but it was also the only thing keeping her alive. With it, she had some leverage. How did her stalker not appreciate that?*

She pushed harder on the gas. *Never look back. That had to become her new motto if she were to survive. Once she got to wherever she ended up, she'd ditch the car too. Start fresh.*

As long as she was on the move, that man couldn't find her. She'd be safe. Logan would be safe.

But what if she got tired of running?

TWENTY

The woman at the front desk of Bernstein at Law had her hair pulled back so tightly, it looked like it tugged on her forehead.

Amanda held up her badge and gave a brief introduction. "We believe that Deb Smith may have been a client of the firm. Does that name sound familiar to you?" It made sense to roll with the alias to start. They still didn't even know what Claire's business might have been here.

"Not off the top of my head. One minute." She clicked on the keyboard, then pressed her lips and shook her head. "No one by that name in our system."

"Try Claire Hunter," Trent said.

"Ah, sure." More clacking of keys. "Yes, I show a Claire Hunter. May I ask what this is regarding?"

Claire had used her real name here. Did that mean anything? "We're working an investigation," Amanda began. "Do you know why Ms. Hunter hired your firm?" They'd looked up the firm before coming, and it appeared they had attorneys on staff with a variety of specialties.

"Looks like Ms. Hunter was interested in criminal defense."

Criminal defense... What business did Claire have with

defense lawyers? Was she about to hand herself over for some-thing and needed representation? Was it linked with all that cash and the gun in her purse? "We need to speak to the lawyer Claire worked with. Are they in?"

The clerk consulted her screen. "That's Duncan McGuire. He's in. One moment."

While she was on the phone, Trent leaned in toward Aman-da's ear. "He's not going to talk to us. Attorney–client privilege survives death of a client."

She stepped a few feet from the counter, guiding Trent with a hand on his elbow but let go when she realized it felt like she was disciplining a child. Not what she was going for. She said, "We need to give it a go. And if we deem it relevant to the case, we can request a court order that will make him talk."

"Detectives? Mr. McGuire will see you now." The clerk directed them down a side hall to the third door on the right.

A handsome man in his forties sat at a conference table. He had his upper body leaned forward to show he was open to talk-ing, but they would have to see just how open.

"Thank you for seeing us, Mr. McGuire," she said while closing the door behind her and Trent, to seal them and Duncan in the room. "I'm Detective Amanda Steele, and this is Detective Trent Stenson."

"If we could make it quick. I have a client meeting in fifteen minutes." Duncan made a show of checking the time on his wristwatch, possibly a Rolex from the look of it.

She dropped into the chair directly across from him, and Trent sat next to her. "We understand you had a client named Claire Hunter."

A pressed smile, arrogant, smug. "Had? That's fine if she went elsewhere, but the firm isn't returning her retainer."

A retainer would confirm that Claire was indeed a client of the firm. "Claire is dead. Murdered." She put that last part out to see if it netted a reaction. All Duncan did was sit back, a grim tightness to his mouth.

"Unfortunate, but attorney–client privilege continues indefinitely. I'm sorry I couldn't be of more help." He went to stand. She held up a hand.

"You could be the link that helps us figure out who shot her, Mr. McGuire," she said, trying to appeal to his humanity. It met with a sour expression. Maybe his work defending criminals had desensitized him.

"I see what you're trying to do, but it won't work. I'm bound by the law."

"That law can be overridden by a judge who issues a court order to make you tell us what was said between the two of you."

"Do what you must."

"That could take a significant amount of time, during which Claire's killer is free." She didn't even know why she bothered continuing to try to break through this guy's armor.

"If you won't tell us what you discussed, will you answer yes or no to some questions we have?" Trent proposed.

Duncan looked at him. "We can give it a try."

"Did you call Claire at Lux Suites?" Trent began.

"I did." Spoken slowly like Duncan was bored and uninspired by their continued presence.

Trent went on. "Were you returning her call?"

Amanda knew where Trent was headed with his questioning, but there was nothing to support that Claire had ever called the lawyer—unless she did it from the phone in the lobby.

"She came in last Wednesday demanding a meeting with a lawyer. No one was available on call like that." He pulled this face like any lawyer who was on call was a loser.

"What time was this?" Amanda asked.

"About ten, ten thirty, in the morning."

That was before she'd checked in at Lux Suites, so Claire

could have made this law office her first stop in Dumfries. "So she was here, and you just sent her on her way?" Amanda was rather offset by this man's arrogance. He gave defense attorneys a bad rep.

"Cindy did."

"And who is Cindy?" Trent asked.

"The receptionist."

"Okay, when did she pay you a retainer?" Amanda knew if money hadn't exchanged hands, Duncan wouldn't owe Claire confidentiality. But he'd already said she had.

"She left ten K in cash right then and there. With Cindy."

"Just like that? Handed it over?" Trent asked, his eyes lit with astonishment.

"Yep. So I made time for a phone call, got some basics."

Duncan's phrasing implied he felt he'd done Claire a favor despite the money. "Didn't you or Cindy find it odd she handed over that much in cash?"

Duncan tilted his head. "Myself and two others in the firm specialize in defense. There are some questions we don't ask our clientele. Where they get their money is one of them."

Don't know, can't tell... "So what did Claire want your help for?"

A crooked smirk and a wagging finger.

"All right, let me ask this then. Did she give you the specifics of what she wanted help with?"

He shrugged—noncommittal, but she'd take it as a yes.

"Did she say that she expected charges would be levied against her soon?" Amanda asked.

"Yes."

"Robbery charges?" Her mind was on all that cash. It had to have come from somewhere and theft seemed like a fast way of getting it.

A slow blink. "Yes."

"But there's more...?" Amanda angled her head, prompting the attorney to continue.

"Ask a question."

Amanda's thoughts shifted to the unregistered gun in Claire's possession. "Did she shoot and injure someone in the course of a robbery?"

"No."

"She..." Amanda had expected a different response. She leaned back in her chair. Claire was involved in a robbery, as confirmed by Duncan. But how the hell did the gun tie in? Or did it? Were she and Trent eager to see what wasn't there? Maybe she'd just picked up the gun along the way for protection—nothing more.

"Listen, I'll save you any more trouble. We didn't get into a myriad of specifics, as I said. We were scheduled to meet yesterday, but she never showed. You said she's dead, so I guess that explains why."

Still no real regard for the fact a woman was *murdered*. "That's all then? Nothing more to share with us?"

"Nope. And don't trouble yourselves with a court order. I'd swear on a stack of Bibles, there's nothing more to say."

"Then we're done here. Thank you for your cooperation today." Amanda gave him a pleasant smile as she stood. She gave him her card—even if it might land straight in the trash. He said there was nothing more to say, and somehow Amanda believed him.

She and Trent left the firm and headed back to Central in Woodbridge.

"There's only one reason you reach out to a criminal defense attorney," she muttered, not even sure where she was going with this or how Trent would pick up from there.

"Claire figured she would need one at some point. That much is clear."

"Yeah." She worried her lip. Her gut was telling her Claire's Glock was more than an accessory she toted around. "If Claire didn't shoot someone and the gun wasn't for personal protection, that leaves one viable possibility. She may have had a partner on the robbery who *did* hurt or kill someone. She might have even planned on turning them in. It would seem she was planning to confess her wrongdoing." Claire getting a lawyer suggested that much.

"That right there could be motive for murder. That's if there is a partner and they found out."

She nodded. "But when did this robbery even happen? Years ago, I suppose we're assuming, and she just held on to the gun all this time?"

"She could have thought it offered her a bargaining chip or protection. But there's a flip side to consider. If that was her intention, and she revealed her hand, she could have been viewed as a liability."

Amanda felt nauseous. "Why Claire was on the run all these years."

"But how did Claire come into possession of the gun in the first place?"

"And, then there's this. What's to say the gun wasn't planted too?"

"For what purpose, though?"

"The killer wanted it to look like Claire was responsible for whatever happened in the past. If it only has her prints on it, for example, we wouldn't even question that, as it was in her purse. Say there is a cold case out there, it would appear closed too."

"I'm curious to see what ballistics come back with. If it is linked to an old case, the killer could have planted Claire's prints on the Glock, like he or she might have on Logan's."

"Let's talk this out then. The killer found out Claire had the gun *and* was back in town—both of which we don't know the how of yet. And let's say Logan's 'accident' in Nebraska was nothing of the sort—which I don't think it was."

Trent shook his head. "Rita's neither. And she kept some things from her husband, such as her history with Claire. I think it's likely whatever got Claire killed ended up getting Rita murdered as well. Along the lines we thought before: the accident wasn't an accident. Must be one hell of a secret they've been carrying around all these years."

"But we circle back. How does the gun Claire had end up getting Rita killed—if that's what happened? Did this hypothetical partner think Claire gave the gun to Rita? Had she held on to it for a while before it wound up in Claire's purse?"

"The husband said Rita and Claire hadn't talked in years, so when would the possible handover have taken place?"

"We'll need to figure out if it even did. I'd like to know if Claire told Rita of her plans to go to the police. And I know I said I would give the lab until tomorrow on the ballistics results, but we need answers yesterday." She pulled her phone, just as it rang. Too much to hope it was the lab with the results, like some sort of telepathic link. The caller ID told her it was someone else. She answered, "Logan?"

"I was just at Claire's estate lawyer's."

"I'm putting you on speaker. Trent's here." She did just that. "You were at her estate lawyer's? How did they even know that—"

"Michelle told them that Claire was dead."

"Usually they require a death certificate before saying anything," Amanda said.

"Which Michelle got from a Hans Rideout."

Amanda hadn't even heard that Michelle had positively identified Claire at the morgue yet. "Okay, so what happened with the lawyer?"

"He called me there, said Claire left something for me."

"Do you know what it is?"

"Yes and no. I mean I got a key and a note. It belongs to a

safe deposit box in Woodbridge at a place called Locked Up Tight. Number seventeen-thirty."

A key... There was a small brass one in Claire's purse along with the hotel key card. Was it for the box too? They hadn't gotten that far. Amanda's pulse was racing. Maybe this development would give them all the answers they needed. Was it too much to hope that Claire left a letter saying that if she was murdered, so-and-so did it? "Did you go there? See what's in it?"

"I haven't yet. I was hoping that you would come with me."

"What did the note say?" Trent asked.

"Just that once I got to the box, there would be a letter inside explaining why she had to leave and everything else."

She did a quick estimate based on how close they were to the police station and considered the drive to Dumfries. "I'll be by to pick you up at the Maxwells' in twenty minutes."

She ended the call as Trent pulled into the station's parking lot. "You want to follow up on the ballistics while I go see Logan? Also watch some video, with your eye on the times the clerk thought Claire took a taxi. Maybe we can find out if Rita and Claire were in recent contact, despite what the husband told us."

"Can do. I'll also swing back to the hotel and see if they recognize Rita. I know the clerk said he didn't remember visitors, but I doubt he works twenty-four seven. Rita could have gone there."

"Sounds like it's worth a try."

"All right, then." He stopped the department car to let her out, then left.

She hustled to her Honda Civic, wanting to get to Logan—and that safe deposit box—as soon as possible. She had one leg in her car when she heard her name.

"Detective Steele." It was Sergeant Graves.

Amanda stood next to her vehicle and faced the woman. "Good day, Sergeant."

"Haven't heard from you since this morning." She thumbed her key fob, and the lights flicked on a Mercedes sedan. She must have made good money with the NYPD because someone on a sergeant's salary in Prince William County wasn't driving one. "What's going on with the case?"

Amanda filled her in.

"Sounds like you're making some progress," Graves said. "It would seem this Claire Hunter had things to hide."

About time she came around to that! "It does, and Trent and I are working to find out what because we're quite certain whatever her secrets were, they wound up getting her murdered." Amanda wasn't getting into Rita's accident with the sergeant.

"Keep me posted. Don't make me flag you down in the parking lot next time." Graves didn't smile, but Amanda swore she detected humor in the sergeant's voice. After all, Amanda wasn't what dragged Graves outside. It would seem it was either her lunch break or she had an appointment somewhere.

Amanda sat in her Civic and watched Graves leave. She and Trent had been so consumed trying to uncover Claire's story that there hadn't been any time to dig into Graves. Now wasn't the time either. Amanda wanted to know what was in that safe deposit box.

TWENTY-ONE

The people at Locked Up Tight were more accommodating once they saw Claire Hunter's death certificate paired with a letter provided by her estate attorney. Amanda and Logan were led to box 1730. It was about four rows up from the floor and center on a wall full of compartments.

The clerk put their key in, and Logan inserted the one he'd picked up from the estate lawyer.

The box was released from its cubbyhole.

"There are private spaces over there for you." The clerk gestured toward two stalls with doors before walking off.

Amanda guessed the spaces were soundproof as well in case customers wanted to make phone calls or received any.

Amanda went to one but turned when Logan hadn't followed. He was holding on to the box and trembling. "You all right?"

"No."

She squeezed his shoulder. "I'm not going to lie and say what comes next is going to be easy. We have no idea what's waiting for us, but you've been waiting a long time for answers. Now you can get them."

"I know. It's just all this makes it feel so final. She's gone. I couldn't save her. Hell, I'm being charged with her murder." His voice cracked on the last word, and it had a lump forming in Amanda's throat.

"I'm working to help you. Now this is what you can do to help yourself. That box"—she pointed to it in his hands—"may give you that. And trust me, you are far more resilient than you think."

He met her eyes, his gaze soft and warm. "Okay, let's do this."

"You got it."

They went into a stall and shut the door. Compact with a table and a chair against the back wall. There was just enough room for that and two people, but it was a tight fit.

Amanda let Logan sit, and she stood to his left.

"Here goes," he said as he lifted the lid.

Her heart picked up speed, but nearly stopped at what she saw. Nothing.

"It's empty," Logan burst out. "I thought it felt light, but... you've got to be freaking kidding me."

It took a few seconds for Amanda to shake the shock, but then she moved behind him and put both her hands on his shoulders. "I'm sorry, Logan."

He took a heaving breath that had his broad shoulders rising and squaring.

She rubbed his arms and leaned over, wrapping her arms around the front of his chest and putting her face against his neck. Her cheek to his, she tapped a kiss there and just let the moment suspend in time.

A couple of minutes had easily passed before he tapped the back of her arm. She returned to full height.

"We'll figure this out," she said. "We'll talk to them at the front. See what they can tell us and go from there. You can stay here for a bit if you want."

"Nah, I'm fine." He sniffled and stood. They returned the box to the cubbyhole where it came from and went to the clerk who had helped them upon arrival.

"The box was empty. Can you tell us when Claire Hunter was last here?" Amanda held up her badge, having had no reason to show it before now.

The clerk's eyes danced over the gold shield. "Sure." She typed into the computer, then said, "Looks like it was this past Friday afternoon. Four thirty."

Mere hours before her murder. "Were you here then?"

"I was."

"Do you remember her? Long brown hair, likely straightened, gray eyes, mid-thirties?"

"Yes."

"Was she with anyone?"

"No, I don't think so."

"Did you see how she got here?"

"I think she walked from somewhere."

This place was a fair distance from Lux Suites for her to have huffed it by foot. She might not have been dropped off right at the doors though. Possibly in the lot or down the street. "Do you have security cameras that cover the lot?"

"Just inside." She pointed to a camera nestled against the ceiling in one corner of the room. "It covers the front desk and door."

Amanda's mind was running wild. Why would Claire leave a note with the estate lawyer for Logan to come here for answers if she was just going to empty the box? Did this letter also implicate someone in a crime, and had that person found out? Had Claire been forced to remove and destroy the letter? And going back to her conversation with Trent, had Claire also held on to the Glock all these years to use against a partner as a bargaining chip? Had it been in the box along with the letter for

Logan? "Thanks for your help." Amanda tapped the counter and motioned for Logan to lead the way outside.

"What the hell, Mandy?" Logan flailed his arms. "She tells me to come here, then empties the box. That's a new low."

"I'm not sure she had a choice."

"Oh please."

Did she tell him her suspicion? "Think about it. Why leave a note if she was going to empty it out? That makes no sense."

Logan looked over at her. "What are you saying? Someone forced her to do it? Why?"

She couldn't disclose too much and risk compromising the case. Logan might be able to help her stitch the timeline together though. "When did Claire leave that note with her estate lawyer?"

"Here's the real kicker. I asked that question. Turns out before we left for Nebraska."

Amanda gave that some thought. "I'll be right back." She went back inside and asked the clerk when Claire had first rented the box. Her answer confirmed that Claire had secrets long before meeting Logan.

TWENTY-TWO

There wasn't much Amanda could say to Logan about Claire because he was no longer listening. She dropped him off at the Maxwells' house, grabbed something quick to eat, and returned to Central.

She found Trent at his desk and went over to him. "The safe deposit box was empty."

"Thought he was told to go there."

"Uh-huh, he was. But apparently, Claire was there last Friday afternoon."

"The same day she died."

"Yes, that tidbit didn't escape my notice either. But it doesn't make sense that she'd send Logan there only to empty it ahead of time." She told Trent that she thought the killer might have forced Claire to do it. And if not that, she could have felt pressured to do so. She then shared what else she'd learned from the clerk at Locked Up Tight. "Claire rented the box when she was twenty-one. That's fifteen years ago. In all this time she's only been back twice. Once the day before leaving for Nebraska, and once last Friday when she removed the contents." She stopped talking as Trent's grin kept growing bigger. "What is it?"

"Oh, let's say some things are coming together, but before I get to the real juicy bits, I went to Lux Suites. No one recognized Rita Flynn."

"All right, so if they were in recent contact, it wasn't there."

"Yep. Now, I called the lab about the ballistics on the Glock. Turns out they were just about to call you." Trent stopped talking there and paled.

"What?"

"They also had the results for the bullet that killed Claire. It was fired from Logan's gun, Amanda."

She let that hit sink in, but she couldn't say she was surprised. "Just means whoever is trying to pin this on Logan has done a damn good job."

"Good enough that unless we find something substantive in his favor, he's going to prison for a murder he didn't commit."

She had promised Logan that she'd help him and so far she was failing miserably. "What were the results on Claire's gun?"

"They're why I was smiling. It's tied to a cold *murder* case."

"Unsolved murder makes you happy?"

"When it could bring answers that take us close to Claire's true killer, it does. We might even close the cold one. Wouldn't be the first time."

"Talk to me."

"The victim was Martin Lawson, fifty-six. He was a wealthy businessman who made a hobby of collecting antiquities, fine artwork, sculptures. He was shot during the course of a robbery."

"Oh. When was this?"

"Fifteen years ago this August."

"Claire opened the safe deposit box that year. Also in August." Chills spread over her arms. The theory about Claire holding on to a gun that was involved in a crime seemed to be firming up. But was she the one who had pulled the trigger, or had an accomplice? One would think the latter as she wound up murdered. "Did police have any strong suspects?"

Trent shook his head. "Of course, everyone in Lawson's world was suspect and interviewed at great length."

"Where was he killed?"

"At his investment firm in Washington. Guess he had an entire floor of his building dedicated to his collection."

"Let's say she'd had the gun in her possession since the shooting, why keep it? Why not destroy it? Was it as we discussed before? She kept it for insurance so if her partner ever turned on her, she could produce the gun."

"You should know only Claire's prints were on the gun."

"The killer planted them for the reason we discussed before. He or she wanted us to dismiss the prints. Then if ballistics were run and tied to the Lawson case, Claire would look guilty."

"Right, while they walk off scot-free. For at least two murders—Lawson's and Claire's. Possibly Rita's."

"Yep."

"Okay, so do you have the investigators at the lab examining it closer? Seeing if they can spot even the teeniest of smudges that could put anyone else's fingers on the Glock? DNA even? He or she might have missed something."

"Yes. I have them doing the same to Logan's gun, just in case the real shooter messed up there too. We still need to answer how the killer knew where to find Logan's gun and ammo. Or did they get lucky? But there's more. I uncovered several reports of valuables stolen in Prince William County and DC areas in the last twenty years."

"Claire would have been sixteen. Rather young if she was involved going back that far. And what makes you think they're connected?"

"I'm not talking stereos and flat-screen TVs. In the cases I'm referring to, the targets were all very wealthy and prided themselves on their artwork and antiquities collections."

"Any witnesses? Video at any of these places?"

"Some described a blond woman who befriended them."

"Claire was a brunette, but she could have worn a wig."

"Thought the same. Other descriptors such as weight and height could fit Claire. We'd have to track down the victims and show them her picture to be sure."

"How many are we talking?"

"Twenty-two heists that I believe are connected in the twenty-year period."

"Wow. What's the estimated value of the items stolen in these heists?"

"North of eighty mil."

"Holy crap."

"That's what I thought."

"Quite a far cry from Claire's twenty K."

"Claire probably kept money in several locations. Also the take wasn't hers alone. There were at least two perps at one heist. You asked about video. There was one. Apparently, the quality is horrid, and the perps were also clad in black. Only thing determined was one was male, the other female."

"Claire and Mystery Guy." As she tagged him with the moniker, she hated how often it was assigned in investigations. "Run me through the Lawson robbery. You said it was at his investment firm. What time of day are we talking about and why was he there?"

"Was about midnight. He left a formal charity event he was attending that night with his wife, Mona Lawson. Police tracked Lawson's calls, but none came in the night of the robbery. So no one called him in to work."

"Whatever got him there went to his grave."

"And likely Claire's," Trent said. "I'm thinking the heist may have been a partial cover for Lawson's murder."

"You think his murder was premeditated?"

"I think it's something we should consider."

"How much was taken from the Lawson guy?"

"Close to thirty-five million in jewels and priceless statues, including a Fabergé egg. That alone had a value of twenty-five mil."

"And I assume that's the case with all these heists... items not cash?"

"That's right."

"These types of goods don't just disappear. It's not like you can turn them into your local pawnbroker."

"Exactly why I figure all these heists were done by the same mystery couple, as I said. Also, I reached out to a few detectives who were assigned to the different heists over the years. Cameras were always taken out the same way—except for that one that had a crappy feed—and as far as they're aware none of these items have turned up."

"For what we're talking about, I imagine there would only be a handful of buyers. I'd also suspect any transactions would take place over the phone or the dark web."

"Well, Lawson's widow is still around, lives in the place she shared with him actually. I thought maybe if we popped over there, she might have something to offer us."

"Let's do it." Amanda sprung up, thinking that maybe this day could turn around. "Did the lab say anything about the lingerie or the lamp?"

"The lingerie is a dead end. Generic label for sale at numerous department stores and online."

"That doesn't sound like anyplace Claire would have shopped. No credit cards for one thing. And the designer jeans... Claire liked the finer things."

"And had the money for them. As for the lamp, they had a closer look and found Claire's prints."

She smiled at that. It always felt incredible when a theory

panned out. "She could have wielded it as a weapon. Any trace from another person?"

"No luck there."

Guess I was being greedy...

They loaded into the department car and headed out.

The Lawson estate was immaculate and set behind a gate with an intercom system. Amanda and Trent were buzzed through, and a woman on staff opened the door for them. Mona Lawson was standing in the marble foyer, at the base of a sweeping staircase. She was beautiful and in her mid-fifties. Amanda went through the formal introductions.

"Detectives, how lovely. You finally find out who killed my dear Martin?" There was a cool demeanor about the woman.

Technically that responsibility landed on the shoulders of the Metro PD, but Amanda said, "Unfortunately not."

"Oh." One syllable, and with it a wave of disapproval washed over her face, tightening her features. "What is it I can help you with then?"

"Well, we are here about your husband's murder, but we have some specific questions relating to the robbery itself."

"This way." Mona took them to a grand sitting room with artwork painted on the ceiling that had Amanda thinking of the Sistine Chapel. Just fewer angels and demons, and more butterflies and flowers. "Ingrid," Mona called out, and shortly after, the woman who had answered the door appeared. "Tea. Sugar, milk... cream?" She looked at Amanda and Trent and didn't bother waiting for a response. "Yes. Cream."

"Yes, ma'am." Ingrid shuffled off.

Mona lowered herself into a wingback chair with the grace and elegance befitting royalty. "Proceed."

Amanda and Trent each dropped into a chair.

Amanda spoke. "We believe your husband's murder may be

connected to a man and woman who worked together on several heists in Prince William County, as well as Washington." *Several* might be a stretch as there was only one robbery that had surveillance footage. But as Trent had mentioned their targets and desired acquisitions set them apart from regular, everyday robberies.

"That's nothing I've heard before."

"Did you hear, then, there was a woman described as getting close to her male victims, working her looks and charm to her advantage?"

"Also news to me." Mona looked at the doorway, pursed her lips and shifted in her chair.

"Were you aware of any women new to your husband's life? Say working in his office?" Amanda wasn't jumping to any immoral conclusions about Martin's character. And Trent did tell her the investigating detectives at the time spoke to those at the firm, inquiring about new hires, etcetera, but no one flagged their continued interest.

"Not that I know of, but the business was his. I never got involved in the day to day or concerned myself with it." Mona primly crossed her legs. "Work brought him pleasure, and I encourage pleasure."

A quick look around this place would support that claim. She had an obvious desire to be surrounded by luxury. "Is that why you thought nothing of him returning to his building the night of the murder?"

"Martin was a busy man, but I knew that when I married him. Much better to have a man with ambition than one that sits around like a lump." Mona leveled her gaze at Amanda, her gray eyes inquiring if Amanda agreed or had something to say on the subject.

"So it didn't bother you at all when he excused himself that evening?" Trent asked.

"No reason that it should."

"Do you know what business he had to attend to at midnight?" Amanda asked.

"As I said, his business was his own and he was ambitious. He was a very proud man. Thought of himself as a young buck still, but those years had long passed for him."

It was with those words that Amanda noted the age difference that would have existed between the couple. Martin was fifty-six fifteen years ago, and Mona was about that now. "So when Martin returned to work, you stayed at the charity event?"

"Yes." Spoken slowly and with irritation.

"You said you don't know why he went to work, but records don't show anyone called him. I'm curious what had him running off at that hour." It would seem Amanda was more curious than the man's wife had been.

Mona blinked slowly. "I don't know why or if someone got him to leave, but you probably saw from the investigation file I was cleared of his murder." Mona leveled a cool glance at Amanda. "And, seriously, why would I have killed—" Mona stopped talking as Ingrid entered the room with a silver tray with a silver teapot, silver spoons, and fine china teacups. It was surprising they weren't silver too.

After Ingrid made up a cup for Mona, Trent and Amanda respectfully declined. Ingrid left the room, and Mona resumed talking.

"Now, you mentioned you had questions about the robbery itself." She lifted her teacup to her lips, her pinkie finger curled.

"We understand that among the pieces stolen there was a Fabergé egg," she began.

"Yes." Mona laid a hand on her chest. "It was Martin's pride and joy."

"I can imagine so. How did Martin come to have it in his collection?" She was hoping to gain some insight into how this world worked.

"He was very much about watching auctions, estate sales. Call it a hobby for him. He also had a collector who worked for him and sourced out good pieces for investment."

"Who was that?" Trent asked.

"I don't remember after all this time. Sorry."

"So Martin would see these pieces and bid on them?" Amanda wasn't sure if Mona was being entirely forthright, but to assume otherwise would imply she may have some items in her home that had been stolen.

"He did. But only if they came with provenance."

"And that is?" Amanda's world couldn't be further from the one in which Mona existed.

"It ensures that the piece is legitimate, including a chronological record of ownership. Without that, the piece of art could be a forgery or stolen."

"Do most people like Martin care about that sort of thing?" This from Trent.

"Those of us who have morals, but I don't need to tell you, Detective, that not everyone is upstanding."

Amanda didn't care for how condescending this woman was being, but from the brief interactions with Ingrid, Mona might have been that way with everyone. "If pieces like your late husband's Fabergé egg, for example, were stolen to be resold, how would the thieves even go about finding a buyer?"

"You're asking me questions that you best ask a criminal." Mona flashed the tiniest of amused smiles.

"Fair enough." Amanda then had the thought that items were stolen to order: a collector desires something and takes out something similar to a classified ad. Only this would be posted, answered, and transacted on the dark web. "We have recently recovered the gun that was used to kill your husband."

Mona gasped and laid a hand over her heart. "Any prints or... something to get you closer to who did this?"

"You can be assured the gun is being examined thoroughly," Trent said, then turned to scribbling something in his notepad.

"May I ask where you found the gun?"

Amanda supposed that was an innocent enough question and one a widow would be curious about. Not that it was a straightforward answer. Amanda pulled up a photograph of Claire on her phone that she had taken from her old Facebook account and walked it over to Mona. "Does this woman look familiar to you? She could have had a different hair color or style when you saw her... even different colored eyes?"

Mona studied Amanda's face, barely glanced at the phone. She snapped her fingers and yelled out, "Ingrid, glasses."

The woman needed a bell...

Ingrid came rushing into the room and handed Mona her glasses. She hooked them on her ears and had them resting on her nose in a flash.

"Let's see what we have..." Mona studied the photograph. A few moments later, she added, "No, I don't believe I've ever seen this girl. What about you, Ingrid?" Mona gestured for Amanda to show Ingrid, who remained on standby. "She's worked with us for years. Back before Martin was killed."

Ingrid looked at the picture, then shook her head. "No, I've never seen her."

Amanda pocketed her phone and thanked both women.

"Who is she?" Mona asked while handing Ingrid the glasses and waving a dismissive hand.

"Her name is Claire Ramsey." Amanda went with her maiden name given that at the time of the heist Claire wasn't married to Logan. Mona took another draw of her tea. Her brow creased. "I've never heard of her, and I'm failing to see how she ties in with Martin's murder."

"We found the gun in her possession," Amanda said, matter-of-fact.

Mona's eyes widened. "That sounds pretty damning to me, Detective. Tell me you've arrested this woman."

"Unfortunately, that's not going to happen. She was murdered last Friday night."

Mona sat back and rested her arms on those of the chair. "My, my."

Amanda hadn't entered this household suspecting anything nefarious of the Lawson widow, but she realized she couldn't just dismiss the woman from suspicion either. Mona was responding to things the way one would expect. Were these reactions genuine or staged? She had money and if Mona believed Claire killed her husband, maybe she got revenge herself or hired a contract killer. "Where were you last Friday evening, Mrs. Lawson?"

"Excuse me?"

Amanda refused to play this woman's puppet and repeat something that she'd heard perfectly.

"I was here. You can ask Ingrid."

Amanda prepared her ears for another bellow, but one didn't come. "We will."

Mona sniffed derision. "Surely you can't think I'm in any way involved with this girl's murder. I don't even know who she is."

Amanda nodded, offered a pressed-lip smile and stood. She withdrew a business card and handed it to Mona. "Call if you think of anything that may aid us in finding your late husband's killer, Mrs. Lawson." Best to revert to Martin's case than poke more about Claire.

She and Trent made the inquiry of Ingrid before leaving the house, and she backed up what Mona had told them—she was at home when Claire was murdered.

Back in the car, Amanda did up her seat belt. "She wasn't fazed at all by her husband leaving the event that night. Even when you brought up there was no record of Martin receiving a phone call."

"She made it sound like business always came first to him, but it's possible he was alerted to a need to go in by someone at the event or via the host's phone." Trent shook his head at his latter words. "Though the file didn't indicate that."

"The lead investigator may not have thought of that avenue. But you brought up a good theory. Was it a setup? If only there was a way to get a list of everyone in attendance at that charity event."

"I can see what I can find out from the file. The lead detective on the Lawson case is long retired."

"We could always ask Mona if it comes to that. She could point us in the organizer's direction."

"In the meantime, we can ask Rita's husband and Michelle about a man Claire might have hung around."

"At some point soon, it might be good to talk with Claire's foster parents too. The ones who had her just before she aged out of the system."

"Sounds like we have a lot of talking to do." Trent smiled.

"Yes, and watching... Doubt you started on the hotel surveillance video yet?"

"Didn't even pop the USB drive into my computer."

Amanda glanced at the clock on the dash. 4:55 PM. They had all these avenues to explore, including hours of surveillance video, but none of them were quick checks off the list. Graves approving more overtime was unlikely, and sometimes it was helpful to get a fresh start. "How about we call it a day? That work for you?" She was thinking she'd get home in time to have pizza night with Zoe.

"Sure. We'll pick up in the morning. But I just had another thought."

She was almost afraid to ask what it was.

Trent went on. "The victims of these heists were high

profile, millionaires. Claire used to work for an art gallery and, yes, I know she was young when she started, but did she get roped into this world during that time?"

"Could have... The dark web is one way for buyers and sellers of fine art and antiquities to connect, but..."

"The art gallery could have been the perfect spot to find buyers who were a little more, let's say, unscrupulous."

She nodded. "Most clients would be interested in the provenance, as Mona mentioned, but maybe not everyone. Definitely an avenue worth exploring. Tomorrow."

"Tomorrow." He smiled at her as he pulled into the lot for Central.

They said good night to each other and went their separate ways. Amanda had Logan on Bluetooth in her Civic before she was pulling onto the street. She asked him about any other men in Claire's life.

"None that I remember."

"Okay, well if someone comes to mind after we hang up, call me."

"Sure." There was silence, but it was filled with hope. She thought of inviting him for pizza night, but it might be confusing for Zoe, and she couldn't ignore the fact Logan was currently facing murder charges on the investigation she was working. She wished him a good night and headed home.

TWENTY-THREE

It was going to be the biggest take of her life to date—if she could pull it off. She knew by now that the easiest way to get the job done was to exploit the weakest link. It wasn't hard to ascertain that was Larry Belt, head janitor at Lawson Investments.

He was seated three rows in front of her on the bus, his destination a matter of routine.

She'd followed him for a few nights already, and the evening always played out the same way: Larry going for a drink or five before heading to work to start at midnight. She usually stayed at a distance, but tonight she was going to get close. The thought grossed her out—he was in his fifties and she was only twenty-one. Him with a pot belly and her a firm body. But the job came first. It always did.

There were times she dared to imagine a different life for herself, but the images were never fully formed. They were always just out of focus. Besides, what would she do if not this? Heists were all she knew since she met Nick, but she'd probably go to her grave wealthy. So there was that.

And Larry here was the key to acquiring the most beautiful piece of art she'd ever seen. One Fabergé egg. Studded with diamonds, rubies, platinum, and gold. Objet d'art. *Priceless.*

She had never seen one of these magnificent creations in person until she'd brought it into the gallery for Lawson's art collector. It was truly the most breathtaking, exquisite piece of work she'd ever seen. She wanted it for herself, and one day it would be hers. She always got what she wanted.

The bus stopped, letting air out of its brakes.

Larry was getting up. She did too.

He entered the bar with its flashing neon signs in the window. She followed him.

It was ten o'clock at night, and the place was packed.

She snagged a chair at a table with a couple in their thirties. They didn't want company, but she convinced them she was just waiting for a friend and wouldn't talk to them. They went back to their own business, chatting each other up. First date, she'd guess by the asinine questions being tossed back and forth.

Tonight she'd dressed to be seen but not remembered, and even if someone recalled a woman in tight blue jeans and a breast-hugging shirt, they'd remember a blond. This wig never let her down. When she'd first followed Larry here, she hadn't gone inside. Her designer skirt and thigh-high boots would have instantly given her away as not belonging. And if they didn't, then the diamond tennis bracelet that kept peeking out from beneath the sleeve of her jacket would.

"What can I get ya?" A female server came to the edge of the table.

"I'll have a draft beer."

"We have several on tap. Which one, and what size?"

She wasn't a beer drinker but went with the largest sign on display behind the bar. "A small draft of Guinness."

The server walked off without a word.

Claire had her eye on Larry, who had bellied up to the bar. From this perspective she was looking at his back, but he'd already slung a shot of whiskey down his throat and now had a glass of frothy beer to his lips.

It didn't stop him from flagging down the bartender. Shortly later another shot and a fresh beer.

"Here." The server had returned with her Guinness and set it down with enough force to slosh some of the liquid over the rim of the glass and onto the table.

"Thanks."

"Uh-huh. Are you gonna have anything to eat? I can get ya a menu."

She shook her head, and the server walked off. Claire was homed in on Larry Belt.

He was going to make this easy-peasy. An alcoholic with another weakness to exploit. He was single and likely hadn't been laid in months.

She grabbed her drink and went over to Larry at the bar. "Hey, there. This spot taken?" She pointed to the stool next to Larry where a man in his seventies was seated. He looked at her, smiled at Larry, and found another spot to sit.

"Not now," Larry said with a crooked grin.

There wasn't anything attractive about the man at a distance, and being up close certainly didn't change her mind. His teeth were yellowed, his eyes bloodshot, and his face pockmarked.

"I see you're drinking Guinness." He pointed at the dark liquid in her glass.

She smiled, pouring on the charm. "Why, yes, I am." She took a long draw on the beer, rolling her eyes back afterward and slowly licking her lips.

Larry was staring at her mouth, likely sporting wood. Filthy man.

"Can I, er, get you another one?"

Her glass was only a third down, if that. "Sure."

He shot back the whiskey and flagged down the bartender again.

"Actually..." She laid her hand on his forearm and instinctively wanted to recoil. His hair was pasted to his sweaty flesh. "Could we, maybe, get a room somewhere?" She flashed her most daring smile.

Larry's arm dropped. "Get a room?" He swallowed so roughly his Adam's apple bobbed heavily.

"Yeah. I mean if you'd like to get to know me better." She traced a fingertip down his arm and felt him shiver under her touch.

He hopped off the stool and slapped two twenties on the counter.

They stepped outside, then he looked around like he was lost. "I don't live near here. You?"

"No, but we could go there." She pointed to a motel sign just down the street.

"Uh... yeah... sure." Larry frowned. "Though I probably shouldn't. I need to get to work in a couple of hours."

She slipped her arm through his and fawned over him with her eyes. "I bet you have a very important job."

"Yeah, I..." He put his hand over hers. "You really want to be with me?"

"I sure do." She grinned.

Larry's eyes dipped to her lips, lowered to her chest. "All right then."

He got them a room while she waited outside in the parking lot. She was in disguise, but she still didn't need to flaunt her face everywhere.

Larry emerged from the lobby dangling a key from his hand. "Let's do this." He held out his arm for her to loop hers through. "Number eleven. My lucky number."

Or not so lucky... She said nothing but smiled again.

He got the door and let her enter first. When he shut the door *behind them, he came right for her. Any reservations or qualms about sleeping with a stranger were certainly gone. He wanted in and out and off to work.*

"Hold it, cowboy." *She inched back and held up a hand before he could put his disgusting mouth on hers. She pushed against his chest.*

"What, baby? I thought we were gonna... You know."

"Drink first? I don't usually do this."

"I'll never say no to a drink."

Something she'd observed. She reached into her jacket and pulled out a flask, unscrewed the top and handed it to him. "Bottom's up."

"What is it?" *Just a glimmer of hesitation.*

"Whiskey."

"A girl after my heart." *He tipped back the flask, and she watched as he gulped greedily.*

Everything was going perfectly so far... She reminded herself not to become cocky and overconfident.

He lowered the flask and gave it back to her. "Your turn, darlin'."

The drug didn't take long to work. His eyelids appeared heavy, and he was squinting. His body swayed, and he reached for her to keep upright.

"Did you put something in that?" *he slurred.*

"Just whiskey." *One teeny lie to keep the situation under control. She put the flask back in her pocket.*

His eyes fluttered, and he stumbled. She helped guide him to the bed and just made it there before his body went limp. He'd wake up with one helluva headache and no memory. But he would wake up.

She rifled in his pockets and came out with the all-access key card. This would give her and Nick free rein over every square inch of Lawson Investments.

"Got it," *she texted into her burner phone.*

A snore erupted from Larry and startled her. She'd never gone quite this far in her efforts before; drugging a man was a new level for her.

And it was time to leave.

She hurried from the room and got into a waiting car. The clock was ticking. She just hoped it wouldn't run out...

TWENTY-FOUR

The night was a warm one, and the AC in Amanda's house wasn't keeping up. Tomorrow she would call to get someone in to look at the thing. Pretty bad when summer hadn't officially started and already the heat was seeping in. It didn't help there was a pizza baking in the oven either. Going another direction with dinner might have been the wise choice, but it was her and Zoe's Pizza Tuesday. Not quite as catchy as Taco Tuesday, but let everyone else conform to the norm.

"What do you say we eat outside? Sound good?" she proposed to Zoe, counting on a breeze.

"I love outside."

"I know you do." That's if her cousin, Ava, didn't have her distracted with something in the house. She'd come to find out Ava was into some new video game and that's what had Zoe glued inside the other day, along with playing some Barbies. "You can head out and play now if you want."

"Yeah!" Zoe squealed and took off through the patio door.

The yard was completely fenced with a gate at the back that opened into the rear of another property—a strange installation that the previous owners had done. But Amanda felt like Zoe was safe there. Still, she watched for a while as the child ran around the grass, barefoot and carefree. She wished the girl could stay that way forever, but that wasn't how life worked. About a month after her sixth birthday, Zoe had been given some hefty baggage. Her parents had been murdered, her father right in front of her eyes no less. Somehow Zoe had kept her light, and while Amanda was there for Zoe, the girl had healed Amanda. She'd helped her move past her grief, or at least navigate through it enough to see a bright future again.

Zoe went to the playset in the back corner and heaved herself onto a swing. Kevin had put in the contraption for Lindsey. It had everything a kid could want—a slide, a climber, swings, and a sandbox. While it had been hard for Amanda when she first saw Zoe use it, now it felt so right. Like there was a part of her daughter that had lived on.

Amanda busied herself cleaning up the kitchen, something she normally did with Zoe. She put the rest of the ingredients away and washed the dishes that they'd used while making the pizza.

By the time she'd finished, she was inhaling the glorious smell of cooking cheese and pepperoni but sweating like mad. *Was the air conditioning working at all?*

A look at the thermostat told her it was seventy-nine degrees. The thing had to be busted. She turned the switch to off and opened some windows. At least a slight evening breeze might save her and Zoe from melting to death when they came back inside. After dinner, she'd fish out some oscillating fans from the basement and the garage.

The pizza was smelling cooked now, and when she returned to the kitchen, there was a minute left on the timer. She pulled it out early and happily flipped off the oven. The crust was golden perfection, and the cheese and pepperoni were bubbling and sizzling.

She peeked out the window again, and Zoe was still on the swing. Amanda called out for her, and the girl came running.

"Pizza!" Zoe burst through the door, a sweaty little mess. Some of her blond hair was pasted to her forehead.

"Here you go..." Amanda made a show of cutting up the pizza and putting a slice on Zoe's plate. The cheese pulled and warranted a *Ymm* from Zoe. "There's some juice in that glass for you." Amanda pointed to where she'd placed it on the counter. "Can you handle it with your plate?"

"I'm not a baby." Zoe picked up the glass in one hand, held her plate with her other one. Amanda got the door and turned to hide her amusement at the girl's spunk.

"Go ahead. I'll be right out." Amanda plated a couple of slices for herself and joined Zoe outside. She gave thought to what summer vacation would look like for the girl. Amanda would probably divvy Zoe's time between all the people who loved her. Libby and her girlfriend, Amanda's numerous siblings and nieces and nephews. She was blessed with a built-in village.

The night was warm, but there was a breeze that provided a welcome relief from the stagnant humid air that was inside. If it was the weekend, Amanda might suggest they set up the tent and sleep outside, have an adventure. It was tempting regardless.

She talked with Zoe about what the girl wanted to do that summer.

"I want a swimming pool. Can I get one?" She was speaking with her mouth full of pizza, but Amanda understood every word while wishing she didn't.

"Be careful you don't choke."

Zoe zapped her with a brief glare and continued munching away.

"I'm not sure a pool is a good idea."

Zoe made a show of swallowing and even pointed in her

now-empty mouth. "Oh, *pleeeaassseeee*." Zoe pouted, an expression she was starting to master.

"We'll see. Maybe a little one. *Maybe*," Amanda stressed.

Zoe smiled, figuring she'd won the debate. She probably had. But there would be rules on when Zoe could use it, and it certainly wouldn't be some huge inground deal. Probably a rather small aboveground one that might not even be suitable for adults unless they wanted to sit in the water just to cool off. Amanda had to admit that sounded like a great idea right this minute.

After dinner, Zoe played in the yard, and Amanda went in search of fans.

The garage had always been Kevin's domain, and she hadn't touched it since his death. They'd never used it for a vehicle. From the day they took possession of the house, it was a space where boxes were moved in. Many of them never moved out. Over time, more and more junk got added, and there was barely room to move in there. Maybe she'd finally take care of this, donate everything she could and move forward. She found the thought something of a relief. She might even use the garage for the purpose it was designed for. Novel concept.

She wedged between stacks of boxes, recalling by some miracle where two standing fans were. With some expert maneuvering, she freed them both of their confinement. She set one up in the living room and another in Zoe's bedroom. If she remembered right, there were a couple of fans in the basement too.

She checked on Zoe and found her playing in the sandbox and talking away to her imaginary friends. They only came out when Zoe was alone. Amanda had asked Zoe's therapist about it, and the woman told her it was completely normal. She also said that Zoe likely saw the relationship with these friends as private, hers alone. There were times Amanda wondered if the girl was communing with her dead parents. Not that Amanda truly believed that possible. But if, and when, Zoe was ready to introduce her friends, Amanda would be loving and accepting.

Amanda went to the basement and found the fans. Both were tabletop ones, but they oscillated. She put one on the dresser in her bedroom and one in the kitchen. Satisfied they were moving the air in the house enough to make it bearable, she called Zoe inside. It was going on seven thirty, and she wanted to make sure that the girl had some time to calm down before bed.

She stuck her head outside and called for Zoe, who was at the back fence line talking to Mrs. Little. They'd had the conversation about not speaking to strangers a few times, but that didn't apply to the neighbor lady. The woman waved to Amanda, and she returned the greeting as Zoe strode across the yard at a decent clip. So much for the fresh air and activity burning up the girl's energy. Hopefully watching some TV would do the trick.

By eight thirty, Zoe was falling asleep against Amanda's shoulder.

"All right, sleepyhead, time for bed." She nudged Zoe, and the girl grumbled. "Let's go," Amanda prompted.

Zoe dragged herself down the hall, slumped, arms hanging at her sides like she was a criminal being led to the execution chamber.

"If you make it snappy, I'll read to you." Amanda hoped that would work as an incentive.

The girl picked up her pace and changed for bed. All tucked in, her stuffed dog next to her, Zoe's eyelids lowered.

Why is she fighting sleep so much? Amanda found amusement in how that was a story on repeat that followed most people through their entire lives. She read for a few minutes until Zoe dozed off. Amanda kissed her on the forehead, turned on the light that cast stars on the ceiling, flicked off the main light, and backed out of the room.

For most of the night, thoughts of the case, even Logan, were far off. But Amanda was curious about Graves's story. Why was she so bent on Logan being guilty? Why had she originally been so insistent that Amanda not go near the case?

She went to the kitchen and grabbed her laptop from the top of the fridge, the new place she was keeping it. Not that Zoe usually got into her things, but it was a safeguard. Kids were becoming savvier all the time, and Zoe showed a natural inclination toward anything with a computer board, which she no doubt picked up from her father who had been a programmer.

She set up on the peninsula and logged on. It opened to the results that came back on her search for Katherine Graves from Friday night. She was clicking on the first article when the battery warning popped up in the bottom right-hand corner.

Figures!

She fished out the cord, plugged it in, and started reading.

Katherine Graves had been a sergeant in Homicide for the NYPD. News that Amanda was familiar with. The piece didn't expose anything scandalous, but it announced the promotion of Callum O'Brien to sergeant. From the looks of it, he took over Graves's position.

She googled his name.

No more articles surfaced to do with Callum O'Brien, but there were plenty about a Seamus O'Brien, police chief of the NYPD.

Had Graves been given the boot to make way for family? Was there favoritism at play in the ranks of the NYPD? Did that explain why Graves was so sensitive to having Amanda involved with this case at all—because Amanda was too close to it?

There was a bang at her front door. *What the...*

Amanda got up. This was the second time someone had knocked on the door while she'd been looking into Graves's background. The first time it had been Trent, but she couldn't imagine who it would be now. She looked out the window in the door. No one was there. But there was something on her top step.

She cracked the door and looked closer at the item.

It was a rock of about three inches in length, and half an inch thick. A string had been tied around it, and she could make out the corner of paper from the underside. Her heart pounding, she grabbed a pair of latex gloves that she knew she had in the pockets of a light jacket by the door. She put them on, picked up the rock, and looked at the note.

One sentence, scrawled in messy handwriting: *Stop or you'll wish you had!*

Shivers spread down her arms and had her going cold despite the high temperature.

The wheels of a vehicle ran over the pavement, and she looked up, feeling vulnerable and exposed. It was Mrs. Little in her Cadillac. But behind her SUV came a silver sedan. It had the body lines of a Toyota Camry. It could have belonged to anyone in the neighborhood, as there were several around, but Amanda had this sickening feeling in her gut. She couldn't make out the driver's face, but she'd swear it was a man, and that he was watching her as he drove past.

She looked at the license plate, but the number was obscured by a tinted cover. Had the driver just left this sinister note on her doorstep?

TWENTY-FIVE

"You need to tell Graves," Trent said, repeating the admonition again and planning to do so until it sank into his partner's stubborn head.

"You don't get it. If I tell her, she's going to remove us from the case."

"Maybe that would be a good thing. This person was at your house, Amanda." He was pulsating, angry and concerned. He wanted to protect her, but he had to be careful how he played this. She'd get her back up, push him away. Lord knew she was strong enough on her own. She'd been through hell, been scorched by its flames, but she had survived.

"I know."

"Where Zoe is," he stressed. Maybe by bringing up the girl, it would help jolt some logic into her. *Maybe.*

"I know. I'll get the lab to run it for prints."

"Graves will find out."

"Maybe say that it was delivered to your door."

"What was delivered to you?" Graves showed up just then, the timing far less than ideal. She leveled her gaze at Trent.

Amanda was watching him, her eyes pleading.

"It's nothing. Just someone must be getting spooked by our investigative efforts."

Graves crossed her arms. "One of you going to tell me what this is about?"

Amanda remained silent, and Trent filled the space. "I had a visitor at home last night. And he left me that." He gestured to the note that was in an evidence bag that Amanda was holding.

"Let me see." Graves held out a hand, her fingers wriggling. Amanda handed it over. "'Stop or you'll wish you had!' Rather vague."

Trent saw little vagueness about it. To him, it clearly had to do with the case they were working. And the person who left it must have been feeling threatened. He wasn't sure why the sergeant didn't find it more menacing. "It was attached to a rock, held there by string."

"I see that." She gave the bag back to Amanda. "Get it printed, see if it lands us anywhere. But I wouldn't hold my breath. I'm sure you've heard that your boyfriend's gun was the weapon that shot Claire Hunter?" Graves looked at Amanda, and Trent noted her cheeks redden.

Amanda set the bag on her desk. "I heard that. I have the lab looking at that gun closely again, along with the one from Claire Hunter's purse."

"Whatever you feel you need to do." Her words were patronizing and condescending.

As the two women stared off, Trent didn't understand why the sergeant was being so difficult and blind. It was like she completely dismissed the threat left on one of her detectives' doorsteps. As if any flags this raised only existed in his and Amanda's heads.

"The victim's gun ties to a cold case," Trent said, stepping in.

"I heard that, and I assume you are both moving on that."

"We are." Amanda nudged out her chin.

"You might find that both she *and* her husband weren't so blameless, Detectives. Keep your minds open to that possibility."

"We are," Trent parroted what Amanda had said just a second before.

"Good, then. Keep me posted."

Trent stiffened. He should just remain quiet, let Graves walk away. "There were several heists in Prince William County and DC that may be tied to Claire Hunter before she married or even met Logan."

Graves pivoted back. "I'm listening."

"We have yet to prove it, but if Claire was one of two perps caught on camera during one of these robberies, she had a male partner. As of yet, unidentified. Detective Steele and I are exploring the theory that this is the man who killed Claire Hunter."

"Did she have something on him?"

If he said *the gun*, it would be met with mockery and the defense that only Claire's fingerprints were on the weapon. "We believe so." Best not to get into the specifics. "We're trying to figure out exactly what and who this person might be. Even if only to shed light on Claire's life."

"Okay. Again, keep me posted." With that, Graves walked off, and Trent was careful not to say or do anything that would bring her back.

"Thanks," Amanda said.

"Don't thank me yet. Just promise me you'll watch your back."

"Always." She smiled, just a partial expression that didn't reach her eyes. He'd guess it touched her he cared enough to say that, but of course he cared about her well-being. She'd have to be blind and stupid to believe otherwise.

"First stop?" He just wanted to get moving. Even if it was to watch video.

"As we told Graves, we need to see if we can find this guy. Let's hit the gallery and go from there. Maybe we can tie the robbery victims to that gallery too."

"All right. I'll get the list of their names on my phone." He did that, and they headed out.

Once on the road to Washington, he turned to Amanda. "By the way, I took a closer look at the Lawson file. The event was a fundraiser for an animal shelter in Washington called Pawsitively in Love. It was held at a rental hall, not an individual's home."

"Unlikely to track an incoming call for Martin then, but it sounds like a big affair. That's good news. It would have taken a lot of organization and that might mean there's a guest list we can get our hands on."

"I've already put a call in to the shelter and spoke to the person who organized the event." He paused there, swearing Amanda's mouth gaped open. "A Paula Ferguson. She said she'll see if she can find the list of those who attended. I gave her my phone and email."

"How early were you in?"

"Seven."

"Impressive." She smiled, and he felt warmed by the expression as he realized how fragile it could be. He hated to think of Amanda ever suffering. She'd been through enough, but damn her pride.

"You really think Graves would take you off the case if she knew you were the one to receive the note?"

"Yep."

"Why so sure?"

"I looked her up."

He shifted in his seat. "You know what brought her to Prince William County?"

"Not that. Just why she might have left the NYPD."

"And..." He stopped at a red light.

"I think she was squeezed out. Her position was filled by a relation to the NYPD police chief."

"That might explain why she's very mindful of showing any favoritism, perceived or actual."

"Yep. To the point I think the pendulum swings in the extreme opposite direction."

"Seems so. By the way, I spoke with Shell last night."

"Oh? And did she know of any boyfriends?"

He shook his head. "Nope."

"Logan neither. He didn't know of any guys hanging around her when they first started dating or after."

"Assuming that Claire is one of the two perps involved with the robberies, she must have done everything to keep him a secret."

"Like most of her life from the sounds of it."

"And now we have a mystery guy who wants to remain a mystery."

She laughed, and he smiled.

"Something like that," she said.

They drove the rest of the way to the gallery in silence. His mind was spinning on the case. How the evidence was stacked against Logan, but Trent agreed with Amanda, it was far too easy, too clean. One thing he'd learned since joining Homicide about eighteen months ago was that murders were messy and complicated, complex, just like the humans who carried them out. But emotion screwed up logic every time and left room for error. That's what they were banking on.

He turned into the lot for the gallery, an impressive building with walls of glass. The environment was quite a far cry from the mobile home park where Claire had her start in life. Along those lines, Shell said Claire was placed in foster homes in

Dumfries, so how had teenage Claire made it to Washington? Did her foster parents set her up with a car? From what Shell told them, she never stayed put in one home for long, so did any of them trust her enough to lend her a vehicle?

At the front counter, they asked for the person in charge. They were told Malachi Walsh managed the place, and that he'd be right with them.

Large sculptures dangled from suspension cables overhead. Trent wouldn't be able to pinpoint their intended representations if he had a gun to his head.

"Detectives? This way." A man in a tailored suit motioned for Trent and Amanda to follow him down a brightly lit corridor. He stopped next to an open door and gestured for them to go inside.

Trent let Amanda go first. It was a modest office with the bare essentials.

"How can I help you? Louise told me you have questions about a former employee."

Louise must be the woman at the front desk.

"We do." Amanda proceeded with the formal introductions, then said, "We understand a Claire Ramsey used to work here."

"When was this?"

"About twenty years ago," Trent said.

"It might be a problem looking up her file, but let me try." Malachi sat at his desk and typed on his keyboard. "Ah, yes. She's in the system. What about her?"

"Do you remember her?" Amanda asked.

"Afraid not. I just came on board two years ago."

"Anyone still work here from back then?" Trent was thinking if they could talk to that person, or persons, they might get a lead on Claire's mysterious male friend and Roo. For the first time, Trent considered that this mystery guy and Roo could be one and the same. They had just assumed Roo was a woman.

Either way, both or one of them could have worked at the gallery too.

"Let's see. I'll search the records." More clicking, then, "Looks like Louise has worked here for the last twenty-one years. But can I ask what this is about? Is there something I may help you with?"

"We'll want to speak with Louise, but you might be able to assist us on another matter." Amanda gestured toward Trent. "Could you read off the list of names?"

She'd be referring to the men who were victims of robbery. "Sure," Trent said, bringing up the list on his phone. "Just let us know if any of these names sound familiar." He read them off.

"Their names are all familiar, but could you add some context? Why are you interested in them?"

"Are these men clients of the gallery?" Trent asked.

"They are, but I can't be discussing their business with you."

"They were victims of robberies in which millions in jewels, sculptures, and artwork were stolen over the last twenty years," Amanda interjected. "We believe Claire Ramsey was part of a heist team that targeted the men my partner just mentioned."

Malachi went white.

Amanda added, "Claire was murdered last week."

"While that's certainly unfortunate, I'm at a loss. This Claire worked here twenty years ago. You're asking about our clients... do you think one of them killed her? And a heist team? Targeted?" That word dripped off his tongue like bile. "Are you implying the gallery itself is—or was—corrupt, wrapped up in this somehow?"

"We're still investigating the matter," Amanda said.

"Oh, this is not good. This can't get out or the reputation of the gallery would be ruined."

"Not to sound unsympathetic here, but the fate of the gallery isn't our priority," Trent said.

"There may be no need to publicize that these men bought from here," Amanda offered, giving Trent a side glance.

"You should know those names you mentioned are fine, reputable men. Loyal clients. Many of them we don't deal with directly, however. They have people who source and curate for them. They have an eye both for value and return on investment. Sometimes this means purchasing work by long-established artists. Other times it's knowing what up-and-comers show promise."

It sounded like the gallery dealt with people who knew the art world well, but were any of them also buyers without scruples? "Do most of these curators and collectors require provenance?"

"Yes."

"But not all?" He angled his head.

Malachi bit his bottom lip. "I couldn't say, but it is something provided with every piece that moves through the gallery."

They wouldn't be getting any names from Malachi, but it was entirely possible that Claire and whoever she was working with stole from clients of the gallery and turned around and sold the pieces to other ones. A built-in supply chain right here. "Do you ever deal in Fabergé eggs?"

"No gallery 'deals in' Fabergé eggs, Detective, at least not habitually. They are exceptionally rare and hardly ever for sale," Malachi said patiently. "That being said, I know the gallery has brokered deals for them in the past, yes."

"Do you know if one such deal involved Martin Lawson?" Trent realized it would be before Malachi's time at the gallery but wondered if word about the purchase had made its way to his ears.

"That's a name I haven't heard in a long time."

"But you're familiar with it?" Trent was curious to know

how, given Martin Lawson was dead before Malachi came to work at the gallery.

"He's a legend around here. Has one of the finest collections on the east coast. He had a very qualified curator working on his behalf, but he had a fine eye himself—so I heard. I never had the pleasure of meeting him. He was murdered several years ago now."

"He was," Amanda confirmed. "It's still an open investigation. How long did Claire work here?"

"Let's see." Malachi looked back at the computer. "Looks like thirteen years."

Claire was sixteen when she'd started working there and thirteen years would make her twenty-nine when she left. Notably that was right around the time she met Logan. Had Claire quit because of him? How many heists had she been involved with? And if Claire and her partner both worked at the gallery, did they have forgeries made which they sold in place of the genuine article? They could have gotten away with even more than he and Amanda had imagined. Trent asked Malachi if he thought that even possible.

"I highly doubt that. Our buyers have everything carefully inspected before taking possession. Most of them bring in skilled experts—whether that be those trained to identify art forgery or a gemologist who can spot a fake jewel a mile away."

Trent nodded. That meant the only way to play the system here was to use the gallery as a garden for picking ripe, rich targets. And possibly, by extension, a client base for turning over the stolen product. "We are going to need the names of everyone who worked here during the time of Claire's employment."

"I can get that for you. It will take a few minutes. Do you want to use that time to speak with Louise?"

"Yes, we'll do that. Thank you." Amanda stood and led the

way from the room. She leaned in toward Trent. "You think that maybe this partner of hers worked at the gallery when she did?"

"It's possible, right?"

"Guess it is."

Not exactly a vote of confidence in his hunch, and he too could see at least one hole in his theory. If Claire and her partner were both at the gallery, surely someone would have caught on. Wouldn't they?

TWENTY-SIX

Louise was still at the front desk, currently on the phone. From the sounds of it, she was wrapping things up. A customer came in the front door, literally looking down her nose at Amanda and Trent, barely even acknowledging Louise. She was carrying a leather satchel that probably cost more than Amanda's monthly salary. Amanda wondered what it must be like to be so wealthy. What a different life from the one she had, but she wouldn't trade hers for a hot second.

She stepped back to let Louise assist the woman. Without a word passing between the two, Louise got Malachi to come out to the gallery floor, and he took the client to his office.

Louise looked at Amanda and smiled. "Something I can help you with?"

"Malachi told us you've worked at the gallery for several years."

"Twenty-one years," Louise replied with a smile.

"Do you remember Claire Ramsey?" Amanda asked. "She used to work here."

"Ah, yes, I do."

Amanda noted the absence of any commentary—no praise

or misgivings. "Claire would have started when she was still a minor. Do you know what she did for the gallery?"

"She started off as a sticker girl."

"A... You're going to have to explain that one for us." Trent smiled with his request.

"We often host galas at the gallery to showcase newly acquired items, and Claire would put a sticker on the artwork labels as they sold."

"That's the plaque posted next to the display listing the specifics of the piece?" Trent asked.

"Uh-huh, that's right."

"Did she get promoted from that?" Amanda asked. "We understand she worked here thirteen years."

"For sure. She started off part-time, doing the stickers and other entry-level tasks when we needed extra staff. Once she turned eighteen, she became full-time and was given more responsibilities, even dealt with some clients and helped advise them and their curators."

That would put Claire in a good spot to identify targets and potential buyers. It would also seem Claire had a natural gift for understanding the art world. There was no record of formal education past high school, and if she was at the gallery full-time, she'd have little hours left to devote to academic studies. "Claire lived in Dumfries as a minor, about an hour away. Do you know how Claire even came to work here?"

"Someone recommended her, but after all this time I couldn't tell you who. I do remember the manager helping the girl out with transportation. She'd pick her up or arrange for someone to if she couldn't."

"Wow, that seems like a lot for a manager to take on." Amanda couldn't imagine any bosses from her part-time jobs as a teen going to those lengths. "Do you remember their name?"

"Rita Cartwright."

Rita... Tingles spread down Amanda's arms. It wasn't exactly a common name.

Trent glanced at Amanda. "How long did Ms. Cartwright work here?"

"She was here a bit. Say about seven years. She quit about fifteen years ago."

That would have made Rita twenty when she had started the gallery. And she was a manager by the time Claire was hired two years later. Rita had climbed the ladder fast. But that might not mean anything. Then there was the fact Rita had quit around the time of Lawson's murder. It could have been coincidental, but Amanda wasn't a huge believer in coincidence. "Why did she quit?"

"She found work teaching art history at a university. The pay was much better than here, of course." She gave the school's name and added, "A job there is the equivalent of winning the lottery."

"It's not easy to be hired there?" Trent asked.

Louise shook her head. "Usually you only get in if you have connections to someone on the board."

"Did Rita?" Amanda didn't even know where this would take the case, but she'd keep tugging on strings until something came loose.

"Not that I know of, but we weren't close. She was also a very private person."

Rita Flynn was a university professor. Was Cartwright her maiden name? If so, the answer of how Rita and Claire met was answered. It didn't fully explain what had led to the two bonding—it could just be their relative proximity in age, perhaps compared to other staff at the gallery, but Amanda had other suspicions. "How would you describe Ms. Cartwright's relationship with Claire Ramsey?"

Louise's lips tightened, then relaxed. "Rita seemed to watch over Claire."

"Like a big sister?" Amanda asked.

"No, I wouldn't say that. More like she didn't really trust the girl."

Interesting that Rita would let Claire continue to work at the gallery then. That didn't gel with what Austin had told them about the women's friendship. Had Rita been involved in the heists too, as she and Trent had considered before? That could be the bond they shared. And had Rita kept Claire close not because there was friendly affection between the two, but because Rita had Claire on a leash? Rita was six years older, a full-grown adult who could hold sway and manipulate a teenager. "If I told you Rita got married and had Claire as her maid of honor, what would be your response to that?"

"Surprise."

"You've been terrific and a big help." Amanda handed Louise her card and told her if she remembered any more about Rita or Claire to call her. "Malachi was to get a list together for us before we left. Could you follow up with him?"

Louise flushed. "I'm sorry, but I'd prefer not to interrupt him with Ms. Wimbledon in there. What was the list? Maybe I could help."

"He was to get us a list of the employees who worked here during the time Claire Ramsey was here," Amanda told her.

"No, I'm sorry, but I don't have access to that part of the system."

"You suggested Claire may have worked with some clients," Trent began. "Could you get us their names?"

"I'm not sure if there's an official list somewhere to print off, but I remember a couple." Louise named a few people—all of whom had been victims of robbery.

Too much to be a coincidence... "Please have Malachi email me the employee list to the address on the card." Amanda pointed it out.

"Will do."

Amanda thanked her again, and she and Trent left.

"It can't be a coincidence that Claire's clients became marks," she said, snapping her seat belt into place.

Trent had the car running, but warm air was still spewing from the vents. She turned hers away, so it wasn't directed straight at her face.

"I don't think a lot of this is coincidence. And Rita..." He pecked on the keyboard for the onboard computer. "Yeah, Rita Flynn and Rita Cartwright are one and the same."

"Rita stretched things when she told her husband she and Claire were friends. Rita was involved in whatever heist ring Claire got pulled into. That's how they met, why Rita didn't elaborate to her husband."

"I think so too. The fact they are both dead, within a day no less, seems to back up that theory."

Amanda felt chilled, but it wasn't the car's air conditioning. "Rita died the day before Claire... Did Claire tamper with Rita's car? Payback for all the years of being used on heists?"

"You make it sound like Claire hated the life, but we can't assume she did. Even after all the grief her secret caused her, she spent money on designer jeans. That tells me she liked having money."

"All right. Payback for Logan's accident then? She could have held Rita responsible—or maybe she was for all we know."

"I certainly don't think we have enough to go there yet."

She hated she agreed with him. How much wheel-spinning were they doing? "So far we can't even put Claire in recent contact with Rita."

"Maybe if we track Claire's movements, we'll come up with something."

"The hotel video might help, but first, it's past time we visited Claire's last foster parents."

"Shell said that Claire stayed with the Hamiltons the longest, and until she aged out of the system."

"They might have something to say about Rita. Also a boyfriend Claire may have had. The mystery man from the robberies?"

"And Roo. Assuming that's not the nickname of her boyfriend and/or the mystery man."

"Hey, I never considered they could be the same."

"Just came to me at the gallery. Now this mystery man could be the final piece we need. He could be who really stands to lose everything. He could have been the one who shot Lawson. The women knew it..."

"Then somehow he found out Claire was going to turn him in. But how does that account for Rita? Was she also going to turn on this person?"

"And I can't believe I'm going there again, but could there be more people who could point their finger at the shooter?"

"We better hope not, because I'm not sure we'll be able to save them in time. Not at this rate." She hated how defeated, yet accurate, that sounded. "Let's hit up the Hamiltons, and we'll go from there."

"You got it." Trent clicked on the keyboard and found Claire's last known childhood address and the names associated with the property. "Looks like Sylvia and Albert still live there."

"What are you waiting for?" Amanda gestured toward the road.

As he drove, her mind spun. How elaborate was this heist team? Had they uncovered the extent of it or was there far more yet to unravel?

TWENTY-SEVEN

Amanda and Trent grabbed a quick bite to eat and arrived at the Hamiltons' house about two thirty in the afternoon. From the records, the couple never had children of their own, and they'd stopped fostering a few years ago. They had a modest, two-story vinyl-sided home in Dumfries. A car was in the driveway, so there was a good chance she and Trent would catch at least one of them home.

She knocked and waited.

"One minute," a woman's voice called out from inside. Then the door opened. "Yes? How can I help you?"

Amanda had her badge up, and so did Trent.

"We're Detectives Steele and Stenson with the Prince William County PD," Amanda said, clipping her badge back onto the waistband of her pants. "We're looking to speak with Sylvia and Albert Hamilton."

"I'm Sylvia." Her brow furrowed as she danced her gaze over the two of them. "Albert's not home right now. What's this about?"

"We have questions about a girl you fostered a number of years ago. Claire Ramsey."

"Oh."

One little utterance, and Amanda wasn't sure what to make of it. "Could we come inside to talk about her?"

A car pulled into the driveway, a man behind the wheel.

"Good timing. That's Albert. I'm sure he'll have things to say. Come on in." She spun, while waving for Amanda and Trent to follow her.

They set up at a dining room table. Sylvia had put on a pot of coffee without asking if Amanda and Trent would want one. Maybe they wouldn't be offered a cup. Albert came into the kitchen, popped open the fridge door and took out a beer, snapped the cap off and drained back a good amount. He ran the back of his hand over his mouth.

"Now, I'll talk. Who are you, and what do you want?" He narrowed his beady eyes on Amanda.

"We're—"

"They are with the police, Bert. They're here about Claire Ramsey."

"Oy." He pulled out a chair and joined them at the table. "Did something happen to her?"

"She was murdered last Friday." Amanda delivered it pointedly as she felt like the couple could handle anything.

Both Hamiltons looked at each other, their mouths curving down into frowns.

"We can't say that surprises us entirely," Albert said.

"Why is that?" Trent had his notepad out and his pen at the ready.

"Claire was one of the most interesting children Sylvia and I ever cared for. But she was a child going on woman."

"She was very smart," Sylvia inserted.

Michelle had said the same thing. And while she might have been intelligent, she'd made some poor decisions along the way, at least one Amanda was certain got her killed. "Why don't you tell us what you mean about 'going on woman?' Did she have boyfriends, possibly someone older than she was?"

"Not under this roof." Albert swigged back more beer.

Sylvia was shaking her head. "He's very stubborn when it comes to young people dating."

"They don't know what they want. They don't even know who they are themselves yet."

Amanda wasn't getting pulled into that debate, and she doubted he had traveled his moral high road when he was a teenager. "So nothing that made you think she was seeing anyone?" She put her attention on the wife who was now fidgeting in her chair, sneaking in glances at her husband. Sylvia got up to get coffee and did offer one to Amanda and Trent. They both accepted.

"Who knows? She could be a wily one." Albert went to take another drink of his beer but set it down with a look of disappointment at the fact it was empty already.

"Mrs. Hamilton?" Amanda prompted.

"I think she was seeing someone."

"Sylvia?" Albert said. "You never said anything to me."

"Because you'd overreact like you are about to now for heaven's sake. She was seventeen when she came here, practically an adult. She stayed with us from the time she was seventeen until eighteen."

"No one else wanted her," Albert said. "I know that sounds harsh, but we weren't her first placement. But then her father had killed her mother so that would screw up any kid."

"You mentioned Claire was quite smart. Did she do well in school?" Amanda asked.

"She got As and Bs," Sylvia said.

It would seem Claire had coped at school even while dealing with the loss of her mother, at the hands of her father, no less. Otherwise her grades would have been far worse. "You said you thought she was seeing someone, Mrs. Hamilton. What gave you that idea?"

"I picked up the phone a couple of times, and she was speaking to a guy."

"Sylvia," Albert barked.

"Well, she could have just been friends with him."

"Then why hold back from mentioning this to me? Oh, you thought I'd overreact."

Sylvia threw her hands in the air as if to say, *Bingo!*

"Did you ever catch what they were talking about?" Trent asked.

"It's been a long time." Sylvia smiled at him. "You're really testing my memory. Let's see..." Sylvia tapped her chin in a dramatic show of summoning recall.

Amanda and Trent remained quiet while Sylvia collected her thoughts. Albert helped himself to another beer and returned to the table.

"Something about work if I remember right," Sylvia eventually said.

"So he worked with her?" Trent asked.

"I'm guessing so."

"You heard the word 'work'?" Amanda inquired.

"I just got that *impression*... Something about an order that was coming into the gallery for a gala that night. He wanted to make sure that Claire had handled it a certain way. Don't ask me now how that was to be..."

It sounded to Amanda that Claire served as more than a "sticker girl" even as a teenager. "You're doing great. But how did any of this make you think they were seeing each other?"

"I asked Claire about the guy, and she blushed fierce and ran out of the house. It could just have been a crush on her side, I guess."

"Did you know she was working at a gallery in Washington while she lived here?" Trent asked.

"Yes, of course. She had the job before moving in here. I dropped her off there a couple of times when she was called in to help with events. That's mostly what she did. Otherwise an hour's drive would have been too much to do on a daily or more regular basis."

"And I laid down the law, weekend nights only," Albert said.

Amanda thought Albert had a tough edge to him, but she didn't sense that he was hostile or even a drunk. He was just one of those people who saw things black and white.

"They must have really liked her there, though. We didn't have to drive her more than a handful of times. They sent drivers for her most of the time," Albert added. "Which I found strange."

But you allowed it, Amanda thought. Claire wasn't even an adult yet, but they let her go with other adults. "You meet who they sent?"

"Nah." Albert shook his head, not seeming to see anything wrong in that he hadn't cared enough to check.

"Sometimes we had Brianna take her." Sylvia took the first sip of her coffee.

"And who is Brianna?" Amanda asked.

"Another girl we were fostering at the time," Sylvia said.

"Yeah, and the poor thing got overlooked because Claire caused so much drama," Albert pushed out.

"What drama?" Amanda had yet to hear of any.

Sylvia held up her hand to her husband, as if telling him she'd be sharing the story. "She'd get in late, after curfew. I caught her a couple of times. Told her Bert and I could put up with a lot but not sneaking around."

"Did Brianna ever know where Claire went at those times?" Amanda asked.

"If she did, she wasn't talking to us about it."

"It was like those two had a freaking pact." Albert made a show of zippering his lips.

Amanda would circle back to Brianna. "Did you know a woman named Rita Cartwright?"

"Her boss at the gallery." Sylvia was nodding. "Met her once when I dropped Claire off for a gala. Seemed like a nice woman."

"Do you know if she and Claire were friends?" Trent asked.

"News to me if so. There were several years between them." Sylvia sipped her coffee.

"So just a professional relationship?" Amanda wanted this fully confirmed.

"Yes." Sylvia narrowed her eyes as if curious why so much discussion was circling around the relationship between Claire and Rita.

"Did you stay in touch with Claire after she left the system?" Trent asked.

"Nope." Albert tipped the bottle to his mouth.

"That's not entirely true..." Sylvia worried her bottom lip.

A fluttering started in Amanda's stomach, telling her that something was coming. Good or bad, she couldn't always be sure.

"You said that Claire was murdered." Sylvia cleared her throat.

"That's right." And as Amanda recalled it, the news hadn't been much of a shock to Albert.

"Do you know who did it? Any leads?" Sylvia asked.

"It's still an open investigation." Amanda would squeeze out all thought that a man had already technically been charged —though wrongly. "We believe, though, that her past may have caught up with her."

"Her past? What about it?" Sylvia set her gaze on Trent.

"Evidence suggests that she was involved with high-value

robberies in Prince William County and Washington, DC," he told her.

Sylvia put her hand on her husband's forearm, and for once it seemed like Albert had lost his voice.

"It also seems plausible that Rita was involved in the robberies," Amanda began. "She died last week too."

Sylvia covered her mouth for a second. "Murdered as well?" She blinked; her lashes wet with tears.

"Car accident." Amanda went with the official record despite her gut screaming murder.

"Oh," Sylvia said, drawing the word out.

"In one of these robberies, a man was murdered. We have reason to suspect that Claire was present at that time," Amanda told them.

"Did Claire... ah... did she...?" Albert's voice trembled and fragmented as he worked to give birth to the question.

"We don't think so, but we believe she knew who did and was planning to turn them in recently," Amanda said. "She didn't get the chance."

"When was this... incident?" Sylvia rubbed her neck.

"Fifteen years ago. Claire was twenty-one, out of your home," Amanda added, and the shoulders of both Hamiltons raised, relieved it wasn't during their watch. The couple's eyes met, though, and it seemed like they were having a silent conversation. "Is there something either of you should tell us?"

Sylvia was breathing heavily.

"We need to tell them, Sylvia." Albert cupped the back of his wife's hand.

Amanda let the couple take a few seconds, leaving them to continue communicating through touch and eye contact.

Tears fell down Sylvia's cheeks silently, not even the trace whimper of a sob. She butted her head toward Albert.

He said, "We received an envelope... Now this was years ago. Say close to seven."

Around the time Claire had met Logan, got married, and ran off to Nebraska.

"There was money inside," Albert went on. "More cash than I've seen in my life. Fifteen thousand, right there in our hands. She left it in the mailbox with a note."

"It said, 'You're good people. Thank you,'" Sylvia inserted. "I knew it was from Claire. She didn't sign it, but the writing gave her away."

"What did you do with the money?" Amanda asked.

"They say never look a gift horse in the mouth." Albert flushed. "We kept it, said nothing."

"That's why I was anxious seeing you at the door and asking about Claire." Sylvia cradled her cup. "I thought you were going to want the money back. But we've long spent it. No way we could come up with that amount."

"We're not here for that." The Hamiltons really had received a gift. Sale of the stolen items were probably handled via wire transfer, or even an early cryptocurrency like Bitcoin. The point was there wouldn't be bills and serial numbers to track. "We asked about boyfriends already, but do you know of a friend Claire had nicknamed Roo?"

"No. Sorry," Sylvia said.

"What about close friends?" Trent spoke up.

Sylvia shook her head. "Claire kept a lot to herself. I'd try to get her to talk, but it never met with much success. But then she had been through so much—her dad killing her mother—how could she trust people?"

Amanda's mind returned to an earlier point in the conversation. "You mentioned fostering another girl at the same time as Claire. You said this girl would cover for her. Her name again?"

"Brianna Shepard," Sylvia said. "And before you ask, we're not in contact with her either."

Amanda thought how lonely and empty that must feel. Sheltering and caring for children at their lowest points then sending them out into the world never to see them again. Fostering must have felt like a thankless job at times. "If you think of anything else that might help us patch Claire's past together, call me." Amanda stood and gave Sylvia her business card. "Thank you for talking with us and for the coffee." Not that she or Trent ended up touching theirs.

They got back in the car. "We need to find this Brianna Shepherd and see what she might tell us," Amanda said.

"No need to even say it."

TWENTY-EIGHT

Trent's paranoia was growing with every minute on this investigation. He kept looking in the rearview mirror, seeing if he could spot anyone following them. Nothing. No one obvious anyhow. He just hated feeling like he was being watched.

He'd found Brianna Shepherd, now Morris, in the system. She was married to a man named Richard and living in Triangle, a small town within Prince William County. It was moving on four o'clock by the time he pulled into the Morrises' driveway.

He knocked, but Amanda was standing directly in front of the door. It was opened by a man in his late thirties. Richard Morris.

"Yeah?"

"We're with the Prince William County PD. Here to speak with your wife, Brianna." Trent held up his badge for the man to look at. He swayed and reached for the doorframe. Trent moved to help steady him. The guy was drunk off his feet. "Let me help you."

The man swatted at Trent. "Let me alone." He was slurring and ogling Amanda. "What do you want with me anyway?"

Trent looked at Amanda, as if to say, *what the hell?*

"Mr. Morris, we need to speak with your wife," Amanda said in a firm voice.

"She's not here. Go away."

"Where can we find her?"

"Probably lying underneath some prick in a hotel somewhere." The man slammed the door in their faces.

Trent banged, but Amanda put a hand on his shoulder.

"We'll come back another time."

"We need to find out where Brianna is and talk with her."

"We don't even know if she's going to have something to tell us."

"So we're just giving up?"

"Just postponing. Let's leave Mr. Morris to sober up, and we'll come back in the morning. He could be more helpful then."

"If you think that will make a difference." He wasn't eager about walking away when it felt like they were so close, but Amanda was right. Richard in his current state was utterly useless. And even sober, he might have no clue where his wife was. "Popcorn and movies then?" She'd know he was referring to the hotel surveillance video.

"Guess so."

They got back in the car, and he took them to Central, an eye out for anyone following them. Again no one he could single out.

Trent got the USB drive ready and the list of times the clerk from Lux Suites remembered seeing Claire leave. He also checked his email, and there was one from Paula Ferguson. It didn't include a guest list from the shelter's charity event but came with the assurance she was still looking. He wasn't going to hold his breath. An event from fifteen years ago. It would be more of a surprise to him if she found it.

Trent could overhear Amanda on the phone with Libby. Her tone of voice gave away how much she hated to tell the woman she needed her to stay with Zoe longer. He could tell the ask hurt his partner, as if she was failing the girl, but being a single parent couldn't be easy. He'd been fortunate to have two loving parents who were there for him and his sisters, but not everyone was so fortunate. Zoe had been through hell after her idyllic life was shot to pieces. Amanda sometimes talked about how the girl was her savior, but Amanda was just as much the girl's.

"All right, we ready to go?" Amanda came over to his cubicle rubbing her hands together, overeager and compensating to hide her disappointment.

"You know I can handle this if you want to go home to Zoe." He paused there, and when she said nothing, he added, "I'd understand." He could have brought up the cryptic note left at Amanda's door. Surely that had to be weighing on her and causing concern. He knew better than to ask why she didn't let Zoe stay with someone else until this case was over. He figured what Amanda's response would be to that: she had things under control, and she wasn't about to cower at being threatened. "Amanda?" he prompted.

"Are you sure?"

"Yes." He added a smile to stamp it home.

"I'll owe you one then. Thank you."

"Don't mention it. We're partners. That's what we do."

After Amanda left, he got himself a coffee and started watching the video, forwarding to the times the hotel clerk had mentioned. He was watching footage from a camera placed at the front counter that also covered just outside the main doors.

Claire entered the camera's line of sight, and she went over to the phone that the clerk had pointed out to him and Amanda.

As Trent waited it out, he wondered who else Claire might have called from the phone.

Claire replaced the receiver after less than thirty seconds, offered a pleasant smile to the man at the desk, and stepped outside. She got into a yellow cab that showed up a few minutes later.

Benji's Taxi, number 2352. Trent wrote this down with the time in his notepad. *Wednesday,* 1:15 *PM.*

He watched as the car pulled out and left. Trent then went to the next time that the clerk gave them. Thursday, Claire made a call and left in Benji's Taxi, number 1510, at 10 AM.

Then Thursday afternoon. *Benji's Taxi, number* 2352 *again.*

Trent forwarded to Friday afternoon, even though it wasn't on the list of days and times he had from the hotel clerk. Amanda had said Claire had been at Locked Up Tight about four thirty that day. About four PM, Claire walked out the front doors, but she hadn't called for a ride at the front desk like the other times.

He switched over to the exterior camera and watched Claire continue down the street. She kept looking over a shoulder until she left the reach of the camera. But Trent caught something else of interest in the Lux Suites parking lot. Claire seemed to have an audience. A person behind the wheel of a silver sedan.

Trent zoomed in, trying to make out the license plate. No luck. It was concealed by one of those tinted plate covers. The emblem on the hood told him it was a Toyota. A Camry like the one he thought was following them the other day? It was likely ridiculous to even think that. There had to be hundreds of silver Camrys in the area.

The person behind the wheel was a man, and he was wearing a baseball cap. The grain in the feed made it impossible to make out distinct features.

Had Claire known she was being watched and picked up a ride farther down the street? Maybe hoping she could lose him?

Trent put his hand over the phone on his desk. He should call Amanda, but to tell her what exactly? He didn't know for sure that the man in the Toyota was Claire's killer. All Trent had was a budding suspicion and a dose of paranoia. Besides, he had sent Amanda home to be with Zoe, and whatever this was could hold until tomorrow morning. He'd mention the car then, and the taxis, and they'd go from there in tracing Claire's last movements.

Though he could get one step ahead and reach out to Benji's Taxi.

The woman who answered the phone sounded older and was polite. "Where would you like to be picked up?"

It must have been the pressure of the day, but Trent found the innocent question amusing, and wondered how many times people gave the woman grief about it every shift. Especially drunks in need of a ride home from the bar. "I'm Detective Stenson with the PWCPD."

The other end of the line went silent for a spell. "If you're not ordering a car, I need you off this line."

"Wait. Could I get the name of the manager or owner and a number to reach him or her?"

"Terrence Phillips. He's not in now. Tomorrow morning eight AM." The nice woman hung up.

Well then... He supposed that was just one more thing that he'd have to stick a pin in until tomorrow. But he could compile the necessary paperwork to request a warrant that would force the cab company to hand over the GPS logs on their cars.

By the time he had all that in order, it was nine and he was exhausted. But he was also starving. He got into his Jeep Wrangler and started in the direction for home but ended up going toward John and Shell's.

He dropped in at a pizzeria on the way and picked up an

extra-large pepperoni. He had more questions about Claire and wagered that arriving armed with a deep dish wouldn't hurt his chances of getting answers.

John was opening the door as Trent climbed the front steps.

"I've got pizza." Trent held up the box as a peace offering.

"So I see." His friend was somber.

"She's not doing so well?"

John shook his head. "She's having a rough go of it. Doesn't know why if Claire was back in town, she didn't at least drop by."

"I'll see if I can help…"

John dipped his head and patted Trent's shoulder as he moved past him into the home. Logan was on one end of the couch, and Shell the other. When he'd made the rash decision to see his friends, he'd forgotten Logan would be here. "Hi, guys," Trent said to everyone in the room.

"Oh, pizza. Pepperoni, I hope." This from Shell, and her eyes lit but Trent could see that it was a shallow expression.

"Is there any other kind?"

"I'll get plates." Logan got up and disappeared in the direction of the kitchen.

"How are you doing?" Trent sat next to Shell. "Stupid question, I'm sure."

"I've been better. Not gonna lie." Shell's chin quivered, and Trent hugged her.

"Sorry that things worked out the way they did," he said as he pulled back.

"Not your fault. Just tell me you're getting some answers. I know Logan didn't kill her."

Trent looked up as Logan came back into the room with the promised plates. He held four beers by the neck too.

"In case you wanted one." Logan held one toward Trent.

"Thanks." He was technically off the clock, so what the heck. He took a long draw, grateful for the cold liquid going down his throat. For that few seconds it was like the investigation and none of the ugliness associated with it existed.

In that time, John had flipped the lid on the pizza box and loaded a slice on a plate for Trent. He took it gratefully and bit off a large chunk.

They must have been watching TV before he arrived—it was on but the volume muted. The four of them scarfed down the pizza in silence, but Trent felt them looking at him to speak, to provide them with something.

Trent set down his plate, a bit of crust from his third slice and some crumbs were all that remained. "We went to the gallery where Claire worked." He stopped there, suddenly aware that maybe he shouldn't be speaking with Logan present.

"What took you there?" Shell dropped the slice she'd been working on.

"I, ah, actually shouldn't get into all of it, but we're making some progress." He flicked a quick glance toward Logan.

"He didn't kill her, Trent," Shell stressed.

"I'm quite sure I know that."

"Quite sure?" Logan barked. "Unbelievable."

Trent felt his anger swell. "I don't know you, all right. But I do know Amanda, and I do know that the evidence, or so-called evidence against you, seems too clean."

Logan's shoulders relaxed and lowered.

"Do either of you know of a Brianna Shepherd, now Morris?" Trent directed the question to anyone in the room who wanted to answer.

"Wasn't she another foster kid the Hamiltons took in during the same time they had Claire?" Michelle said.

"So Claire told you about her?" Trent was curious why Shell hadn't mentioned this Brianna long before now, like when he and Amanda were asking about Claire's friends on their first visit. Though he supposed, Shell had a lot to process with her

estranged sister showing up dead after years of being absent
from her life.

"Not really. I sort of pried it out of her after she let it slip
that she had to share a room with someone."

"Were she and Claire close?" He hoped that Shell would
give him reason to be excited about speaking with her. Sometimes working an investigation was so infuriating with all the
spinning in circles and backtracking. But a new perspective
often lent clarity to a previous scenario.

"No idea really."

Shell's uncertainty about Claire's relationship with Brianna
could be why she never thought to mention her. But it would be
hard to be in that proximity and not be privy to some of the
other person's affairs. And the Hamiltons seemed to think
Brianna covered for Claire. He had no doubt Brianna would
add value to the investigation. "I don't suppose either of you
talked to Brianna after Claire disappeared?"

Shell glanced at Logan and gestured for him to speak.

"Yeah, I found out about Brianna from one PI along the
way. I went to her years ago when I first got back to Dumfries. I
thought she might know where Claire was."

"Why? You thought they were good friends?" Trent's
insides were buzzing because he could have pointed them in
Brianna's direction a long time ago.

"I had—and have—no idea."

"Okay, so when you spoke to Brianna, what did she tell
you?"

"That she and Claire hadn't been in touch for years."

Trent felt the air leave his lungs. *Too much to hope for
answers...* "Is there anything more you can tell me about Brianna?" What he really wanted to ask, he felt he couldn't. *Was
Brianna part of a heist ring? Could she be Claire's killer?* Not
that he knew where that left the male perp captured on that

video years ago or explained the man in the Toyota. And were they the same man?

Logan set his now-empty plate on the coffee table. "She also told me she liked Claire from the beginning."

Did that mean anything that moved the investigation forward? The two could have bonded just because they had similar stories. They had both landed in foster care. Had Brianna made similar choices to Claire and gotten involved with the wrong people? Was that why she covered for Claire? "When you met Brianna, did you get the impression she was involved in anything illegal?"

"I don't know her enough to make that call."

"Why are you so interested in this Brianna person?" John asked, speaking for the first time since the pizza box was opened.

Leave it to John to go there. And there was no answer that Trent could give him. It's not like he could come out with the fact Claire had secured a defense attorney about a robbery, and that the gun she had in her purse was connected to a murder. "Just a name that came up. I can't say much of anything. Sorry. Well, I should get going. It will be another long one tomorrow."

He saw himself out and wondered if he'd stopped by more to offer his friends comfort or to feel some himself. Like some consolation that he was doing all he could, even though it felt like his hands were tied. And now he was walking out with more questions. Why had Brianna protected Claire's secrets? Had Claire cut her in? And the big one: did Brianna know anything about Claire's murder or the man in the Toyota?

TWENTY-NINE

Amanda picked up two coffees from Hannah's Diner on the way to Central. She was beyond grateful that Trent had let her go home on time yesterday and had volunteered to handle the video on his own.

She set the extra-large cup on his desk, and he didn't even look up at her. He was staring at his monitor. "Trent?" she prompted him.

"Oh, sorry." He leaned back in his chair. "I'm just right into my work I guess."

"I see that. I brought you a coffee." She gestured toward it.

"Thanks. The best too, I see."

"Only the best. So what are you looking at?"

"Let's just say I got a lot accomplished last night." He peeled back the lid on the to-go cup and took a sip.

"Tell me everything." She perched on the edge of his desk, and when his eyes met hers, he looked exhausted. "You slept, though?"

"I got some. So I watched the video, starting with the times the hotel clerk told us that Claire ordered a taxi. Company's Benji's Taxi. I have the unit numbers. Turns out three fares from the hotel but two units. I filed for a subpoena last night—"

"You did all the paperwork too? Not just a verbal one?"

"I did the paperwork."

"Whoa." She tried to bury her surprise at his initiative as she didn't want to insult him.

"The manager at the cab company, a Terrence Phillips, was in this morning at eight. So was I. And so was the approval from a judge. So I'm reviewing the GPS readings from the two units." He motioned toward his screen.

"And what have you found out?"

"Really? I stayed late, did all that, and you think I have the answers already? I just got the records a minute before you got here."

"I didn't mean to—"

Trent laughed and lifted his cup to hers in a toast gesture. "Relax, I'm giving you a hard time."

She touched her cup to his and took a swallow of her coffee. "What else is there?" It was just something in the way his laughter was cut short, like it stopped before its natural conclusion.

"Friday afternoon around four, Claire left Lux Suites. She didn't get into a vehicle but walked down the street. I found it because she was at Locked Up Tight at four thirty that day. You didn't figure she'd walked there."

"Correct. It's quite a distance from the hotel."

"I'm guessing she caught another ride from someplace else. But when I was watching her walk away, I spotted a silver Toyota Camry in the hotel's lot. There was a man behind the wheel, and he was keeping an eye on Claire."

A silver Toyota Camry... Amanda set her cup on Trent's desk and rocked back and forth, just slowly.

Trent added, "And I never mentioned this because I thought I was making more of it than was there, but... the other day, I swear I saw a silver Camry following us. I'm guessing you noticed the same?" He raised his eyebrows.

She shook her head. "Nope, but I saw one pass my house after I got my *special delivery*." She added finger quotes to the latter two words.

"That does it for me. Whoever is driving that Camry must be connected to Claire's murder."

"Did you get a plate?"

He shook his head. "It had one of those tinted covers."

"As did the one I saw on my street."

"Has to be the same car, same person. Baseball cap?"

"Don't remember that." But she recalled seeing a silver sedan someplace else along the course of the investigation, but she couldn't pin down where. Maybe she had subconsciously picked up on the one following them like Trent had. "We need to see if anything came out of the interviews with Logan's neighbors. Maybe one of them mentioned a silver Toyota Camry and got a plate, even a partial."

"We can thumb through them again to be sure, but I don't remember coming across it before."

Amanda's mind returned to the timing of Claire's departure from Lux Suites. "So she left on Friday at four to empty the safe deposit box at four thirty—we know she was there then. And she's killed three hours later. Did he just keep an eye on her for a while? He might have even known what her business was at Locked Up Tight. But why would she risk taking the box's contents with him watching her?"

"She might not have known he was that close, or she could have felt there was a greater risk to leaving the letter in the box, and the gun too, assuming that's where it was."

"Okay, but what happened after she emptied the box? Did that man catch up with her then?" As Amanda asked the questions, she could surmise one answer. "She told her estate attorney there was a letter explaining everything for Logan. Did she find out where Logan lived somehow, go there, wait and see if he slipped out, then let herself in with the hide-a-key?"

"All right, I see where you're headed with this. Then the man in the Camry, let's say he's the killer, goes into the house afterward thinking he's got the perfect solution to get away with murder."

"Yeah." She bit her bottom lip. "The only thing that doesn't fit is the lingerie. I highly doubt he was walking around with it in his pocket."

"He could have seen her waiting to go into Logan's. Then took time to concoct his entire plan, which ended up with him buying lingerie. He could have guessed her size or if he is Claire's old heist partner, he might have known it."

"Just insane. How did he even know she had the gun or proof against him?" Amanda shook her head. "Don't know about you, but I look forward to having answers for a change." She got off his desk and looked at his screen. "Let's see if we can get some."

"All right. Going back to Wednesday..." He scrolled down the document on his screen. "At one fifteen, via unit twenty-three fifty-two, she went to this address." He wrote it down, then met Amanda's gaze. "I think we both know where that is."

"The Flynn house."

"Claire paid Rita a visit Wednesday afternoon, and by Thursday night, Rita's dead." Trent paled. "Did Claire exact revenge and tamper with her car then?"

"Don't know but even if she did, it doesn't answer who killed Claire."

Trent raised his eyebrows. "Someone who knows she took out Rita."

"We're getting ahead of ourselves. What's the next ride Claire took?"

"Well, she returned to her hotel Wednesday afternoon at three thirty. The next afternoon, Thursday, and sticking with cab twenty-three fifty-two, she goes to Woodbridge Inn. Now, this specific cab didn't return to Claire's hotel, but she could have gotten a ride back in another unit."

"And what about Thursday morning? She go anywhere?"

"Yep, unit fifteen ten. One second." He opened another file and scrolled down. "Here it is. Looks like Claire was dropped off at—"

Amanda looked closely at the address on the screen. "Mona Lawson's? What was Claire doing there?"

"I don't have a clue."

"Well, we're going to find out. So much for Mona not recognizing Claire."

"Playing devil's advocate here, but that place is humongous. Could be Claire paid someone else there a visit. We also need to figure out what had Claire going to Woodbridge Inn. Was she visiting someone there too? And, if so, who?"

Amanda and Trent were buzzed through the front gate, but she had to bang on the door before it was opened. It was Mona Lawson herself, the picture of calm.

"Detectives? What is so urgent?" Mona let her gaze dance over the two of them, settling rather judgmentally on Amanda.

"We just have a couple of questions for you. Could we come in for a minute?" Amanda plastered on a smile, hoping it would translate as sincere but highly doubting it.

"Sure." Mona opened the door wider and led the way to the sitting room they'd sat in before. "Just be a dear and get the door behind you."

Trent got there before Amanda. She leaned in close to his ear and said, "We need to play nice here." She didn't know if the reminder was more for him or herself.

"No problem," he mouthed to her.

They really had nothing on Mona except for her possibly

lying about knowing Claire herself, but Mona could have paid someone to take Claire out. Not that they were anywhere close to having enough to justify warrants for her financials.

"Would you like a tea or coffee? I can get Ingrid," Mona said, slipping onto a chair.

"Not necessary." The offer felt superficial, and Amanda wanted no part of it. She brought up a photo of Claire again, the same one she'd shown Mona the other day. "Just confirming that you've never seen her before."

"Let me take another look." Today, Mona took reading glasses from a pouch on the table next to her. She put them on and looked at the screen. "No, as I told you. Never seen her before."

Amanda put her phone in a pocket. "Does anyone else live with you, Ms. Lawson?"

"No, but I have staff often on the premises. Ingrid you've met, but I also have groundskeepers."

"Could we get their names?" Trent asked.

"I don't see why you'd need them. Could you explain to me what is going on?" Mona asked, leveling her gaze at Amanda.

"Claire Ramsey had a taxi drop her off here on Thursday morning."

"And that's the woman in the photo you showed me?"

"Yes." Mona wasn't stupid, but she was working to portray herself that way. Amanda would bet the woman was hiding something.

Mona added, "I have no idea why she'd be here."

"Could we speak with your staff?" Amanda remembered clearly that Ingrid said she didn't know Claire, but she wondered if her answer would change if they got her away from Mona.

"They are all busy with their duties," Mona peacocked.

"Their names then. We'll reach out to them after hours."

"Certainly." She rang a bell that was on her table today, and Ingrid came running.

"Yes, ma'am."

"See to their request." Mona gestured toward Amanda, then said, "If you will both excuse me, I have an appointment."

About a half hour later, Amanda and Trent were leaving the estate with the list of people.

"We'll pull backgrounds on all of them," she said. "First, I want to get over to Woodbridge Inn and see if we can find out what had Claire going there Thursday afternoon."

"And I hate to point this out, but who knows where else Claire went in her final days? After she leaves the hotel, it's hard to know."

"Only thing I can think of is to check any pickup requests for the places she was dropped off."

"There could be something to that, but something occurring to me is Claire survived off the grid for years. She knows how to cover her tracks. But she didn't seem to work at hiding her steps in town. Which seems crazy. She knew she was being watched. Just the way she was looking over her shoulder... but I can't swallow that she didn't go to see Shell."

"Maybe Claire simply ran out of time." She hoped that brought Trent some comfort. Not that she necessarily bought it. Why wasn't Michelle Claire's first stop? Had the thought of dropping in on her sister after all these years been too much to handle? Or had she feared putting her sister in harm's way? It could have been any number of things, and all Amanda had were assumptions and theories. She might as well be banging her head against the wall.

THIRTY

Amanda rang the bell on the counter. The Woodbridge Inn wasn't as nice as where Claire had been staying, but it was considered a four-star hotel. No one was at reception when she and Trent went inside.

"Good morning." A lean man in a black suit paired with a salmon shirt came out from an office in the back. "How can I help you?"

"We're detectives with the PWCPD." Amanda pulled up a picture of Claire and held it for the clerk. "Do you recognize this woman?"

He took her phone and scrutinized the photo. "She looks familiar, but I don't think she stayed here."

"We think she visited one of your guests last Thursday afternoon."

A strange smile. "But you don't know which one."

"Do you?" Trent countered.

The clerk pressed his lips.

"Could we get the names of your guests who had rooms last Thursday?" Amanda asked, hearing the long shot of the request. Longer still was that one would mean something to her and Trent.

"If you can get me a warrant."

Amanda held up her index finger and spun. She made a call to Judge Anderson to see if he'd extend a verbal warrant. He did. She pivoted toward the counter, put the call to *mute*, and said to the clerk, "I have a judge on the line, if you'd like to confirm, but we have legal approval to look at your guest list."

The clerk reached for her phone, and she took the call off mute. "This is Emanuel Acosta with Woodbridge Inn... yes... okay." He handed the phone back to Amanda. The judge had hung up.

"All good?" she asked Emanuel.

"Yes, ma'am. One moment." He tapped on his keyboard, and the printer next to his monitor whirred to life. "Here you go." He snatched the page off the machine and laid it on the counter, a move he'd no doubt made a million times when presenting room bills to clients.

Amanda moved down the counter with Trent when a customer came in. None of the names were meaning anything to her until she got to Brianna Morris. She pointed to the entry and across to the column that showed her checkout date was open-ended.

"So Brianna's husband wasn't far off the mark when he said she was shacked up in a hotel somewhere," she said.

"Sure, but here's the thing... It would seem that Claire came here to see Brianna. How did Claire know where to find her? Claire didn't have a phone that we know of, and she didn't make calls from the hotel."

"Not from her room. She could have called from the lobby or used a payphone somewhere else and got the information out of Brianna's husband. Still, that would raise the point that Claire must have kept tabs on her all these years. And if she watched over Brianna, maybe she watched everyone else too—

Michelle, Logan, Rita. It must have broken Claire's heart leaving behind her husband and sister, more than you and I can imagine."

"I'll reserve judgment on that for now. Let's see if Brianna's in. Room eight fifteen."

They loaded onto the elevator and went up to the eighth floor. Room 815 was to the left.

Trent knocked, and there was no way Brianna wasn't hearing it if she was inside.

"Try again, I guess." Amanda had this horrid feeling that something might be wrong. Claire, then Rita. Had their killer got to Brianna too?

He banged again, this time even louder, if possible.

"She's not in there," he concluded.

"I hope that's what it is."

"You can't be thinking that—"

"Excuse me? Get away from my room."

Amanda turned. "Brianna Morris? Prince William County PD." She didn't have time to pull her badge or say they wanted to speak with her. Brianna was on the run.

She hit a woman on the way, and her purse fell to the floor, items spilling everywhere. Amanda sprung over the mess, Trent right at her heels.

The door to the stairwell clanged open, the metal of it hitting the brick wall behind it. Amanda was close to Brianna, just a few steps away. She had to push just a little harder... pull from deep inside, from her younger days on her high school running team.

"PWCPD!" Amanda shouted, repeating it for anyone that might be within earshot. "Stop, Morris!"

The footsteps slowed. Amanda didn't think for one second it was because the woman was surrendering. Just catching her breath more likely. She was a smoker, that much Amanda picked up on her trail.

The stairwell came out in the lobby, and Brianna steamed right through.

Amanda and Trent were right behind her.

Amanda pushed a little harder, the muscles in her legs burning, threatening to cramp. It's not like she ran much these days. Usually only when a suspect resisted arrest.

"Stop! PWCPD!" Amanda yelled again.

People in the parking lot were staring at them. Most motionless, their mouths gaped open, catching flies. Would be nice if just one of them would help.

"Holy shit!" Brianna screamed as she flew forward and landed hard.

One Good Samaritan. A man, in his sixties, had put his leg out to trip Brianna. He tipped his fedora at Amanda and Trent. "Happy to be of help."

"Thank you," she told him with a smile.

Amanda and Trent hauled Brianna to her feet, both taking an arm and lifting. Brianna tried to shrug them off. She succeeded with the arm Amanda had been holding. The woman was strong and doped on adrenaline, but it was more than that. Something that Amanda saw on Brianna's forearm had her grip loosening. A tattoo—*Roo*.

"We need to talk to you," Amanda said firmly. "You have a choice. Here or down at Central Station."

Brianna flicked a finger toward the hotel. "My room."

Amanda nodded, and the three of them went back to room 815.

"You didn't need to run," Trent hissed. He was still winded, and Amanda figured it wasn't because he had bad cardiovascular health, but rather pain. She had a suspicion he'd twisted his ankle during the pursuit. He was behind her, but she'd heard him grunt in pain and had glanced over a shoulder.

"If you were me, you'd run too."

"You're afraid of cops," Trent volleyed back.

"I'm not afraid of anything. But cops can't be trusted."

Amanda imagined her dislike for cops was linked to her winding up in foster care. "You were Claire's best friend, Roo." She added that latter bit and looked at Trent as she did. "I saw the tattoo on your arm."

Brianna twisted her bicep, showing off the ink. "What do you mean I *was* her best friend? Did something happen to her?"

"Might be best if you took a seat," Amanda told her.

Brianna sat on the edge of the bed.

Amanda continued. "Claire was murdered last Friday."

Brianna gasped and started shaking furiously. "I told her. I told her to just leave it all alone. There's no good that comes from digging around in the past."

Amanda's stomach fluttered. "Tell us everything you know."

"I don't know everything, that's the thing. Just enough. I know she got herself caught up in something bad. Illegal," she added under her breath.

"A robbery ring that targeted wealthy collectors of artwork, jewels, sculptures...?" Amanda put it out there as if Claire's pastime was of little consequence. She wanted to encourage Brianna to continue talking.

"That's right, though I'm not sure if you could call it a *ring*. I don't think there were many people involved."

"It was connected to the gallery where Claire worked in Washington?" Trent said.

"Yes and no. I mean I don't think the place is corrupt, just some people who worked there were. Not sure if that's still the case." Brianna rubbed her cheek with her shoulder. "It was the worst place for Claire, but she couldn't get away from them."

"Who is *them*, and how did they force her hand?" Amanda was trying to understand, putting herself in the mind of a sixteen-year-old who had just lost her mother and father. She'd be looking for a place to belong, a surrogate family. Was that all it took, and that desire kept her tethered to those people and that lifestyle even when she became an adult?

"I don't know names. Claire didn't want me involved. She wanted me far away from all of it."

"Did they control her somehow, hold something over her head?" *Michelle. Logan.* What if these people had threatened their welfare? Amanda could imagine that would compel Claire's cooperation. It would seem she'd viewed Logan's accident as an attempt on his life.

"They groomed her. They gave her nice things, handed over wads of cash. I'm telling you I just had a bad feeling about the entire thing. So did Claire, but there were times she tried to convince me they weren't so bad. I wasn't sure it was me she was trying to convince or herself."

"Did you and Claire stay in touch?" Amanda was following a gut feeling. In what turned out to be Claire's last week alive, she hadn't gone to her sister or Logan, but saw Brianna.

"Yeah, I'd get letters in the mail, no return address. She'd use postal outlets in the towns she passed through. I never knew where she was staying. And I knew better than to ask."

"You never told any of this to Logan Hunter, Claire's husband." Trent's face was a resting scowl. "He came to you looking for Claire."

"It hurt me to keep quiet, but Claire made me promise. She said for Logan's safety, he could never find her or uncover her past."

"Claire was discovered in Logan's house," Amanda said.

Brianna's eyes watered. "Because of me."

Amanda stiffened. "Why because of you?"

"I found out where Logan lived years ago and passed that along to Claire. She asked if I could find out."

That answered one question they'd had since near the beginning—how Claire even knew where Logan lived. "When

Claire left for Nebraska, did she stop being involved in the robberies?"

"She stopped when things between her and Logan became serious."

"I'm guessing her quitting wasn't received well by the others," Trent said.

"She ran off to Nebraska. What do you think?"

A small pulse ticked in Trent's cheek at Brianna's sharp remark, but Amanda was more interested in how the pieces were starting to fit together. As long as Claire was part of the heists, she wasn't a threat. When she wanted no part of them anymore, she became a liability. Even more when the killer must have found out Claire was holding on to the Glock. There were still many questions, though. "Do you know why she returned to Prince William County last week?"

Brianna met Amanda's gaze, blinked slowly. "She was dying from cancer. She wanted to set everything right before..." She paused, sniffled, her eyes glazing over. "She hated what she did to Logan, to her sister, even to me. We might have been in some contact, but she was my rock before she left town. She knew that. Most of all, her conscience was eating her alive."

"About?"

"She saw something bad happen and had the evidence to back it up. She never gave me the details. I always got the feeling she'd witnessed a murder." Brianna presented it as if she expected that news to be a shock to Amanda and Trent. "That doesn't surprise you?"

Trent said, "We've put some things together. Like the fact she came here last Thursday to see you. How did she even know how to reach you?"

"As I said, I'd get the odd letter. She kept tabs on me. She called the house two weeks ago and found out that I'd left my husband. She did her thing and tracked me down, called all the hotels in the area, figuring I wouldn't have gone far. She didn't believe Dick when he told her I'd cheated and shacked up with some guy."

Amanda wondered if that was always how she abbreviated her husband's name, or if it started with their marriage problems.

"He passed the same story on to us," Trent said.

"What a shit." Brianna clenched her jaw.

"What did she tell you when she came to see you here?" Amanda prompted, wanting an answer to Trent's other question.

"That was when she told me she was dying and tired of running. Also how she wanted to atone for her life choices, somehow make up for the heartbreak she caused. I tried to talk her out of it."

"Out of what exactly?" Goosebumps raised on Amanda's arms.

"She was going to confront her past. Head on. But she was all about second chances and wanted this person to know she was turning them in."

And herself, Amanda thought. "Do you have any names?"

"No."

"What do you know about Rita Cartwright?" Amanda figured Brianna would know Claire's boss from the gallery.

Brianna bunched up her face like she was going to spit. "Isn't it Flynn now? She was a manipulative bitch. She thought that by including Claire in her wedding, it would make Claire feel indebted to her more. It was all a mind game."

"We know Claire reported to Rita at the gallery. They weren't friends though?" Amanda desired to reinforce what they'd already found.

"Heavens no."

"Claire paid Rita a visit on Wednesday," Trent put out there, matter-of-fact. "Would you know why?"

"All I can think is she was doing what she told me. Giving

this person she spoke of the chance to turn themselves in. Could have been Rita, I suppose. Did Rita kill Claire?"

Amanda shook her head. "Rita died on Thursday, the day before Claire."

"The day after Claire saw her?" Brianna was trembling. "Was she murdered too?"

"Her death is certainly suspicious." Amanda felt that was the truth yet also vague enough. "Do you think that Claire might have—"

"No," she snapped. "Never. Claire wasn't her biggest fan, but she wouldn't have killed her. But Claire goes to talk to her and then she's dead? Seems a little more than a coincidence to me."

While it was impossible that Rita had killed Claire, it seemed rather apparent that Rita had been involved in the heist ring. Maybe Claire visiting her had panged her conscience or had her cowering in fear. Rita had built a pretty good life for herself. She had a nice home, a husband, children. She wouldn't have wanted to lose it all, and she wouldn't want to bring shame on them. Had she killed herself by tampering with her car? Or was the answer even darker than that? "You said Claire wasn't her biggest fan, but did you sense Claire held animosity toward Rita?"

"I'd say more fear."

"Do you know why?"

"Claire never got into that with me, but I think it factored into her going to Nebraska and running from there a couple of years after. Claire did say to me once, 'I think they found me.'"

They... Was that Rita and the mystery man or also others with the heist crew they didn't know about yet?

"And you have no idea who Claire might have been planning to confront?" Trent asked.

"As I said, no names. Claire said that was for my safety."

As frustrating as it was for the case, Claire had probably

made the right call for her friend's well-being. "Did Claire have any boyfriends that you knew about?"

"Besides Logan? No. I'm why they even got together. I was trying to get her into a normal life. Guess I could have saved everyone a lot of pain by butting out."

"What about any other men hanging around?" Trent turned the chair from the vanity around and sat down.

"Sure. At the gallery. One also picked her up to take her there a few times. He was good-looking, but several years older than Claire. Say in his early twenties when she was seventeen?"

Someone older, influential, possibly charming. "Do you know his name?"

"I don't. I asked her, but she wouldn't tell me. Told me even then the less I knew the better."

When they left here, Amanda would call the gallery again if the list of employees wasn't in her inbox. "When was this?"

"Not long after she started to work at the gallery."

Amanda wondered if this man didn't groom Claire to help him in the heists. She'd seen pictures of the younger Claire. She'd been pretty, and a few people told them how smart she was. Looks and brains would make her an asset. Also factor in her vulnerability from just losing her parents, and she was ripe for manipulation. "And all this was going on when you two lived with the Hamiltons?"

"Uh-huh. The Hamiltons never knew of course. Claire ended up getting a cell phone from the gallery people. They called at all hours. Claire was downright protective of that phone too. I never got my hands on it. Not for the lack of trying. Hey, do you think I could be in danger?"

"It is possible. But we need to know more," Amanda said.

"While I what? Sit around and see if I'm next?"

"Do you have any reason to believe you're a threat to who killed Claire?" Trent asked.

"They might have figured out that Claire and I were in contact, even though we were careful. You found me here."

"We'll get you protection," Amanda offered.

"Okay, but I'm not hiding."

A-plus for courage... "You and Rita weren't the only people Claire saw in the days leading up to her murder."

"Are they dead too?"

"No, nothing like that," Amanda rushed to say. "Claire went to the Lawson estate. Does that name mean anything to you?"

Brianna's expression went blank.

Amanda went on. "Martin Lawson was a wealthy businessman who was murdered during the course of a robbery." Brianna was watching her, soaking up every word; this was coming as news to her.

"I've never heard of him," she ended up saying.

"So no idea why she'd go to his estate?" Trent asked.

"You still refer to it as *his* estate even though he's dead. Does his widow or family live there?"

Trent nodded.

"If I was right and Claire witnessed a murder, maybe it was this Lawson guy. She could have gone to tell the family that she knew what had happened? Confess? Just an idea."

"She never talked about this with you? She went there Thursday morning, before seeing you that afternoon," Amanda said, wishing for more.

Brianna shook her head. "She never mentioned the name at all, or even what else she'd done that day."

"Okay, you've done great, Brianna." Amanda pulled her card. "You have my number and can call me any time."

"You were getting me protection?"

"Yes, and I will the second I step out that door." Amanda pointed toward it and went that way. She stepped into the hall with Trent and spoke once they boarded the elevator. "Between you and me, I'm surprised she's still alive. The killer seems to have been watching Claire's steps. Why take the chance on what she might have disclosed to her best friend?"

"Can't kill everyone."

"Let's hope that's the truth. Now if only we could ID the man involved with the heists. Was he the one who took Claire to the gallery? Is he also the mystery man in the silver Camry?"

"I think that's a solid bet."

"As for Brianna, I believe her when she says Claire withheld a lot from her."

Trent pressed his lips and shrugged. "People can be good actors. Look at Rita Flynn. I'd say she lived a lie and sold it to her husband and children."

"Me too."

The elevator dinged their arrival on the ground floor, and they unloaded and went to the department car. Amanda pulled her phone and made the call to Graves to get protection detail on Brianna. Hopefully, she wouldn't end up needing it.

THIRTY-ONE

It took time and convincing, but Amanda finally got it through Graves's thick skull that Brianna needed protection. Minutes passed, an hour, two, before a cruiser pulled into the hotel's parking lot. Officer Wyatt was behind the wheel. Amanda got out of the air-conditioned department car and filled him in, not trusting that he was fully briefed. "You'll need to watch her room."

"Okay, I wasn't told that."

Amanda felt anger heat her blood. Watching the hotel from the parking lot wouldn't accomplish anything. "You need to go inside."

"I'll pass it by my sergeant, see if that's what he wants me to do."

"Do that. Morris could be in danger." As Amanda stressed the importance of sticking close to Brianna, her thoughts went to the note left on her front step. "Tell me you'll do it."

Wyatt seemed to hesitate. "I'll see what he says."

She raked a hand through her hair, looked at the clear, blue sky. Then back to Wyatt. She let out a deep breath. "Do what you must. But if you aren't going in, watch for a silver Toyota Camry."

"A newer model," Trent added. He must have walked over while she was speaking with Wyatt.

The officer nodded and got on the phone.

She didn't want to leave, feeling tethered to the hotel, to watch over and protect Brianna. But her job was to catch the killer. "Let's go. We need to press Austin Flynn some more. Find out if he knows more than he told us—about his wife's past, about her last contact with Claire."

Trent hobbled a bit and let out a wince. Stopped.

Amanda turned. "You all right?"

"Yeah. Just twisted my ankle a bit when we were chasing Brianna. Nothing that's going to kill me."

"In our line of work, don't even joke about that." She grinned, and he smiled back.

Trent's ankle hurt like a son of a bitch, but he wasn't sitting out any bit of this investigation. He was invested. His top priority wasn't to clear Logan's name; he just wanted to solve the mystery. There was an incessant need in him to get answers, solve the puzzle. And after speaking to Brianna, he started seeing Claire as a young woman whose entire life course was charted for her from the age of sixteen. Just a child who an older man and woman saw fit to groom for their purposes. They were bullies and abusers, even if they offered Claire a world she no doubt found exciting—at least in the beginning.

It made him think of his Aunt Gertrude and how easily charm and luxuries could blind a person—even an intelligent, fully grown woman. His aunt had lost the love of her life and was won over by a charlatan who morphed into a woman-beater almost overnight. But there were always signs, red flags, if one was open-eyed enough to see them. His aunt hadn't been, and he and his family had been too late. And if she'd succumbed to such scum, Claire hadn't stood a chance. And once she was in, she was just running forward, trying to make the most of what she had to work with. She might have felt there was no other choice.

He knocked on the Flynns' door. There were the same vehicles in the drive as the other day, so someone should be home.

Austin answered the door. "Detectives?"

"We'd like to ask you some more questions," Trent said, shoulders squared.

"Is this about the accident?"

"If we could just come inside for a minute..." Amanda intercepted and spoke kindly to the man.

Austin stepped back to let them enter without a word. He shut the door behind them. The three of them stood there in awkward silence for a spell before Austin told them to come with him.

He took them to the living room and sat on the couch. Trent and Amanda dropped into a couple of chairs.

"Her accident wasn't an accident, was it?" Austin's chin quivered, and Trent felt for the man. It was possible he had no idea how much his wife had hidden from him.

"As you might remember, we're investigating the murder of her friend Claire." Trent swerved, thinking it was best to steer clear of Rita's fate just yet. The truth was they didn't know what Austin did, and for all they knew he was in on the heist ring too. Though Trent doubted that. He struck him as a strait-laced character who played by the rules.

"I told you, I have little to say on the topic."

"Claire reported to Rita at a gallery in Washington," he said.

"I'll trust you on that."

It would seem Rita hadn't even enlightened her husband to the fact she and Claire had worked together. "You told us Rita hadn't seen Claire in years." Trent studied Austin, and his body language was slightly tense but not closed off.

"That's right."

"Then you have no knowledge that Claire was here, at your house, last Wednesday?" Trent asked.

"I know of no such thing."

"Then you don't have any idea what might have been said between your wife and Claire?" Amanda chimed in.

"As I said, I didn't even know that they saw each other. Hey, maybe Rita wasn't even home. What time of day was this?"

"One fifteen in the afternoon."

"Oh."

Trent angled his head. "*Oh?*"

"I tried reaching her at work. They told me she went home for the afternoon on Wednesday. She could have been here, I suppose."

There was no *suppose* about it as the taxi Claire took from her hotel came straight here. Claire must have reached out to Rita and brought her home. But why not just go to her?

Trent's eyes glanced to the mantle and the wedding photo. He and Amanda had to be missing something. Brianna had said the maid-of-honor gig was given to Claire as a manipulative tactic. But why was Claire's photo still on the mantle? That would suggest a bond that Rita had felt toward Claire—even after her disappearance from Prince William County. Then again, maybe Rita was trying to keep up appearances. But the question was why and to whom? Her husband? If so, Trent would see that as a sign Rita had more to hide or in the least a guilty conscience to assuage. "We have reason to believe that your wife may have been caught up in something, as we brought up before."

"Here we go." He rolled his eyes dramatically. "She was a mother and art professor. Hardly some mastermind criminal."

"Before all that she worked at the gallery in Washington I mentioned, where it seems her love for art and the finer things might have gotten her into trouble." Trent did his best to present the facts as they saw them without shoveling a ton of blame on the man's dead wife. If he did, Austin would shut the conversation down fast. Call it a hunch.

"Did she have other friends at the gallery? Anyone she brought over for dinner maybe?" Amanda asked after several seconds of silence.

"By the time we got together, the gallery was behind her, so no one... well, except for Claire. You said she worked at the gallery. She was still around from time to time."

Had Rita kept herself involved with the ring after leaving the gallery? Or was there more depth to the relationship between Claire and Rita than Brianna had known about? Rita had been Claire's first stop. Did it show that Claire had a soft spot for her, wanted to give her time to get things in order before Claire turned her in for her role in the robberies?

Austin went on. "Rita rarely talked about her time there. But it doesn't mean anything nefarious was going on—then or after." Pain saturated Austin's voice like he was battling with accepting his wife may have been a criminal.

Trent glanced at Amanda, and she nodded. Their knack for silent communication was growing stronger by the minute. "Claire was in a heist ring. She targeted wealthy collectors, many of them through the gallery, but she wasn't working alone."

"Rita." Let out on a hitched breath.

"We believe so, and others," Trent said. "At least one person besides Claire. A man."

"And we think their relationship might have continued after Rita got a job at the university," Amanda inserted.

"Now you're telling me Rita was cheating on me?"

Amanda shook her head. "Not at all. We don't have reason to suspect things between them were more than platonic."

"There was a robbery that resulted in a murder." Trent figured that was the best way of putting it, even if he and Amanda toyed with the murder being premeditated. "His name was Martin Lawson."

Austin shut his eyes and pinched the bridge of his nose.

Amanda leaned forward. "You know the name?"

"Of course, I do. Martin was Rita's stepfather."

"He was..." Trent couldn't finish. Just when they thought they had things figured out, there was another twist. "How did she take his murder?"

"I don't honestly know. We weren't together then, but any time he came up over the years, she shut the conversation down quick."

"Because it hurt?" Amanda asked.

Austin shook his head. "Honestly, I never got the impression she was that broken up about it. Rita and her stepdad weren't close." He paused, chewed his bottom lip. "It was worse than that, and she had every reason to hate him."

Had Rita been the one to pull the trigger on her own stepfather? But how did that explain Rita's death, Claire's murder the following day, the man in the silver Camry, the threat left on Amanda's doorstep...? "What reason?"

Austin let out a deep breath. "Lawson sexually abused her."

That right there could be motive to want Martin dead, but why wait so long after leaving the family home to exact revenge? Rita would have been twenty-seven at the time of her stepfather's murder. Had resentment built up over the years only to be finally triggered somehow? "Where was Rita the night Martin Lawson was murdered?"

"I don't know... Again, we weren't together then. Are you suggesting that she killed her own stepfather now?"

Amanda shot Trent a brief look. "We're not saying that was the case. Did your wife ever talk to anyone about what happened when she was younger? To her mother?"

"Her mother died a few years after marrying Lawson when Rita was just young. He continued to raise her. Martin ended up marrying a woman named Mona, but by that time, Rita was already out of the house. She and Mona still built a relationship, though, which continued after Martin's murder. Mona's who got Rita the teaching job at the university."

Rita had lived alone with her abusive stepfather until she became an adult. That was a lot of years for hatred to build. Trent got to his feet. "Thank you for your time, Mr. Flynn. We'll be back if we have any more questions or information about your wife's accident."

"Wait, you can't go now. Do you think one of the people you say Rita was mixed up with came back and killed her after all these years? That it wasn't an accident?"

"I'm sorry, but we can't say with any certainty at this time." Amanda rose, and the two of them left Austin.

Trent got them headed to Central. "Never saw that coming," he eventually said. "Martin Lawson was Rita's stepfather."

"And Mona her stepmother..."

"You know, it feels like something's off with her. Not that I can put my finger on what."

"Well, I think Mona knows very well that Claire went to her house. I wouldn't even be surprised if it was to see Mona herself for some reason."

"I don't think we have enough to make that leap yet, but when we get back to Central, I'm going to reach out to Metro PD and see if Rita was ever questioned after Martin's murder."

"Smart idea."

"Did you ever get that employee list from Malachi Walsh at the gallery?"

"Oh, I was going to follow up on that." She pulled out her phone and said, "No email. I'll call now."

While she was on the phone, he pressed the gas. He was hungry for answers and had every intention of getting them.

THIRTY-TWO

He told her not to worry, that he had everything under control.
That she was a real natural. She did have a talent for manipu-
lating things to go her way. She kept replaying his many compli-
ments in her head, but they were overrun with images of Larry's
limp body on the bed.

"You did great." Nick flashed one of those smiles that had his
dimples deepening. After all these years, they still had a way of
making her go weak in the knees.

He parked the van in a 24-hour underground garage, and
they got changed in the back. They had jackets with numerous
pouches and hid them beneath coveralls—the latter, the same
uniform as the custodial staff wore at Lawson Investments.
While her job was getting the key, Nick was procuring the outfit,
including employee badges on lanyards. But both their jobs were
far from over.

Once suited up, they walked toward the Lawson Investments
building. Claire's nerves were on high alert, making her shake.

She took a few deep breaths; an exercise Nick had taught her
to ground and calm herself.

The high-rise now in front of her was intimidating, with

most of its windows darkened against the skyline. Just the flashing lights on the top to warn aircraft of its existence.

Nick flashed the key card in front of the pad next to the doors. The pad flashed green and beeped. He got the door for her.

A security man sitting at the front desk nudged his head at them.

"Hey, there," she said, with a smile, impressed with how she'd kept her nerves from altering her voice. "Larry's just not feeling well tonight. We were called in."

"Have we met?"

"We're new hires."

"Nice to meet you, Miss...?"

She lifted her lanyard showing her employee card. "Nadia. You?" she purred.

"Charlie." He put his gaze on Nick.

"We need to get to work, Charlie," she said, tossing out a wink. "I'm sure you understand."

"Most certainly do."

They left Charlie at the front desk. One of two security guards for the entire building. Martin Lawson, who owned this place, must have had confidence on par with God.

They first hit the janitor closet and got a cart each. Then they took the elevator straight to the top floor, number twenty-eight. The entire floor was dedicated to Lawson's collection. Artwork, jewels, priceless sculptures... that Fabergé egg.

She had her list of specific items to grab, and she'd been instructed to take nothing in addition.

"Got it," Nick said, talking to the contact on the other end of the mic in his ear. He said to her, "The cameras are out."

She barely nodded in acknowledgment. Adrenaline blanketed her in a sense of serenity, dampening the rational fear that always lingered in the background. The repercussions if this went bust. She'd be headed to prison. The trick was don't get caught.

But she kept doing this, and not just to please Nick—heists were a high like no other. As much as she toyed with the thought of leaving this life, she never would.

The elevator doors opened, and a security guard was stationed there. He stepped toward them, his face contorted in surprise. "What are you doing up here?"

"We're here to clean," she said, nonchalant, doing her best to play up her femininity.

"It's not Thursday."

She stood still as Nick lunged forward and shot the guard with a taser. The large man fell to the floor and twitched like a fish in oil as the volts kept running through him. Nick released the button and got down next to the man to hold a chloroformed rag over his mouth. Next, he dragged the man's limp body into a storage closet.

"He'll be fine," Nick assured her as he rejoined her.

They moved down the corridor where he again flashed the key card and doors unlocked.

Display cases and gilded frames housing artwork from the Renaissance era. The collection went on as far as she could see.

"Beautiful, eh? But keep your focus. You know what we're here for."

She nodded, but she was absorbed, captivated by the beauty that surrounded her. Such a treasure trove belonged in a museum, not squirreled away as part of a greedy man's private collection.

The two of them stayed close but moved through the room, checking items off their "shopping" list and putting them in the various pockets in their vests. What wouldn't fit on their person, they tucked away in the janitorial carts.

She stopped in front of a display case. Inside was the Fabergé egg. Her heart, she swore, skipped a beat. "It's incredible."

"Get in, get it. Move it." He spoke like he was in a hurry, but he was moving slower than he normally did.

He carried on to the next item while she continued to stare at the egg. The case could have been rigged with an alarm, but she never saw evidence of that. Again, Lawson's overconfidence would be his undoing.

She lifted the glass enclosure and slowly set it on the floor. The egg was just inches away from her. As she picked it up with her gloved hands, she couldn't imagine ever letting it go.

"Where the hell is the security guy?"

Her breath froze, locked in her lungs. It was a man's voice, but it wasn't Nick's. He was standing only ten feet from her. The voice had come from the hall.

"It's so nice of you to take the time out for this, Dad." A woman's voice that she'd know anywhere. Rita Cartwright, her boss from the gallery, but she wasn't supposed to be in on this job.

"Least I could do. You got me out of that dull charity event at least."

Claire slipped the egg into the largest compartment in her vest and moved toward Nick.

He pulled a gun, and her heart raced. But it wasn't real. Just a replica made to look real. They'd used it before when the heists got dicey.

The man stopped when he saw her and Nick. Martin Lawson. And Rita had called him... Dad?

She had this sick feeling in her gut, the one that always warned her something bad was going to happen. She'd had it the day she left for the bookstore all those years ago, the day her mother died.

Martin pulled out his phone. "I'm calling the police!"

Before Martin could hit a button, Nick pulled the trigger. A loud boom.

Blood blossomed from Martin's chest, and he collapsed to the floor.

Claire spun, gripping her head. "It's real?" she screamed.

"I couldn't let him call the police."

"I thought the... the gun... Oh, I'm going to be sick." *Claire clutched her stomach as bile shot up into her mouth. She swallowed reluctantly.* "What the hell have you done?"

Rita just stood there, staring at the man she'd called Dad a minute before. Her mouth was curled up in disgust. "He deserved so much worse."

Martin's mouth opened and shut, blood bubbling out. Then there was this loud rasp from his throat. A death rattle.

"We can't just leave him here." *Claire's chest was squeezing.*

"Going to," *Rita said, and the three of them fled the building.*

Rita went out the front, while Claire and Nick exited through the rear door.

She expected police sirens but heard none. The night was quiet except for the sound of her pounding heart.

THIRTY-THREE

"If you're not careful, you're going to set your keyboard on fire." Amanda looked over the partition between their desks. He was pounding away at the keys without mercy.

"Just trying to compile a list of places Claire went in the taxis. Then I'll send a request to all the cab companies in the area to see if they dispatched any cars to the drop-off locations Claire had gone with Benji's Taxi." He spoke but didn't stop typing.

This was his way of passing time while he waited on a detective at Metro PD to send any notes they might have made on Rita.

She planned to work through the list of employees from the Lawson estate and started pulling backgrounds on everyone—men and women. While they were aware of a mystery man, there could be others they didn't know about. She still didn't have the employee list from Malachi at the gallery, even though he'd promised to get it over to them "immediately" when she'd chased him. Apparently, he ascribed a different definition to the word.

Amanda's phone rang, showing Libby's name on the screen. "Hello there," Amanda answered.

"Mandy?" It was Zoe.

"Give me that phone you little worm." It was Libby in the background, and she was laughing despite her words. She got on the line. "She took it right out of my hands she wanted to talk to you so badly."

Amanda was smiling. She felt Zoe was growing up too fast and was going to forget about her, but that wasn't happening just yet. "What's going on?" She glanced at the clock mounted on the wall. It was just four o'clock. Zoe and Libby would have made it to the house just a few minutes prior.

"She wants to know if she can go over to Ava's and play some video game with her. Your sister said she'd feed her dinner, and you can join too if you want."

Amanda considered all the work that could keep her busy here. This request could save her a call she might have made in about an hour. "That's fine. Can you put Zoe on the phone a minute?"

Some scuffling, then, "Mandy?"

"Hey, sweetie. You have a good day at school?"

"Always."

And that would most likely change... "You can go to Ava's."

"Yippie!"

"But don't rot your brain with that game. See if Ava will play in the yard with you. Get some fresh air."

"Okay." One word. Extreme disappointment.

"Love you. Have fun."

"Love—" And Zoe was gone.

"They grow up too quick," Amanda said under her breath. Not that Trent would likely have heard a word of her conversation the way he kept hammering on his keyboard.

With Zoe's care arranged, the bulk of the evening spread before her. She started with the backgrounds. There were eleven people who worked at the Lawson estate, serving in different capacities. Next, she revisited the reports from the canvassing officers in Logan's neighborhood. Not a single mention of a Camry hanging around, which was understandable. There were a lot of them, and they didn't exactly stand out. By the time she'd finished, hours had passed. Somewhere in there Trent surfaced and confirmed he'd sent the request to the taxi companies and received the information from Metro PD.

"No criminal records for those employed at the Lawson estate," she said.

"Not on the one I pulled either."

"Didn't know you were pulling any."

"I had to know more about Mona Lawson. And I found out that she has a daughter. Leanne, currently twenty-one and attending university in Washington. Anyway, Leanne was just four when Mona married Martin. Austin told us Lawson sexually abused Rita. Maybe he did the same with Leanne. Could have been the trigger Rita needed to kill her father."

"Let's the hell hope not. And maybe Mona isn't so innocent when it comes to her late husband's demise. Come to think of it, I don't remember seeing a single picture of him anywhere in the house. Though maybe that doesn't mean anything." She was sorry she'd brought up that point the moment she had. She didn't have a bunch of photos on display of Kevin and Lindsey. She had a family portrait in her bedroom, but that was all. Would it still be there eight years from now? Hard to say, and Mona could have her pictures of Martin secreted away.

"Still, I think that woman is sketchy."

"What came back from Metro PD?"

"The original lead on the case spoke to Rita, but from what I see didn't find anything suspicious about her. It didn't help that she had an alibi. She was at the charity event the night of the murder, where several people spotted her."

"Isn't that convenient? She probably lulled her stepfather from the event to his building."

"Feels like it. And I think it would be worth our time talking to Leanne. We could ask her about Martin."

"We can. Tomorrow." It was too late to drive to Washington and back tonight. In fact, a rumble in her stomach had her looking at the clock. It was going on nine at night. "Let's catch some rest and start fresh."

"Sure. Not much else happening tonight." He got up and left.

Something was weighing on him, and she wasn't sure exactly what, but ever since they spoke to Brianna it felt like the case had become personal to him. She couldn't think of any direct correlations to Trent's life—unless the talk of domestic violence and sexual abuse had his mind weighed down with thoughts about his aunt.

THIRTY-FOUR

Amanda didn't pick favorites among her family, but her brother-in-law Erik was taking a lead. It didn't faze him to slap a nice chunk of beef onto the barbecue with a cob of corn—just for her —after nine at night, no less. She was satisfied and happy, but not at ease. There was this dread crawling over her skin and burrowing into her gut. It had something to do with the case, that note left on her doorstep, leaving Brianna at the hotel. She sure hoped that Wyatt and whoever came on for the following shift watched her room and not just the parking lot. Saving grace was she and Trent had only found Brianna by tracking the taxis Claire took. Guess it depended on how closely the killer was sticking to Claire, whether he followed her to Brianna's hotel.

Zoe was in the passenger seat and hyper. It was going to be a challenge getting her into bed tonight, but once the child surrendered, Amanda suspected she'd fall hard. She had her stuffed dog, Lucky, in her lap, but it was getting less attention every day. Amanda saw that as a good sign. When Zoe's parents were murdered last fall, she'd had the doll with her, and

Amanda believed it had taken on the qualities of a talisman to the girl.

Amanda passed lots of looks in the rearview mirror as she drove. She was becoming obsessed thinking about silver Toyota Camrys and spotting them everywhere. She could swear that she saw one after leaving her sister's, but she hadn't seen it since.

She pulled into her driveway and got out of the car and went around to Zoe's side. She was already out, a huge grin on her face, rocking her little torso side to side. "Thanks for letting me play with Ava."

"You're very welcome, sweetie." But Amanda wasn't winning any parenting awards tonight. Zoe had school tomorrow, and it was already way past the girl's bedtime. She glanced over a shoulder, doing her best to keep it as discreet as possible. A light-colored vehicle was parked under a maple tree down the block. Was it a silver Camry? Was there someone inside? Amanda felt chills run through her, and the night was warm. "Let's get you inside."

Zoe rushed and tripped over her feet, lunged forward, but managed to keep herself upright. Lucky went flying a few feet ahead of her, and she fumbled over him and started laughing. The sound was contagious, and it had Amanda smiling too despite this bad feeling rolling through her.

She and Zoe went inside, the girl taking off down the hall toward her bedroom. Amanda peeked through the window in the front door. Definitely a sedan. Silver. Could be a Camry. There was a person behind the wheel.

She had to get Zoe out of there. She called Becky who agreed to collect Zoe from the back gate in five minutes.

Next call was to Trent. He said he'd be right there. Amanda told him to hang back and not spook the guy.

"Mandy? Where are you?"

Amanda went to Zoe's bedroom and found her changed for

bed already. *Figures...* "Honey, there's something I need you to do. Interested in another adventure tonight?"

"I guess." A big yawn.

Of all the nights for the girl to admit she was tired and cave, it had to be this one. "Becky's going to come get you for a sleepover."

"Why?"

Amanda did her best to think fast. "She misses you."

"Okay." She slouched, her arms dangling long at her sides. "Do I need to change?"

"No, just go as you are. But I'm going to pack you some clothes for school." Amanda was doing her best to keep calm and rational while thoughts rushed her to move faster. Who knew when that creep from the car would make his move? He had told her to stop days ago now, and she hadn't. She had Zoe to think about, and she wasn't taking any chances with her daughter's life or her own.

There was the pinhole of light—small enough to be from a phone's flashlight—at the back gate by the time Amanda had Zoe corralled.

"All right, sweetie. Becky's there. See?" Amanda gestured. She'd walk Zoe to the fence line, but she didn't want to leave the house in case the man got inside. When he did, she wanted to be ready for him.

Her phone pinged with a text from Becky. *Be careful.*

She fired off a quick reply that she was armed, and Trent was on the way over. They really should get the entire cavalry, but the risk the guy would run off was too great. He could be the killer they were after.

After Becky and Zoe disappeared from view, Amanda returned to the front door and peeked out. The car was still there, the figure too.

He's still here, she texted Trent. *Going to turn the lights out and pretend we're asleep.*

Zoe?

With Becky. Safe.

She went around and turned out the lights. Next, she positioned a dining chair against the living room wall, so she had a line of sight to the front and the back. She brought out her Glock, resting her gun hand on her lap. Her phone rested on her other leg.

She waited, sweat dripping off her brow. She hadn't had one minute to call someone about the air conditioner.

A text came through from Trent, confirming he was down the street, and the figure wasn't in the car. She muted her phone.

She stiffened, readying herself. Her father always told her to trust her instincts, that they'd never steer her wrong. And she had listened. It was why she'd gotten Zoe out and called in Trent.

A scraping noise came from the back of the house. He was at the patio door. She stayed still. She wanted him to come inside, so she could trap him.

She waited some more. The door slid open.

She saw his figure silhouetted in the moonlight coming through the windows. She held her breath, trying to be as quiet as possible.

He reached the peninsula. He didn't appear to be holding out a gun, but that didn't mean he wasn't armed. She had to surprise him, spring on him when he would least expect it.

He entered the hall that branched off the living room. If she could go after him when he was down the hall, she would have him cornered. There were only two doors that led outside, and neither was accessible from where he was headed.

She had to move to keep an eye on him. She avoided the

creaky floorboards, living in this house for long enough she knew it like her own body.

He still didn't appear to have a gun out. He ducked his head into Zoe's darkened room.

Seeing this man about to enter Zoe's private space, an unmitigated rage steamrolled through her.

She crept up on him and readied her gun. "Stop right there."

The man's arm started toward his waist.

"I have a gun trained on the back of your head."

He froze, then barreled into the room. He grabbed Zoe's chair from her crafts table and threw it through the window before leapfrogging out behind it. The base of the window was about six feet off the ground. He moaned, and she heard the wood trellis for her roses snap.

"Crap." She holstered her gun and went to the front door. She wasn't following his lead.

She came outside to see him running toward the Camry. The headlights came on, and Trent was standing halfway between her house and the car. She bridged the distance.

"Trent!" She waved her arm wildly. "He's getting away."

Trent brought up his gun. "I'll shoot the guy before I run."

"No." She put her hand on his arm, lowering it. "We need him to talk." She ran toward the car, and the Camry's engine growled as the man floored the gas.

"Come on. Let's go." She changed course, headed to Trent's Jeep and jumped into the passenger seat. Let Trent drive, let her be in charge of when to shoot.

He was slower getting there, but he hopped in and gunned the engine, peeling down her street. Everyone in the neighborhood was likely awake now.

"Go! He's right there." She pointed to where the Camry had taken a sharp right turn.

"I see him."

"Son of a freaking..." She clenched her teeth, angry about leaving her house wide open, and the broken window, the murdered rosebush. "Hope he got some thorns up his ass!" she mumbled. God, she loved that rosebush. She wasn't a gardener, but it had been there from the time she and Kevin had bought the place.

"I'd say he's got at least two." Trent was swerving through the streets, following the perp's every move.

She called in for backup. "Get close. Let's get his plate. Hey, you didn't get it, did you?"

"Would have been a good idea, but I was distracted when I heard your window break, saw a chair flying out, with a guy following it."

Another shiver of rage ran through her. "He went right to Zoe's room. What was he going to do to her?" She gripped at the dash as Trent took another corner.

"As long as he stays in town— Ah, shit." Trent gestured ahead of him. "He's getting on the highway."

She called in to dispatch to let them know about the silver Toyota Camry heading north on Interstate 95. "We're in a black Jeep Wrangler. License...?"

Trent rattled it off as he tore after the Camry.

Sirens roared from behind them, and the officer riding shotgun was waving his arm, signaling for Trent to pull over. "Someone with the state police needs to know what's going on," he said through clenched teeth.

"I'm working on it." Amanda ran through what was going on with the PWCPD dispatcher to pass along to the state police. What felt like forever later, the state police pulled away, leaving Trent's Jeep in its dust. "Are you kidding me? Get this thing moving!"

"Foot is flat to the floor."

"We're standing still. Shit." She slapped the dash.

Trent weaved through traffic that was lighter this time of

night than it would have been midday, but she was cringing with every near miss.

"Are you intentionally riding people's asses before pulling out?" She was typically a good passenger. She let Trent chauffeur her around all the time, but the speed and the lane changes were causing that steak and corn to churn in her gut.

"I'm doing my best here."

She couldn't even see the tail end of the sedan. How the heck was it pulling away? The guy had to have retrofitted the thing—it would explain the growl when he'd pulled away on her street. Camry's didn't typically sound that way or have that much pep.

"I can't see him at all," Trent lamented.

"Me either." Amanda's phone rang, and she answered.

"What the hell is going on?" It was Graves, and she was pissed. She must have heard about their predicament from dispatch. No one could say the rumor mill worked slow at the PWCPD.

"I was going to call. It's just—"

"Talk to me this minute."

"Right there!" Amanda pointed wildly. The Camry was pulling off the highway. It must have been hiding among the other vehicles on the road, and that's why she'd lost sight of it. "I've gotta go." She ended the call and dropped her phone in the console. It rang almost immediately.

"You should probably get that."

"Not doing it. Just catch that guy." If she could manifest him into custody this instant, she would. Instead they just kept moving.

Trent took Exit 1, as the Camry had. This route merged onto US-1 North, taking them into the heart of Washington. People and traffic would be everywhere.

Wow, Washington had come fast at the speed they were going. Forty-five minutes in the blink of an eye.

"Shit." She finally picked up her phone and accepted the call from Graves. She filled her in, then said, "Make sure that the Metro PD know we're incoming. We just got onto US-1 North into Washington."

"Steele, this is—"

"Please, just do it. I'm quite sure this man killed Claire *and* tampered with Rita Flynn's car. He just broke into my home." She swallowed roughly as she recalled him skulking into Zoe's room.

Graves swore several colorful adjectives, then hung up.

"Yikes. The sergeant has quite a mouth on her," Amanda said to Trent.

"Wonderful. I so look forward to hearing it when this chase is over."

"We catch our bad guy, and things will work out."

"*If* we catch him."

"Don't even think like that."

The state police had left the pursuit, but she and Trent were joined by Metro PD cruisers. At first Amanda wasn't sure if they were on their side or coming for them. But it was made clear rather quickly that they were there to help.

The pursuit through the city's streets lasted an hour, but then it was like the Camry just vaporized into thin air.

"No. I can't accept this." She was shaking her head. Frustrated. Angry.

Trent pulled to the curb and parked. "Not much we can do about it."

"You still have gas in this thing? Let's move."

He stayed put.

"What are you doing? Go."

"We'll get him another way. A traffic cam or maybe the state guys caught the plate? We'll get him somehow."

She punched her right fist into her left palm and let out a growl.

Trent didn't say anything, but she could feel anger and frustration emanating from him too.

"You're right. We will get him," she said. "Somehow, some way. I won't stop until we do."

"Good. That makes two of us."

"Take us back to Central. I'll call Graves to let her know to expect us."

"Just when I didn't think this day could get worse."

She thought of her murdered rosebush, the failed apprehension of a murder suspect. Shit-can day, to be sure.

"My ankle's worse than I thought," Trent eventually said. "That's why I wasn't running after the guy."

"You get a good look at him, though? We didn't even talk about that."

"Nope. Too dark to make out any features. Say about six feet tall, average build. Beyond that—"

"Yep, useless."

As Trent drove them to Central, she wished they had met with a better result—the Toyota driver in cuffs, answering for his crimes. Instead they were going to be forced to answer for theirs.

THIRTY-FIVE

"Whose idea was it to handle this without the proper backup?" Graves's cheeks were a bright shade of red, her glare pinned on Amanda.

Obviously, her question was redundant. Amanda, Trent, and Graves were in her office, along with the police chief. Buchanan looked the least happy of all of them. They'd already run through the basics that got them to where they currently were.

"I called my partner," Amanda said, as if that were a defense worth trying. "If I had called in everyone, he would have gotten spooked and fled."

Graves peered into Amanda's eyes. "And how would we be in a different position than now?"

Amanda's heart was thumping. She had nothing to say to that.

"If you'd followed correct protocol, we could have this guy in an interview room right now. Instead, who knows where he is?"

She bit back the urge to say something smart and remained quiet. So did Trent. It was best to just take the heat when a superior lashed out. And Graves's mind certainly wasn't open to much. Amanda didn't hold out much hope that Buchanan's was either. Not given the way his arms were crossed, and his mouth was fixed in a grimace.

"And you got that note the other day." Graves nudged her head toward Trent, then turned to Amanda. "And you have this guy show up at your home tonight, and you don't call it in." She flailed her arms in the air. "I just don't understand either of you. It was a complete freaking circus out there tonight. And no one even came away with a license plate."

"You got a note?" Buchanan directed this at Trent, as if he were catching up on all that had been said.

Trent flicked his gaze to Amanda.

"Actually, I did, Chief," Amanda said, drawing herself up.

"You?" Graves hissed.

"I asked Trent to say it was him."

"Why on earth?" Graves clasped her hands on her desk. Her eyebrows were corkscrewed like she had a migraine.

"I thought you'd take me off the case if you knew *I* got it."

"Damn right I would have."

"Then I made the right decision." She laid it out there calm, cool, and respectfully. She didn't make eye contact with the sergeant or the chief.

Piercing quiet.

"Huh." Graves about sixty seconds later. "I would have removed you from the case, but now I want your badge. There's only one thing stopping me. I think you're close to getting this guy. You bring him in, Steele, then we'll talk. But if I hear about any more road rage being carried out by my detectives, you're both on the street. Hear me?" She dragged her pointed finger between Amanda and Trent, pursed her lips like it was something she was born doing.

"I hear you," Amanda and Trent said in unison.

Amanda dared to look at the chief. He was watching her.

His cheeks were flushed, and she could tell she'd disappointed him. He certainly hadn't jumped in to her or Trent's defense.

"That all, ma'am?" she said to Graves.

"For now. Go home. I don't want to hear any more about this case tonight."

"But—" Amanda shut her mouth at Graves holding her hand up, silencing her.

"Go. Before I decide to have that discussion about your badges now." She pointed to her office door.

Amanda and Trent got up and left. They walked to the parking lot without a word.

"Want a ride home?" Trent's question intruded her thoughts. How she just wanted to get that mystery man in the Camry.

"Might be nice. Or I could call a taxi."

"Ridiculous. Hop in." Trent patted the hood of his Jeep as he circled it to the driver's side.

They went to her house, not speaking a word. He pulled into her driveway. Her eyes went first to the broken window but quickly landed on the trampled rosebush. She pointed it out and said, "Think it's dead."

"Plants can be resilient."

"I never gathered you were much of a gardener."

"I'm not, but I think I've heard that said." He laughed.

Neither of them seemed in a hurry to go anywhere.

"You ask me, Graves is eating some humble pie," he said. "She has Logan charged for murder, but then openly admits in front of the chief that you and I are getting close to solving this mess."

"She never called it a mess."

He smiled at her. "It was implied."

She laughed and gestured to the front of her house. "*That's* a mess."

"I can help you board it up right now."

"It's not just the window."

"It's about the rosebush again. It means something to you?"

"Yeah, I guess. The trellis too. Looks like the idiot trampled over it. The plant was here when Kevin and I bought the house, but we made the trellis together."

"Impressive. You have carpentry skills?"

"No. Kevin cut, I nailed."

Trent laughed, then went serious. "I meant it when I said I'd help with the window. You can't go to bed with it like that."

She wanted to come up with a slew of excuses that would have Trent leaving, but she said, "I'd appreciate it. Kevin has some boards in the garage. One might work."

"All right then."

They got out of Trent's Jeep and found a piece of plywood that suited the job perfectly. He held it in place, while she nailed it into the frame. She flashed to the past when she'd worked around the house with Kevin. They'd laughed more than they fought and when they did, it was always fun making up.

They finished up and had Zoe's chair back in her room, and were in her kitchen facing each other.

"Thank you, by the way. How about a beer? Least I can do." She moved and swore that just as she had, Trent did. He had come toward her, though, while she'd stepped to the side, headed to the fridge.

"Sure, ah, a beer sounds good." He flashed a smile, moved aside awkwardly.

Was he going to kiss me? She swallowed roughly thinking that's exactly what he might have been about to do. She fished out two bottles and stuck one into his waiting hand. "Here you go."

They snapped off the tops and clicked the bottles.

"To catching this guy tomorrow," he said.

"Amen to that."

They went out to the patio and looked up at the stars. They didn't say much. Something was about to happen in her kitchen before she'd messed it up—or maybe the universe had stepped in to save them from making a huge mistake. Not that she really put faith in things manifesting to plan or by intent, or in some grand being directing affairs on Earth. But she and Trent could never be more than friends, no matter how many times she fantasized about more.

THIRTY-SIX

The next day, Amanda was up before the sun with a case-breaking epiphany. But maybe she was getting her hopes up too high. She knew where else she'd seen a silver Toyota Camry and with any stroke of luck at all, it would get them to their mystery man.

She met Trent at the station at eight in the morning, and they went over in a department car to Lux Suites, where Claire had been staying. She beelined for the front desk, Trent sticking right with her.

"You're sure?" He had asked that question a few times on the way over and the drive wasn't a long one.

Oh, she was sure. Now whether it was *the* silver Camry in question, she couldn't be certain until she looked at the hotel surveillance, but she was following her gut. She'd seen the car from the window in Claire's hotel room. What they had at Central didn't cover the Monday when they were here—the time in which she was interested.

She held up her badge to the clerk, a different man than the one they spoke with before. "Detectives Steele and Stenson with Prince William County PD. You have camera surveillance that covers the lot. We need to see it from Monday afternoon." She gave the clerk the approximate time of when she watched two police cruisers enter the lot. They had passed a silver sedan. Her mind had tucked it away as useless information until she woke up this morning.

"Not sure if I should hand that over without a warrant."

"You may have heard by now that the PWCPD is investigating the murder of a woman who stayed here, at your hotel. We already received approval for some footage, but what I'm asking for now could very well lead us right to her killer."

The clerk licked his lips and shifted his posture. "Sure. Come back."

The clerk took them to a tiny room with a few monitors and a chair. He sat down and brought up the time Amanda was interested in.

And there it was—a silver Toyota Camry, a person behind the wheel. "Right there." She pointed at the screen. "Can you zoom in on the driver's face?"

The clerk took a few minutes to figure out how to do that. The person's face wasn't clear, but it was unquestionably a man.

"Try moving in on the license plate," she said.

Finally luck was on their side. Given the positioning of the late afternoon sun, the tinted cover was useless at concealing the digits.

Trent scribbled them in his notepad and was on the move through the lobby back to the department car. "I'm on it."

"Thank you," she told the clerk.

She caught up with Trent at the vehicle and got in the passenger seat. He was clicking away on the onboard computer.

"Nick Clayton, forty-one. Lives in Dumfries," he told her.

"Nick Clayton. Are you serious right now?"

"Yeah, not exactly the time to be joking around."

"He works at the Lawson estate. Think he helps with the landscaping. We need to get cars to his apartment right away.

We're doing this by the book." She made the calls while Trent drove.

He was pulling to a stop down the street from Clayton's about ten minutes later. Cruisers were already there, as Amanda could see ahead of them. Strategic Weapons And Tactics, better known as SWAT, came up on their rear. They'd go in first, with Amanda and Trent on standby once it was confirmed the place was clear. This was the safest way to handle a search and arrest when a suspect was considered armed and dangerous.

One officer came over to Trent and Amanda about a half hour after SWAT entered Clayton's house. Trent lowered his window.

"No one is inside. We'll have the place swept of course, see if there's anything we can use as evidence against him."

Amanda nodded but wasn't confident they'd find anything. And after last night, Clayton was probably on the run... or hiding in plain sight. She touched Trent's arm. "We need to get to the Lawson estate immediately."

"Ma'am, do you want another team to follow you?" asked the SWAT officer who was still standing there.

"Yes." She gave him the address.

"On it." He pushed off the car, and Trent hit the gas.

They sped through the streets and hit the intercom at the gate. They announced themselves to Ingrid, and she said, "I'm sorry, but Ms. Lawson is unavailable."

"Open this gate," Trent barked.

Nothing for several seconds, then the buzzer sounded, and the gates opened.

Trent sped down the lane to the front doors. Ingrid was standing in the open doorway. Tears were streaked down her face.

Amanda went right to her. "What is it? Where is Ms. Lawson?"

Ingrid pointed toward a staircase that went to the basement. Her eyes were widened with fear. "She... she..."

"Take a deep breath. She what?" Amanda spoke calmly, though her heart was racing.

"She has Nick..."

"Nick Clayton?"

The maid nodded.

"Is she armed?" Trent asked.

"Yes," the woman whispered.

Amanda made a call to the officers outside, and then she and Trent headed down the stairs.

They followed the sound of a man and woman talking. The man's voice was strained.

"They don't know everything. I swear. How could they?"

"You should have just left it alone," the woman said.

Amanda and Trent stopped beside a room with an open door. Peeked in.

Mona was pacing and holding a gun.

"Claire had *the* gun," Nick pleaded.

"So what?"

"It was all the evidence the police would have needed to put me away. I don't want to go to prison." His voice took on a high shrill.

"Do you think I give a crap if you go away? But, no, you had to go and make a big freaking mess. The police have been here twice, and you decide to race through the streets of Washington. Do you have a brain at all? What in the world did Rita ever see in you?"

"Claire was going to turn us all in. I did what I thought was best."

"That's the problem, you didn't think. Well, I'm not going down for her murder or yours. They'll never find your body when I'm finished with you."

Amanda burst through the doorway, gun raised, Trent at her side. "Stop! Police!"

Mona froze for a second. "Why should I be surprised? You idiot!" She turned on Nick and pulled the trigger.

Nick screamed, and in that split second, Amanda had put a bullet into Mona's arm.

Mona's gun clattered to the floor, but even wounded, the older woman scurried to get ahold of it again.

"I wouldn't, if I were you." Trent stood over Mona, his gun in her face.

She lifted her uninjured arm in surrender. And just as all that happened, footsteps were coming down the hall. The cavalry was here.

Amanda called for an ambulance for both Nick Clayton and Mona Lawson. Then she went over to him.

"Claire... she was going to bring us all down." His eyes rolled back in his head, but his chest continued to rise and fall.

Thankfully for Nick, Mona was a bad shot. Just a few feet away, and she'd hit him in the shoulder. It was likely Nick would survive his injuries to serve time in a federal prison.

All's well that ends well.

Then Sergeant Graves stepped through the doorway, a scowl on her face.

THIRTY-SEVEN

The next day, Amanda and Trent were headed to Nick Clayton's hospital room. She and Trent got to keep their badges and even warranted a "well done" from the police chief. Charges against Logan were being dropped. As she'd thought, Nick was going to pull through just fine—except for he would be going to prison. That was a foregone conclusion given the case they already had against him. A search of his place had turned up a receipt showing a purchase at Betty's Boudoir for lacy lingerie early Friday evening and a quick trip there had confirmed it was the set Claire had been wearing. Malachi from the gallery had finally come through with that employee list—a day late, a dollar short—and Nick had worked there at the same time as Claire and Rita.

They found him awake and hooked to a couple intravenous lines. He still had a bruise on his forehead from when Claire had struck him with the lamp.

"We're looking for a lot of answers." Amanda hoped his date with a bullet made him talkative. "You can begin with why you killed Claire Hunter."

"I was never supposed to get caught."

"But you did." There was satisfaction in pointing that out.

"You might have gotten away with it if you hadn't left the Glock from the Lawson heist," Trent said, looking up from his notepad.

Nick bunched up his face and shook his head, disgusted by his slipup. Amanda could piece together what his grand plan had been. The short of it was he'd intended to pin Claire's murder on Logan and Martin's on Claire. A win-win. Only Nick hadn't been able to let it go there. He had become obsessed with the progress of the investigation.

"You staged everything for us to believe that Logan killed Claire. So well, in fact, that it nearly worked," Amanda said.

Nick wasn't looking at her or Trent, but twisting the top hem of the bedsheet.

"Why did you want to frame Logan?" This question struck personal and was hard to swallow.

"It seemed perfect. Claire had left him, broke his heart years ago. You don't think I didn't notice the guy running around town asking anyone who would listen if they'd seen Claire?"

"And the lingerie?"

"A nice touch, don't you think? Spouses reunited, but then things go deadly wrong."

This guy had a big ego considering he was caught, but she could work that to their advantage. "It was pretty smart. What we can't figure out is how you got Claire into Logan's house." Benji's Taxi had responded to Trent's request, but it hadn't led them anywhere. They were still awaiting responses from the other cab companies.

"That part fell together. I followed her there Friday evening. She took a cab, got dropped off a few blocks away and walked. She waited until he left and let herself inside. I kept at a distance, got the idea, bought the lingerie, and returned. By that time, Logan was gone and Claire was in his house. It was perfect timing."

The way Nick spoke so lightly about killing Claire, a person who had been his former partner in crime, was nauseating. His head wasn't screwed on right, and might not have been for a long time. Now, she and Trent had theorized that Claire went into Logan's by herself. But that raised the question of what had her going into his house in the first place. "Why was she there?"

"How should I know?"

"How did you know Logan would have a gun and ammo?" Further to that, the fact Logan's weapon would accept 9-millimetre bullets like the Glock.

Nick smiled. "Just got lucky."

Spoken as if the gods approved. "And if he hadn't had a gun?"

"I would have shot her with a gun I'd brought, wiped the prints, left it behind. It still would have made Logan suspect."

Amanda would have expected Nick to be charming, but he was just annoying. "You could have used him to lure Claire out." Her mind was on the "accident" Logan had in Nebraska.

"She never would have fallen for that. Besides, she had cut him out of her life when she left Nebraska."

Amanda smirked. "So, you knew she went to Nebraska."

Nick drew a deep breath, winced, glanced over at the morphine drip. "I figured it out."

"How?" Trent asked.

"Claire wanted out, no more heists. But it doesn't work like that. I had my eye on her and followed her to the airport, found out she was headed to Nebraska."

"She could have gone there, then hopped on another plane," Amanda pointed out.

"She could have, but she didn't."

"You followed her to Nebraska, eventually found her. Then you tried to kill Logan."

Nick stared through her. "I never intended to kill him; I wanted to send a message to Claire."

"It seemed to work because Claire hightailed it out of there," Amanda said. "She was on the run for the last four years."

"She never should have come back to Dumfries."

"How did you even know she was in town?" Amanda paced the end of the bed, keeping her attention on Nick.

He seemed hesitant to answer.

"Did Rita Cartwright tell you?" Some pieces were clicking together. Brianna said Claire believed in second chances. She'd gone to see Rita to let her know she planned to turn her in for the heists and Martin's murder. Had to be.

Nick shrugged.

She'd take that as a yes. "Were you and Rita partners before bringing Claire into the fold? Were you more than—"

"Leave Rita out of this," Nick snarled.

Mention of her name had obviously angered him. She'd push just a little more. "Did you kill Rita too? Do your best to make it look like an accident?"

"No!" Spittle flew with his outburst. "I loved Rita. I've always loved Rita. And I wasn't going to kill Claire... I didn't want to but..."

"What? She made you?" Trent pushed out.

"She backed me into a corner."

"What happened to Rita?" Amanda sensed Nick knew the answer, and that it might align with a theory Amanda had before.

Nick sniffled. "Claire should have just left well enough alone!"

"It seems you're the one who wouldn't do that," Amanda hurled back. "She wanted out, but you wouldn't let her go."

A single tear fell down Nick's cheek, which he was quick to swipe away with his good arm. "Rita killed herself. She called me before and said she couldn't bear the thought of her past coming out, putting her husband and children through a trial, her going to prison." His voice turned gravely. "She said they were better off with her dead."

Amanda and Trent let a few moments pass while Nick sobbed. She was the one to speak first.

"You're the one who shot Martin Lawson, aren't you? You can tell us. One murder, two, not much difference in sentencing." A lie, but she hoped that Nick would be naive enough to buy it.

"No one was supposed to pay for it."

Amanda leaned forward. "Is that a confession? She was Rita's stepfather, the woman you loved..."

"Martin was a pig and deserved worse than what he got."

"Then you did shoot him using that Glock you left with Claire?" she pushed.

"Yes! Okay? For Rita. She got him there, and I killed him. I don't feel sorry about it. Not knowing what he put Rita through for years. Her entire childhood he abused her, going into her room at night, touching her places he had no right to touch." His facial features darkened with each word.

"You must have wiped your prints from the gun, made sure that Claire's were the only ones on it. Was that the same time you added her prints to Logan's gun?"

"Why ask what you know."

A pregnant pause.

"I couldn't let Claire turn us all in," he said, filling the silence.

"And by *all*, that includes Mona Lawson?" Amanda asked, but knew that answer as well. They'd already questioned her in depth—lawyer present, of course. She would be charged with abetting the murder of her husband, for shooting Nick, and for her part in the heists. As it turned out, Mona Lawson had been the mastermind. Not that Claire had known that. Mona confessed Claire had come to see her to apologize and say she knew who killed her husband and had proof.

"Yes," he hissed.

"Who else was part of the team?"

"I'm not dying, Detective, and about to make a full deathbed confession."

"You knew Claire was sick," she countered.

"She told Rita, who told me."

It seemed the longer they spoke, and the more time passed, Nick was getting comfortable accepting himself as a killer. Or maybe he justified his actions as self-preservation and soothed his conscience because Claire was dying, regardless.

"What I'd like to know," Trent said, pen poised over his notepad, "is how did Claire get the gun from that night in her possession, and how did you find out she had it?"

"She—" He smirked. "*She* thought by telling me she had leverage, i.e. the gun, that I'd leave her alone, but I couldn't have that hanging out there."

"And Detective Stenson's other question. How did Claire get the gun?"

"I asked her that because I didn't understand, thought she was just bluffing. After the shooting, I had tossed it into a dumpster that was blocks from Lawson Investments. She said that she went back and got it. By that point, I couldn't verify it. I had every reason to believe her."

"Not that it worked in making you leave her alone," Amanda said. "You saw her as a liability."

Nick licked his lips, not needing to say anything in response. And that was it. Another murder investigation wrapped up. Two, counting the cold case of Martin Lawson. Amanda had expected the resolution to have brought more satisfaction. Instead, it left her with a gnawing sadness. If Claire had never disclosed that she had the Glock from that fateful night, would she and Logan still be married happily ever after?

THIRTY-EIGHT
THE DAY OF THE MURDER...

When Claire had found the key in the rock, she was touched that Logan had kept it after all these years. That told her he still loved her, but she was even more convinced when she found their small wedding album in a chest in his living room. Between the pages would be the perfect place to leave her message, the letter she'd originally put in the safe deposit box for him. It would explain everything, doing the job for her.

The cancer had pushed her to want to make amends for her past, but she really didn't think she could find the courage to face him. But at least he should get the letter.

She could feel Nick breathing down her neck almost from the second she returned to Dumfries. But she realized her mistake too late. Visiting Rita. Her old mentor let it slip that she and Nick were still in contact. Claire hadn't any way of knowing their relationship had survived after Rita had gotten married. She'd wanted to give Rita a chance to come clean to her husband before the police became involved.

Claire had found out about the sexual abuse—a little girl who only wanted a stepfather's love and admiration—but he had been even more monster than man. He'd touched her, defiled her.

Rita had said she'd tried to warn her stepmom about what her stepdad had done to her, if only to save the woman's daughter from the same fate. But she hadn't listened until it was far too late and her daughter too was sexually assaulted. It was then that Rita's stepmom had decided to take out Martin and make it look like a robbery gone wrong. Rita was to get close to her stepfather at a charity event he was attending that night and petition to see his art collection. This was all so Rita's lover, Nick, could shoot her abuser and stop the cycle from continuing with her stepsister.

Not that Claire had known about Mona's involvement until two days ago when she put it together. She hadn't even known about the connection to Rita until then either. Mona hadn't been at Rita's wedding.

She heard footsteps in the living room. She wasn't alone, but it wasn't Logan. She'd have heard his truck pull into the driveway. She thought of the Glock in her purse, but she couldn't touch it without gloves, and it wasn't loaded anyway. She'd tossed the remaining bullets years ago.

She quickly looked in Logan's closet. He used to have a gun when they were together. She found it just as Nick stepped into the bedroom.

"Stay back." She held the gun on him.

He had one on her too.

She pulled the trigger. All she got was a click.

Nick laughed. "This one's loaded, so I suggest you do as I say."

She was trembling. She'd seen him kill before, and he was no longer the man she used to know. He was unpredictable and that terrified her. "What do you expect of me, Nick? You killed a man in cold blood. I can't cover for you forever."

"That's all I asked for. Loyalty. But that turned out to be too much. You made Rita kill herself. Yet you think you're better than me," he spat.

You made Rita kill herself...

She'd seen the piece on the news about a university professor who died yesterday when her car went off I-95—Rita. It was why she'd emptied the safe deposit box and come here. She planned to leave the letter for Logan, and take the Glock with her and go somewhere far away.

"Hand me his gun."

Her mind could assemble his plan. He intended to kill her here in Logan's bedroom and now with Logan's gun, it would really look like Logan had done it. And Nick had something lacy draped over his arm too. Lingerie? "Please don't do this."

"Here. Now." *He held out his hand, and she set it in his gloved palm.*

Gloves. *She looked down at her bare hands. Her prints would be on the gun. Would that confuse the police investigation or make it more damning for Logan?*

"Step back."

She did as Nick asked, her mind racing to find a way out of the mess but nothing was coming to her.

Nick pulled a small box of ammunition from the closet, a smirk on his lips, and started to load the gun. To do so, he had to relinquish his hold on his own.

She had an opening. But what could she do? She looked around, eager to find something with which she could defend herself, but the space was pristine, not a thing out of place. All she had within reach was the lamp on the nightstand. It was a rather bulky number but if she could lift it and swing it at his head fast enough, she might have a chance to run.

Nick had his tongue sticking out as he continued loading the magazine.

"You don't need to do this. I haven't gone to the police yet."

"I can't take the chance that you haven't or that you won't. You're running your mouth all over town!"

If he really thought she was going down without a fight, he was a complete idiot. She turned in a swift movement and grabbed the lamp from the table and swung it hard and high. The blow was a glancing one, and only with the shade rather than the base. Nick rolled with it.

She drew back to take another swing, but he punched her. Hard. Right to the side of her forehead.

The lamp dropped from her hands, and she fell to the bed. Her head was pounding, and her vision flashed white.

"You stupid bitch." He raised Logan's gun on her.

A loud crack. Deafening.

Time slowed.

She felt the thud as the bullet entered her chest, tearing through tissue and bone. Intense pain, burning. She put a hand over her heart, her blood warm against her palm and fingers. She pulled her hand back and saw the wedding band Logan had given her—for just a brief passing in time. She had loved him so much.

Her arm fell heavy to the bed.

As she lay there, Nick was moving her arms and legs, undressing her and redressing her, but she couldn't get her body to fight back.

Instead, she surrendered, praying that God would forgive her, even more importantly, Logan, her sister, and Roo. She hoped Logan found the letter she'd left for him, in which she had laid everything out, including a recent postscript that said should something happen to her it was Nick Clayton or Mona Lawson. And with it was a key that would give him what had been her most valued acquisition.

All these thoughts raced through her mind as her heart slowed.

That night at Lawson Investments came flooding back. Martin lying there, taking his last breath...

Her eyelids fluttered shut, and she heard her own death rattle. Then all went quiet.

THIRTY-NINE

"At least you didn't get yourselves shot or killed." That's what Graves had told Amanda and Trent not long after she entered the room at the Lawson estate. Two days later, it was still repeating in Amanda's head.

Zoe was playing in the backyard, while Amanda was slicing apples for a snack in the kitchen. She smiled as she watched the girl giggle and run through the yard.

This was a happy moment. What she lived for. Well, that and closed cases.

She'd thought a lot about Claire as a young girl in the past week. She'd had it rough and made decisions based on the options available to her. Some might judge her, and she certainly wasn't innocent, but which of us were?

She'd just loaded the sliced apple onto a plate and was going to grab some cheese from the fridge when a knock at the door stopped her.

She answered and found Trent holding a small rosebush.

"For you." He nudged it toward her.

She took it. "Why?"

"I thought you'd like one."

She smiled at him. "Want to come in?"

"Sounds nice."

"Beer? I was just getting a snack ready to take out back for Zoe."

"That sounds nice too." He was walking closely behind her as she went to the kitchen.

"How's your ankle by the way?"

"Much better. Thanks."

She set the pot with the rosebush on the peninsula and went into the fridge. She had two bottles by the neck when she turned around. Trent was right there. He didn't budge. She could smell his cologne, feel the heat from his body.

He looked from her eyes to her lips and moved in before she had a chance to thwart what was about to happen.

The kiss was tender but heated. Brief. But it had her stomach filling with butterflies.

"What did you just do?"

"Something I've wanted to do for a while. I'm sorry. I shouldn't have. I should have asked if it was okay with—"

She put her mouth back on his. *What the hell am I doing?* She stepped back, brushing a fingertip to her lips. "This isn't going to work. You and I." She could barely catch a decent breath.

"I know." His eyes were pained. "Trust me, I know. Probably why I've been a grouch to work with lately. But let's just forget what happened. We'll go back to normal. You can do that?"

She hesitated, not sure if she could. Those kisses... her lips were still on fire, and it had ignited other parts of her too.

"Amanda," he prompted.

She swallowed hard, then nodded.

"Good. Let's never speak of it again." He turned away, but just before he did, she caught the glimmer of anguish in his eyes.

They were at a defining crossroads. Straight required a sacrifice, but so did any turn they might make. They could petition for a change in partners and pursue this, whatever *this* was. But it could all blow up in their faces, and their partnership and friendship could be gone forever. Or they could just forget about the kiss, about their growing feelings for each other, and continue putting killers behind bars. As a team they made a real difference in the world.

She held out her hand toward him. "Friends and partners?"

He shook on it. "Always."

She handed him a beer. They had just snapped the caps off when there was another knock on the door.

"Feels like Grand Central Station here these days. One minute." She went to the door.

A large white delivery truck was at the curb out front, a man in jeans and a T-shirt at her door. He was holding a clipboard. "I have a delivery for an Amanda Steele."

She read the logo on the truck. *Patio Leisure & BBQ.* "I didn't order anything."

"Well, it says right here that you have a six-burner with a side searing station."

"What?" Amanda turned to Trent, ready to vent more confusion, but he was smiling. "You? *You* did this?"

"Maybe," he dragged out.

"Why?"

"You know the answer to that."

She studied his eyes, hoping this wasn't somehow intended to bait her into a relationship with him. But he said he understood they couldn't be together.

"Ma'am? Are you Amanda Steele?"

"Yes, I—"

"Good." The delivery man turned around and went back to his truck, where another man had now come out the back. They unloaded a huge box with a picture of a barbecue on the side.

"I'm going to need a little help to understand why..." She gestured toward the delivery men.

"This case was a little personal for me with Claire being Shell's sister. You never gave me a hard time. Never once asked if I could be objective."

He was referring to the past when he'd questioned that of her.

"Maybe consider it an apology too." He smiled, but it faded as Logan's truck pulled into Amanda's driveway.

"I should probably go." Trent stepped outside. "But I'll come back and put it together another time."

"No you won't. You're not going anywhere."

He'd already gone down a step. He turned around. "Why not?"

"Because you're doing it right now."

"I don't want to get in the way."

"You won't be. You'll be putting a barbecue together. I'll go get Kevin's tools out of the garage."

Logan got out of his truck with a box in his hands. What was with the men in her life bearing gifts today?

She waved at him. He smiled back, but the expression dulled at the sight of Trent.

She backed up, letting them into her house, after directing the delivery men to take the barbecue through the side gate into the backyard.

"How are you holding up?" she asked Logan.

"Better than you might think, but I have my answers."

"All of them?" She was surprised. There were answers that even she and Trent didn't have, and might never. For one, where had all the stolen goods ended up from the heists? They had asked Nick for the names of his buyers before they left him, but he had refused to talk.

"I found a letter from Claire. She must have found time to hide it before... well, you know."

"Probably the one originally in that safe deposit box," Amanda said. "Where did you find it?"

"She stuck it between pages in our wedding album. I was feeling a little melancholy and looked at it this morning."

"So happy you have your answers." Claire must have been able to hide it before Nick got to the house. The lab ended up confirming yesterday that Claire's prints had been on Logan's house key, and even as Nick had testified, she had been inside before him.

"There was more." Logan lifted the box he held. It had a lid. "Open it."

She hesitated but did so. Inside was the most beautiful sight. A Fabergé egg, encrusted with gold and platinum, diamonds, and rubies. Trent stepped closer to her.

"Where did you get that?" he asked Logan.

"With the letter, Claire left me a key to another safe deposit box. Different place than we went, Amanda."

She wondered if the key Claire left was a duplicate to the small brass one in her purse. They never did confirm where it belonged.

Logan went on. "The egg was inside with a card. It's there if you want to read it."

Amanda lifted the index card.

To the love of my life. I thought this was the most valuable treasure until I met you. Now I want you to have it.

"You can't keep this," Trent said firmly.

"I'm well aware. And I don't want it... or anything to do with Claire's shady past. I'll choose to remember the times I know weren't a lie. Like when we were holding each other and talking about our plans..." His eyes flicked to Amanda's, and he cleared his throat.

"I'm happy for you," she repeated, and she truly was.

"There was an envelope in the box too with numerous safe deposit keys inside. Each had a label saying where they belonged. Another note explained the boxes hold all the cash she had left from the heists." He handed her a large manilla envelope she hadn't even noticed he'd had stuffed under an arm.

"We'll make sure this is sorted." She paused, considering the invitation she was about to extend, and thought *what the heck?* "Trent and I were getting ready to go outside for a beer. Now, he has a barbecue to assemble. But, Logan, you and I can have a beer and watch him work."

"Sounds good to me," Logan said.

"And how about I cook you dinner when you're done, Trent? Well, for both of you. But one of you will need to teach me how to use the thing."

They both volunteered, fumbling with their words. She laughed.

"Guess I'm covered."

She grabbed a third beer from the fridge, and when she came out with it, the men had already gone outside. She touched her lips again, thinking of kissing Trent. It felt so right. Magical, dare she say.

"Mandy, I'm hungry." Zoe came storming through the patio door.

"Coming, sweetie." She handed Zoe the plate with apple, which had browned some, and grabbed a piece of cheese from the fridge quick. "There you go."

"Thanks."

The girl ran back out the door and sat in a chair next to Trent.

"Heya, Trent." Zoe waved at him and smiled.

"Hey, Zoe."

Amanda was quite sure Zoe might have a crush on her partner, and she couldn't blame the little girl. But Logan was great, too, and Amanda and him had worked as a couple before... well, until they didn't. But they made more sense than she and Trent.

A romantic relationship with him would just cause far too many complications.

Trent smiled at her, and she hadn't even been aware she'd been watching him. He held up his bottle. She mirrored the action.

Maybe one day things would be different...

A LETTER FROM CAROLYN

Dear reader,

I want to say a huge thank you for choosing to read *Last Seen Alive*. If you enjoyed it and would like to hear about new releases in the Amanda Steele series, just sign up at the following link. Your email address will never be shared, and you can unsubscribe at any time.

www.bookouture.com/carolyn-arnold

If you loved *Last Seen Alive*, I would be incredibly grateful if you would write a brief, honest review. Also, if you'd like to continue investigating murder, you'll be happy to know there will be more Detective Amanda Steele books. I also offer several other international bestselling series for you to savor—everything from crime fiction, to cozy mysteries, to thrillers and action adventures. One of these series features Detective Madison Knight, another kick-ass female detective, who will risk her life, her badge—whatever it takes—to find justice for murder victims.

If you enjoyed being in the Prince William County, Virginia, area, you might want to return in my Brandon Fisher FBI series. Brandon is the boyfriend of Becky Tulson, mentioned in this book, but you'll be able to be there when they meet in *Silent Graves* (book two in my FBI series). These books are perfect for readers who love heart-pounding thrillers and are fascinated with the psychology of serial killers. Each install-ment is a new case with a fresh bloody trail to follow. Hunt with the FBI's Behavioral Analysis Unit and profile some of the most devious and darkest minds on the planet.

And if you're familiar with the Prince William County, Virginia area, or have done some internet searching, you'll realize some differences between reality and my book. That's me taking creative liberties.

Last but certainly not least, I love hearing from my readers! You can get in touch on my Facebook page, through Twitter, Goodreads, or my website. This is also a good way to stay noti-fied of my new releases. You can also reach out to me via email at Carolyn@CarolynArnold.net.

Wishing you a thrill a word!

Carolyn Arnold

www.carolynarnold.net

facebook.com/AuthorCarolynArnold

twitter.com/Carolyn_Arnold